FEELS LIKE FALLING

A BLACKSTONE FALLS NOVEL
BOOK 1

ALEXANDRA HALE

Melissa –
Welcome to Blackstone Falls!
A. Hale ♥

To my readers, thank you for not giving up on me.

AUTHOR'S NOTE

Please be advised that this small town story is an open door romance containing explicit detail and language. There is also an on page medical incident that may be sensitive to some readers.

PROLOGUE

MONTANA

ONE MONTH AGO

"Dammit, Grandad!" I yell across the field as the old man on the seat of the *very* stuck tractor turns to look at me with a toothy smile and a wave.

"Montana, my boy!" He gestures toward the wheel with a shrug. "I seem to be a little stuck."

"Yeah, Grandad, looks like that mud puddle jumped up and got ya," I say as my lips twitch and his eyes sparkle.

"Damn things been poppin' up all over the place," he agrees, amused and not the least bit worried.

"Incoming," I murmur as a woman in her sixties comes into view. I'd originally hired her to look after Grandad, but she'd taken to lookin' after me too.

The woman is a saint.

"Oh for heaven's sake, Hal," Miss Celeste huffs as she hustles across the grass in her apron, wavin' a hand towel around like she's trying to land an airplane. "Montana, I am so sorry. I was gettin' supper ready and he told me he was headin' in to lie down." Lowering her voice, she mutters, "the rascal," before returning her attention back to my grandad. "Well Hal? What do you have to say for yourself?"

She slams her hands onto her hips as the old devil grins at her from his perch.

"You're lookin' lovely today, Miss Celeste. Is that a new apron?"

"You know darn well, you old loon, that this is the same one I wear every day." She shakes her finger at him, but her lips are fighting a smile. Grandad just has that way about him, and it's one of the many reasons I knew I'd never let him live anywhere but here.

"Help an old man down, wouldya?" he asks, finally turning to me with a grin, and like always, I help ease him down until he's found his footing. He pats my face with his palm, the skin rough from years of farming this very land. "You're my favorite, you know that, right?"

"I do," I say, returning his grin even as emotion clogs my throat. Nodding, he turns and holds out his arm, Miss Celeste shaking her head as she loops her arm through his offered elbow.

"Don't tell your sisters I said that!" he hollers over his shoulder.

"It'll cost ya," I yell, and he waves a hand without looking back.

"Put it on my tab."

Chuckling, I watch them walk across the field and back onto the path that leads to the house I grew up in.

The house Grandad did too.

It's home.

It's the reason I'll never lay my head down anywhere else. The soil under my boots and the way the wind whips through the cotton is a part of me just like the blood flowin' though my veins.

My sisters never understood it, and my parents couldn't wait to get out of here after Vienna and Aspen left for college. They all couldn't wait to leave, but the only way I'd be leavin' is when the good Lord calls me home.

I watch until I know he's safely inside before turning my attention back to the tractor I know isn't comin' unstuck anytime soon and pull out my phone.

There's no greeting as the line picks up, just a grunt of irritation from my friend—the new owner of the Rusty Fender, the mechanic shop the next town over—and that makes me smile.

"Hank, you're never going to believe what happened..."

1

MONTANA
PRESENT DAY

S tepping out onto the back porch, I take a deep breath and smile, the steam rising from my coffee mug as the sun peeks over the horizon. It's my favorite time of day.

It's fresh starts and new beginnings. It's my time to recharge in the quiet before the chaos each morning.

People joked that I'd been born in the wrong decade, preferring to spend time out in the fresh air with the sun on my face and dirt on my boots. But I liked the way being in the fields settled my nerves. I didn't need to be anyone else but me—didn't have to prove myself because *here* my skills and knowledge spoke loud and clear.

The grass is green on my side of the fence, and I wasn't about to dwell on the glory days when I'm happy each and every day to be able to do what I love.

We even managed to keep Blackstone University on the edge of town, effectively preserving the quaint and cozy atmosphere—neighbors helping neighbors, the requisite busybodies, and a community that rallies for the people they love.

Why would anyone need anything else?

The roads are sometimes paved, sometimes dirt, and almost always flanked with crops or cattle. Tennessee is known for raising soybeans and cotton, my family harvesting mainly the latter, but we still have enough variety here to be a well-rounded agricultural cornerstone.

We also have animals to keep us busy, but it isn't something I am interested in expanding. Not yet at least.

> ELLISON: Can I dress up the cows for Christmas?

I SNORT as I read the text from my best friend, her left-field question completely throwing off my morning musings.

> MONTANA: You remember how big cows are, right?

> ELLISON: (picture of cow wearing red and green antlers)

> ELLISON: (picture of two cows wearing Santa hats and scarves)

> ELLISON: Won't that be so cute??

> MONTANA: You already ordered everything, didn't you

> ELLISON: It's en route to your house

MONTANA: It's July

ELLISON: Can never start too early

SHAKING MY HEAD, I pocket my phone, my smile stretching wide across my face. It has been a long time since Ellison Mills lived in Blackstone Falls, and in just a few short weeks, she'll be back in our hometown.

Hopefully for good.

As far as I'm concerned, as long as she's coming home single—and until she tells me otherwise—she's coming home to me. We'd only given in that one night, but Ellison Mills has always been it for me.

There'd been a time where we'd drifted apart, but like a compass finding north, we found our way back to each other. She's been one of the many that needed to stretch their wings beyond the county lines.

I understand it.

But I don't *get* it.

Growing up had been idyllic, and I never understood why everyone couldn't wait to leave. My parents had been childhood sweethearts who'd gone away to college and come home to run the farm.

Mama had been obsessed with geography which is how she'd ended up naming me and my sisters. Being the firstborn son, I'd been given a state name. My sisters had been blessed with cities—Aspen for Mama's love of the mountains and Vienna who had been a welcome surprise.

Vienna's name had been a game-day decision in the hospital room. Mama had gone in thinkin' she'd be naming my sister "Salem" but she said one look at the baby's face and she knew that wasn't right. She'd been delighted to learn that Vienna, in addition to being the capital of Austria, is also a small town in Virginia.

That last bit of information had been all Mama needed, and I'd been over the moon to have another sister. Most guys wanted a brother, but I'd loved my girls fiercely and had been proud to see them grow up with confidence and grace and a proper fighting stance.

It made Mama roll her eyes, but if I was letting my baby sisters outside our little slice of heaven, I had to make sure they knew how to protect themselves.

Even though I still worried.

Somehow, they'd both ended up in the lowcountry of South Carolina—Aspen in Magnolia Point and Vienna in Love Beach. Both sounded suspect but that was the big brother in me. Basically, any place they lived that wasn't Blackstone Falls would most likely give me an ulcer.

But they were happy, and I was trying like hell to be happy for them. They deserved it and so did I.

If my life had a theme song it would be "This Ole Boy" by Craig Morgan, and just thinking about the catchy tune had my boot tapping on the porch, the buzz of my phone adding to the soundtrack in my mind.

Smiling, I pull the device out expecting to see Ellison's name, but my hopes are quickly dashed with one single message from my friend who lives with his brother on the farm in the cottage out back. And who thankfully helps around here from time to time.

MASON: Someone left the paddock open and we've got a couple cows in our backyard.

WELL, hell, time to go to work.

2

ELLISON

"Are you sure we can't get you to reconsider?" my mother asks as she picks an invisible piece of lint off the pristine white tablecloth.

"No," I say firmly. "I gave my notice at work and I've accepted a job in Blackstone Falls." My mother sniffs at the mere mention of the place I grew up. There had been nothing holding us there—we could have moved at any time. But for some reason we'd stayed, and then they'd followed me once I'd left for college.

My mother had been thrilled to leave Blackstone Falls even though I reminded her that I was a grown woman and didn't need my parents micromanaging my life. Her undisguised hate for the small town never made sense to me.

Probably why I love it so much.

"But the academy has been so good to you, taking you when you were fresh out of college."

It's another reminder of how long I've allowed her to have her hand in my life. It didn't take long to realize I'd been hired at the private academy, not based on merit—

although I had the grades—but because of my mother's generous donation.

And continued annual donations.

"You'll stay at the house," my father says, trying to offer an olive branch. "I'll tell the realty company to cancel all reservations for the duration of your stay."

"I've already rented a place," I say with a shake of my head, causing my father to frown. I hate seeing him sad, but he's out of his mind if he thinks I'm going back to my childhood home.

My father opens his mouth and then closes it while my mother takes another sip of her mineral water, her expensive salad untouched on her plate.

I look between the two of them and for the millionth time try to figure out why he's stayed all these years. He wasn't the best father, but he tried.

Especially while I was in high school. I decided to play tennis my freshman year, and he'd sneak away to watch me play at the away matches. Even in college, I'd turn around and find him sitting in a folding chair with the biggest smile and a *don't tell your mother* shrug.

I wouldn't dare.

It was the only time I felt like we were a team—like there wasn't this mountain of unknown between us. In those moments, he was just my dad and I adored him. We'd go to dinner and just *talk* about the match, school, things we were looking forward to, but we never talked about my mother.

And those were the happiest childhood memories I had.

"I've set up a dinner at the country club for the Tuesday after you get back," Mother starts as she dabs her smudge-free lipstick. "Dustin is so excited to see you."

No she didn't...

"Mother," I say as calmly as I can manage at brunch time

in this *very* pretentious restaurant, "I will *not* be meeting Dustin for dinner. Or breakfast. Or lunch." My voice rises with each word, and I have to take a couple of deep breaths before continuing. "After what happened..."

"Oh Ellison, that was *years* ago. Surely you've gotten over that by now."

My father's eyes widen, and his mouth opens to speak but I shake my head. He doesn't need to be subjected to her reign of terror when I leave. His jaw clenches like he's physically trying to stop himself from defending me, and just that small act of support gives me the strength I need to get through this.

"I will not be having dinner with Dustin or *anyone* from the country club. No dinners. No meetings. Once I leave Savannah, I will not be a part of this world." I subtly motion around the room, and her only reaction is the slight flaring of her nose. "Please do not schedule *anything* for me at the country club or elsewhere."

"How could you be so ungrateful after everything I've done for you?" Her voice is cold, and short of getting up and walking out, there's nothing I can do but placate her through the rest of this meal.

"Sherri Ann," my father says gently, "Ellison is a grown woman and we need to let her—"

"We have a reputation to uphold," my mother hisses, and I nudge my father's leg under the table with my foot. He rolls his eyes when she's not looking, and I hide my snicker by shoving an unladylike bite of ravioli into my mouth.

God, I'll miss the ravioli.

I want to laugh at the ridiculousness of that statement, but there's no use in drawing more unwanted attention to myself.

My phone buzzes in my purse, and it takes everything in

me to ignore it. There's only one person who knows where I am right now.

He also knows it will drive me crazy not being able to check the damn thing until I'm out of here.

"While I appreciate everything you've done for me," I say calmly, "I don't fit into all this. It's not who I am and it never has been." I sigh as I look around the lavishly designed space. My mother would probably have a heart attack right here at the table if she found out that I'd sold or donated most of the designer clothes that had lined my oversized closet.

I'd kept my favorite pieces and a dress that I'd worn once and couldn't seem to part with, but there was nothing else I'd need from that era of my life when I returned to Blackstone Falls.

"You have a long drive ahead of you," my father says, and my mother huffs before taking another sip of her drink.

With agonizing slowness, we manage to finish our meals —my father and I polishing off the meager servings and my mother never once raising her fork more than a few inches off her plate before setting it down again.

It was a routine I wouldn't miss.

Walking out of the restaurant and handing my ticket to the valet, I turn my face up to the sun with a smile.

I'm free.

"Happy looks good on you, kid." My father's voice is low, but sincerity rings in his words.

"I'm excited to go home," I say and he nods, completely unsurprised by my declaration. "Come watch me play tennis?"

His lips tip up in the corner and he dips his head. "I'd like that."

"Evan." My mother's voice is shrill as she steps out of the air conditioning of the restaurant as their car is brought to the front. "It's time to go. Ellison,"—she gives me an air kiss —"let me know if you change your mind about that dinner."

I give her a placating expression as the valet holds open her door and she climbs inside. Turning toward me, my father opens his arms, and I step into them without hesitation.

"Why won't you leave her?" I ask quietly, and my father's body stiffens before he pulls back to look at me.

"It's complicated." Taking a deep breath, he forces a smile as he adds, "And right now we're focusing on you getting settled and then seeing what your tennis schedule looks like."

"It's a deal."

Hugging me once more, my father places a kiss on the top of my head before tipping the valet as my car is brought up. It's not until they're out of sight that I take my first full breath of the morning. Pulling out my phone, I grin as I read the message from my best friend.

> MONTANA: Your ass looks great in that dress (heart eye emoji)

> ELLISON: How do you know I'm wearing a dress?

I SNICKER as I look down at my floral-printed dress and snap a picture.

MONTANA: Your ass would look great in pants too

MONTANA: But it's summer in Savannah and you always wear dresses to brunch

ELLISON: (selfie showing off dress)

ELLISON: It's cute you know brunch attire

MONTANA: Told you your ass looks great

ELLISON: You can't even see it

MONTANA: I don't need to see it to know it looks great

ELLISON: (eyeroll emoji)

ELLISON: You're such a guy

MONTANA: Guilty. So, when are you coming home?

ELLISON: Should be the day after tomorrow.

MONTANA: Well hurry up, we've got plans

ELLISON: What plans?

MONTANA: You and me plans, Eddie.

ELLISON: I'll be home soon, Max.

EDDIE AND MAX. Childhood nicknames that meant a whole lot more to me than a fancy dinner ever would. And just that thought alone has me smiling all the way back to pack up the rest of my apartment.

3

MONTANA

"Mornin'," I say, climbing out of my truck at the Kettle & Kiln and stretching my arms over my head. Archer nods as he walks across the gravel lot and grabs the pressed-tin door, holding it open for me. "You're such a gentleman."

"I haven't had enough coffee for you yet," my cousin grumbles, but it's all in good fun. At least that's what I tell myself.

"Aw...don't be like that," I say stepping into the space with the white painted walls and hanging green plants. They'd taken out half of the second floor, accentuating the light and openness of the space with vaulted ceilings and making the other half a lofted sitting area.

Nicolette and Karina had done a lot of the work themselves, and they'd done a hell of a job. The make your own pottery and coffee shop hadn't been open very long but it was already a town favorite.

The transplants from Virginia had made Blackstone Falls their home not more than a year ago. They'd hit the mark with offering customers the chance to really maximize their experience either painting pre-fired mugs or entirely making their own. I'd yet to do either, but still stopped by a couple times a week to support them.

The couple brought a certain kind of energy that was as enthusiastic as it was organic. They'd wooed locals and tourists alike with caffeine, clay, and a whole lot of love. It made me proud, and a little relieved, to see them embracing —enhancing—small-town living instead of trying to make Blackstone Falls something it wasn't.

Archer grumbles again, bringing me back to the present. His brown hair is a little more unruly than usual and his matching brown eyes are tired. If I were a bettin' man, I'd say it has something to do with his girlfriend and the fact that they spend the night together more times than not.

"Late night?" I ask, and he grunts but otherwise doesn't respond aside from the slight twitch of his lips.

Good for him.

I like seein' him happy.

I just don't need this cup of coffee like he does. Celeste always has the coffee brewing for Grandad in the morning with enoug' eft for me. Call me spoiled but I like the routine

Like it but don't *need* it.

I learned a long time ago that banking on a plan led to either headache or heartache—sometimes both—and a man in my position couldn't afford to wallow in either.

Life is too unpredictable. Hell, I have to call Hank no less than once a month to pull the tractor out of the mud. It always eats up half a day, but nobody gets hurt and my friends go home with their pockets a little fatter.

Still, it's just neighbors helpin' neighbors.

Hank Thayer had been workin' at the Rusty Fender since getting out of prison more than a decade ago. His wrongful conviction and the ensuing scandal had been the biggest news either of our towns had seen probably ever.

His family was big and loud and easily some of my favorite people on the planet. Frowning, I try and remember the last time I'd been down to his mama's house for a just-because picnic.

"Well, it looks like the coffee's a brewin' and trouble is too." Karina chuckles, pulling me from my wayward thoughts. "Morning, boys, what can I getcha?" she asks with an exaggerated flutter of her eyelashes, causing Archer to blush beside me as he clears his throat. Flustering Archer is one of my favorite pastimes too, and I don't hide my smile as he glowers at me.

"Miss Karina, you are lookin' *lovely* today, and I couldn't help but notice that you've changed up your wardrobe choice to gray over black. Bold choice on a Wednesday."

Karina narrows espresso-colored eyes at me even as her lips twitch. Later in the day, when the sun is higher, the light will pull the gold to mix with the almost-black color. Her skin is a rich caramel, and her dark curly hair meticulously frames her face, landing at her shoulders and drawing my eyes back to her very plain shirt.

"I wanted to mix it up," she says, following my gaze with a shrug. "Besides, Nicolette is all the color I need."

And she's not lying.

Karina's wife is her complete opposite with blonde hair she usually has tied up into some sort of braid, bright teal eyes that would look unnatural on anyone else, and porcelain skin. While Karina brings a sassier edge, Nicolette is all sunshine with bangles lining her wrists. I have no idea how she manages to keep them out of the clay while working—I'd been covered in the stuff every time the unit came up at school.

"Y'all are adorable."

"He's choosing violence today, huh?" she says as she stares around me and pops her hip.

"She's talking about you," I stage whisper to my cousin as I elbow him for emphasis.

"Each and every day," Archer manages and Karina snickers.

"All right," Karina says, pointing a purple manicured nail at me. "You having your usual?"

"Of course, you have a usual," Archer says, speaking unprompted for the first time since we walked in.

"What can I say? I'm unforgettable."

"I was going to say exhausting but…" Archer trails off as Karina bustles around. After placing my order on the counter—a western wrap with homemade salsa on the side and a large coffee with sugar and a dash of cream—Karina turns her focus to Archer. He blinks a couple of times then rattles off a boring black coffee and a bagel. She nods then turns, and I let my gaze sweep over the specials board.

"Is Nicolette still in Virginia?" I ask and Karina hums as she works.

"She'll be back next week. We finally sold the house, nightmare that was, but she's spending some time with her parents before she comes home."

Home.

I know she means home to *her* but I still love that Blackstone Falls holds that title too.

"Well, make sure you come to the house. I know Celeste and Grandad would love to have you for dinner."

"That would be really nice," she says, and it's perhaps the least sassy thing she's ever said. I don't know what it's like to be an outsider, but I *do* know what it's like to fit in and to want to be part of something bigger than yourself.

"Good." I snatch one of the business cards from the counter while Archer pays for our breakfast and I shove a twenty in the tip jar. "I'll talk to Celeste and let you know."

"That would be great, and here," she says, holding out a white cardboard box with her logo stamped on the top in green ink, "these are Hal's favorite."

I don't have to open it to know that Karina has placed a couple of strawberry muffins inside. We share a secret smile before she wanders off toward the kitchen, and Archer and I finally walk to a small table off to the side.

"Rock and Roll" by Eric Hutchinson plays quietly through the space as we settle in, and I waste no time taking a massive bite of my wrap. I realize my mistake almost instantly, but I'm too committed now, even though this thing is *one level down from surface of the sun* hot. Archer stares at me in disbelief, his own bagel halfway to his mouth as he watches me try, and fail, to cool down and chew my breakfast.

"There is seriously something wrong with you," he mumbles and I shrug.

"Coulda been worse," I say, washing everything down with equally hot coffee.

"But you literally watched her make it. You—" He shakes his head. "You know what? Never mind."

Snorting and somehow managing not to choke, I decide to move to a safer subject. His girlfriend. "How's Bea?"

"She's good." His smile is tender as a blush creeps up his neck.

Good for him.

"Heard her business has been doin' real well." My cousin met his girl at a local vendor event earlier this year. He'd had his jams and canned goods and she had homemade soaps and lotions. Her business, Bea's Bubbles and Balms, has taken our little town by storm, and she's already managed to get her products in a lot of the local stores.

I've never used goat milk soap but I am happy to support family—and that's what she is, bein' with Archer. Family.

"It is but she wants to get some goats, not just source the milk," he says pointedly at me.

Expectantly.

"Hell no. You find someone else to house those mean fuckers." My head shakes with a vehemence only those four-legged little demons can bring out in me.

"Oh, come on. You have plenty of room. And she's going to do most of the work and then pay one of the guys you have to help."

"No," I say again even as Archer stares at me. "Brother, I do *not* want goats. Getting bitten in the ass at eleven was enough for me."

He snickers and his eyes sparkle at my discomfort. Huffing, I take the last bite of my wrap and ball up the garbage. Sobering, Archer rubs the back of his head with his palm, and I wait like I always do until he's gathered himself enough to speak because seriously, what could be worse than goats?

"I told her about us—about Sundown Realty."

Internally, my heart rate slows to a more acceptable rhythm and I shrug, unfazed because I kind of figured. "I trust you."

Archer opens his mouth and closes it before nodding. "Right. Of course. Well, anyway, she asked if we were looking for someone to run the office front—handle the emails and scheduling for housekeeping and maintenance, streamline the calendar for the rentals or something."

"You want to hire your girlfriend to manage our secret multimillion-dollar business?" I deadpan as he shifts nervously in his chair. We've grown the business over the last several years from a handful of properties to well over a hundred in Blackstone Falls, Clementine Creek, and a couple in the neighboring towns. We'd picked up a good variety of cottages, vacation homes, apartments, and cabins for both the college crowd and tourists alike.

With any luck, we'd be expanding all the way into Nashville within the year, and having Bea on the front line would definitely help us do that.

Slapping my hand against the table makes him jump, and I chuckle. "Dude, that's your girl. You gotta be like, 'hell yeah, I want to hire my girl—she's the best damn woman for the job and she's going to fucking kill it.' Seriously, man, have I taught you nothing?"

"I mean—"

"Grandad always said when you find the girl that makes the sun rise and set, you make her your whole world. You're her shoulder to cry on and her number one fan. And if you're pitching her for a job that risks our anonymity when all our dealings have been entirely online or third party, then I need you to give me a little more than *or something.*"

Grabbing a sugar packet from the container, Archer flicks it at my head with a grin. "You're an idiot and *damn straight* she's the best one for the job. She's really smart and she's good with the marketing piece too. You should see her social media—runs circles around us."

I snort and take a sip of my coffee. "Well, that last part isn't hard. I like sendin' memes, not makin' them."

"Exactly. She started talkin' about algorithms and aesthetics and..." He trails off and I don't have to be a genius to figure out how he got her to stop talking about all those things.

"I'm happy for you." His eyebrows raise over the lip of his coffee cup, and when he swallows, the sound is audible.

"Thanks." Rubbing the back of his neck, he looks down at the butcher-block table and grins before looking up at me. "It's crazy, right?"

"Being happy? Naw, man, you just hadn't met the right one."

"Speaking of the right one..."

I shrug. "I gotta wait and see how it goes. She broke up with her boyfriend not long ago, and I just want to make sure she's ready before I start something."

"That's...very adult of you," he says as he tries—and fails—to hide a smile with his coffee cup.

"Honestly, I hate this new side of me."

"No, you don't," he says with a laugh and he's right. I don't. But things with Ellison Mills have always been the kind of complicated you see in the movies. She had a well-to-do upbringing, and my mama used to swat at me for tracking mud into the house.

"I just want her to be all in, and she can't be all in with me if she still has feelings for some douchebag in Savannah."

"How do you know she still has feelings?"

"I don't, but I can't take that chance." My fist rubs at the ache in the center of my chest. "I lost her for a long time, you know? She wasn't totally *gone* but she wasn't *there* either." Archer stares at me like he's tryin' to figure out a puzzle. He's never had something like Ellison and I had back then, really not until he got together with Bea.

But Ellison and I have always been something special. She'd been the center of my world for so long it was hard to reconcile the time when she wasn't. I'd hated every second of the distance between us and every wall erected. We weren't *us,* and that's something that left an irreparable hole in my heart.

"Not that I'm an expert,"—I smirk and he rolls his eyes —"but I think you're supposed to talk to her. Women like that sort of thing."

"I don't think that's just women. I'm pretty sure that's supposed to be a universal rule."

"Hell if I know," he mumbles and I can't help but chuckle. Getting actual words out of Archer has always been a trial in patience, but seeing him open up over the last few months has brought me a kind of joy I didn't know existed.

Despite most people's best intentions, there's always a judgment when you meet men like us. Archer is quiet and reserved—often shy—and yet he's cast as standoffish or rude, while I'm just the guy lookin' for a good time who can't take anything seriously. Sometimes I think it's easier than people thinking I'll never make anything of myself. I've maintained and even expanded the success of the farm and, with the man sitting across from me, managed to build a profitable empire in Sundown Realty.

We're more alike than most people think, shyness aside, but that's a battle for another day.

I take a sip of my coffee and stare out the window before returning my attention to Archer. "Hire your girlfriend and let her pick the storefront. She can furnish it." My mouth opens and closes as my brows furrow. "Just make sure it looks manly—like us but you know, not us."

"That makes literally no sense."

"Sure it does. We want it rustic and country and shit without having every available wall covered in shiplap."

"And you just trust Bea to do this?" he asks in disbelief. I get it—I do—but he's never seen himself the way I do. He's my cousin, a title I gave him based on love and respect rather than blood, and that means something to me.

"I trust you. You love her." I pause and wait for him to dispute it. He doesn't, so I continue, "So by extension I love and trust her, and when you're ready to make it official, I'll call her family just the same."

"I'm not sure I'll ever truly understand you."

I shrug and school my expression even as I feel the tips of my ears heat. "Life's too short to be upset over things that don't matter. Love hard, live big, and find what brings you joy."

"Like you pining over Ellison?"

"I still love her. I always have, and her being in Savannah didn't change that. I just never let myself really fall for her the way we both deserve."

I meet his gaze and watch as his lips part the smallest amount. I've shocked him almost as much as I've shocked myself saying that last part out loud. But no one who truly knows me can look at me and not know I'd do damn near anything to have what my grandparents had.

Sure, my parents are happy and still in love but it's different. It's generational. It's the stories Grandad told me with a glass of sweet tea on the porch and Nan yelling her version from behind the screen door.

It's the love and affection that comes from having nothing and building something with your bare hands that sustains more than just a moment in time. It's knowing that the land brings me comfort and peace. It's knowing I'll live and die by the land.

And it's the hope to love one woman for the rest of my days.

One woman in particular.

"You all right?" Archer asks, and I have to shake my head to clear the daydream.

"Yeah, just thinking."

"Is it about getting goats? Because I'm sure Bea can help facilitate that in between finding and furnishing a storefront."

"I will disown you," I warn, but I'm not joking and he knows it. Or he should.

His lips twitch as he pushes back from the table and stands. "No goats—got it."

"I'm serious, man." My whole body shudders at the memory of being chased around the paddock as a kid and being thankful I could clear the top of the fence in one leap.

He clasps me on the shoulder as we discard our now empty cups and head out into the parking lot with a wave at Karina. The air is already heavy, but it feels like home and there's nowhere else I'd rather be.

Sitting in my truck, I watch in my rearview mirror as Archer pulls out and disappears from view. It's already a good day, and as I flip on the radio, I can't help the smile that stretches over my face.

"Chicks Dig It" by Chris Cagle plays, and hell if I can argue with that.

4

MONTANA

ASPEN: Heard Ellison Mills is coming back to Blackstone Falls…

VIENNA: Uh-oh…

VIENNA: Do I need to book a ticket home?

MONTANA: Why would you need to book a ticket home?

ASPEN: We remember Ellison-gate big brother

VIENNA: It wasn't pretty

MONTANA: What are you talking about? Nothing happened

VIENNA: (side-eye emoji)

ASPEN: (gif of woman making a faux surprised face)

MONTANA: Couldn't y'all just come home because you love me and not because you think my life is about to implode?

> VIENNA: It's hard getting time off work right now–gotta spend that PTO wisely

MONTANA: I'm so proud of you but I still miss you

> VIENNA: Awww

ASPEN: Focus people. Big brother, the girl of your dreams is moving home. What's your status?

MONTANA: There is no status. Everything is fine.

Three dots appear and then disappear. Sighing, I take a sip of my sweet tea and try unsuccessfully to move my thoughts away from my best friend. I'd expected the interrogation from Archer but not my sisters. They should have been too young to understand what had gone down between Ellison and me.

More accurately, what *hadn't*.

There was no *us*—just a friendship that we'd both let fade into the background. I hated thinking of it like that, but at the end of the day we'd left our relationship out in the rain. We'd rescued it from the elements worn and faded and in need of repair.

It was in rough shape, but it wasn't broken.

Still, times like these had me forgetting my sisters were

well into their twenties instead of the two hell-raising princesses with dark hair and green eyes.

VIENNA: We're just worried about you big brother

ASPEN: We hated seeing you so upset when she left

MONTANA: Should have seen me when my baby sisters moved away never to return

ASPEN: (gif of woman looking annoyed)

VIENNA: Did he just…

ASPEN: He did

MONTANA: Love my girls

MONTANA: (gif of guy blowing a kiss)

VIENNA: Ugh we love you too

MONTANA: Then I don't know why you need to gang up on me

ASPEN: Stop being so sensitive

ASPEN: Listen—I have to go to work but I'm going to need updates

VIENNA: Definitely updates. I'm friends with Ellison on social media—she's still super pretty big brother…

MONTANA: I'm gonna say goodbye now

VIENNA: You're no fun

MONTANA: Literally no one would agree
with you

ASPEN: So you're saying we get the
serious, boring side of you?

MONTANA: Aren't you supposed to be
working?

VIENNA: (gif of woman cackling)

ASPEN: (kiss face emoji)

TOSSING my phone on the table, I'm relieved when the screen stays dark. No doubt, they're having a side conversation about me right now, but that's not something I can worry about.

Closing my eyes, I let my head fall back, thankful for the small reprieve of the quiet house.

"Oh, Lord. Montana, have you seen Hal?" Celeste says on a huff as she comes bustling into the kitchen, our silver Labrador, Hermie, hot on her heels, his nails clicking on the hardwood. I open my eyes slowly, my gaze finding the paneling on the ceiling as I swallow the sigh that wants to escape.

It's been a day.

"I just got in the house," I say as she studies me a beat longer, absentmindedly stroking Hermie's head while his entire body wags and not just his tail. The three-legged brute is still very much a puppy and barely notices his missing limb. We'd taken him in from the shelter in Clementine Creek, Vetted Paws, after they'd rescued him from a hoarding situation.

Hermie had taken to Celeste immediately, and she never missed an opportunity to fuss over him.

"I swear, that man," she mumbles under her breath. "I turn my back for two seconds and he..."

Her words die off as the sound of a pickup truck grows louder coming up the driveway. Dirt and rocks kick up behind it, and I roll my eyes as I realize I'll have to tell Mason to slow down. I swear it wasn't too long ago that Grandad was hollering at me for the same damn thing. Scrubbing my hand over my stubble-covered jaw, I try and remember when I got to be so old.

Mason hops out of the driver's side and hustles over to where Grandad is already closing his door and waving Mason off. I can practically hear the grumbling from my grandfather that he doesn't need help as he saunters toward the house.

He's not even halfway up the porch steps before Celeste is throwing open the door, hands on her hips and a scowl that has Mason's eyes going wide.

"Where have you been?" she snaps, and Grandad's lips turn up at the corners.

"Can't an old man go for a walk on a beautiful afternoon?" he asks as his head tilts to one side in question.

"He can," Celeste draws the last word out but no one dares to speak, "*if* he tells people where he's going so he doesn't die of heat stroke out there."

"Woman, I have been farmin' these fields for—"

"Don't you *woman* me. Now get inside and take a seat,"

she demands before smoothing her hands down the front of her apron. "There's a drink and a snack on the table."

Mason's lips part, his eyes wide with wonder as he watches Grandad walk to where Celeste is still standing. He places a quick kiss on her cheek before whistling his way toward the kitchen.

She sighs before turning her attention to Mason. "Come on, there's a plate in there for you too."

Mason scuffs his worn boot against the dirt, looking even younger than he actually is. "Oh, I couldn't—"

"Inside," she says again, shooing him with her hands this time. He barks out a laugh and hustles through the doorway. I follow because this falls under *if you can't beat 'em join 'em* and I don't need Mason getting roped into anymore of Grandad's shenanigans.

Celeste closes the door behind us, and I'm almost to the table when my phone buzzes in my pocket. Wrestling it from the denim pocket of my jeans, my smile is immediate as the message lights up the screen.

ELLISON: Maybe we can put the cows on the Christmas card

MONTANA: What Christmas card?

ELLISON: Ours silly (eye roll emoji)

MONTANA: Do best friends send out joint Christmas cards?

ELLISON: Are you saying you don't want to send out joint Christmas cards, Max?

ELLISON: I could always send the other ones...

ELLISON: I think I have like 500 or so left

MONTANA: 500??!! How many did you fucking order??

ELLISON: My finger slipped and it went from 100 to 1000

MONTANA: That's a hell of a whoops

ELLISON: But so worth it

MONTANTA: Wait...

ELLISON: (angel emoji)

MONTANA: Who the hell did you send 500 Christmas cards to with me in my boxer shorts wearing cowboy boots and a Santa hat?

ELLISON: It's hard to remember

MONTANA: Who would even WANT to see that?

ELLISON: The entire female population

ELLISON: Probably most of the men too

MONTANA: But seriously—you've sent 500 of those???

ELLISON: I think it's a compliment honestly

ELLISON: You should be flattered

> MONTANA: You're in so much trouble when you get home

ELLISON: Can't wait!

ELLISON: (kiss face emoji)

SWALLOWING A HUFF, I look up and meet three sets of eyes and matching grins, and dammit all to hell, I forgot I wasn't alone.

"Anything you'd like to share?" Grandad asks as Mason snickers.

"Not even a little," I grumble, dropping into the chair next to Mason and stealing a cookie off his plate. He's about to protest when Celeste places another in front of him. He beams at her, and it's so genuine I can't be mad.

But I also can't let him win, so I swipe that cookie too and shove it in my mouth. Celeste gasps, Mason pouts, and Grandad barks out a laugh, holding his stomach and drawing Hermie's attention from his bed in the corner.

Leaning back, I smile and chew, feeling remarkably better than I have all day.

5

ELLISON

"The Whiskey's Gone" By Alli Walker plays loudly for the fourth time through the speakers of my car as I drive the last hour home to Blackstone Falls. The energy drinks and candy bars are wearing off faster than the miles ticking down, and we've passed jittery and are headed straight for loopy.

But it's the good kind of loopy. The high-on-life kind that can only come from being so close to something you've dreamed would be your forever.

And now it's finally within my grasp.

I'd thankfully been able to terminate my rental agreement with the stipulation that I wouldn't be getting my security deposit back. But joke's on them because I probably would have given them my kidney if it got me out of Savannah.

The thought should be troubling but it's not.

I'd made any number of excuses over the years for why I couldn't come back to Blackstone Falls. I was mad at Montana for seemingly throwing us away, giving up on a future I wished could be ours. The abruptness from loving to indifferent had destroyed me, making it impossible for those wounds to heal.

And in the dead of night, I was mad at myself for not fighting harder—against him *and* my parents. Those nights, whispers of doubt played through my mind, hinting that I'd missed something and that Montana would never have let me go.

Not like that.

But they'd always been gone before morning, disappearing like dew on the grass when the sun comes up.

The anger had eventually morphed into hurt, and I'd been too ashamed to come back to the only place that would ever be home. Somehow the longer I stayed away, the easier it was to push Blackstone Falls, and Montana, from my mind.

Deep down, I knew I couldn't run forever.

But shame still tried to swallow me whole, knowing that Nan's death was the only thing I couldn't ignore. She may have been Montana's grandmother, but she'd made me feel like hers too. Our relationship had been too precious, too full of love, for me to not. It'd been the catalyst for rearranging my life—for taking a stand for myself and purging the things that no longer suited me.

My parents—my mother especially—had been part of that. Or at least as much as I could manage.

But Nan's voice had been so clear in my head the day I'd donned all black and stood next to Montana, my hand clenched in his at her gravesite. I never said a word about it, but I'd bet the trust fund I couldn't access that I'd heard Nan say *welcome home, my darling girl* as if she was standing right next to me.

I'd always teased her about the nickname and the way she always said the *g* in darling when so often her accent was heavier than her homemade poundcake. It made me feel special and I'd loved it. I loved the care and the adoration I felt whenever she greeted me. I felt *fancy* being her *darling* like being in one of those old black-and-white movies she loved so much.

Nan and Grandad taught me so much about love and life and the kind of person I wanted to wake up next to every morning. My young girl heart didn't understand back then the complications of the world I'd grown up in—the things that would prevent me from being able to fall in love with my best friend.

I'd confided in Nan—more during the years that Montana had been achingly absent from my life. My heart had broken when I left Blackstone Falls for college, but I was still so hopeful we could make it. We weren't dating, but that didn't mean I didn't consider him mine.

And with high school behind us and my eighteenth birthday in the rearview mirror, I thought we could finally break free of the things holding us back. But I'd been wrong.

And to this day, I still didn't truly understand *why*. There'd been no dramatic falling out or declaration of distaste toward each other. He'd simply been there one day and had all but vanished the next. I'd wanted to go home—to leave Georgia and return to Tennessee—and finish school where I could see Montana every day, but my parents had put a stop to that real quick. They'd somehow managed to make a new life down the road from my school in Georgia, renting our house in Blackstone Falls in the next breath. I hadn't left my life behind—the parts I hated most had followed me.

And the parts I loved had stayed away.

Montana stayed away.

The distance between us obliterated what was left of the organ in my chest and with it the hope of home.

Nan had filled the void the best she could, never giving up on me even when I wanted to give up on myself. She loved me more when Montana loved me less, making weekly phone calls and video chats with her a priority.

A lifeline.

The abrupt end to our Tuesday night ritual left a hole in my heart that was still gaping two years later.

He'd lost his grandmother, but it was me who needed the support and strength to get through the service. I owed it to her.

There were a million things I should have been here for, but the longer I was away, the harder it was to come back.

I missed so much.

Swallowing the regret, I take a deep breath and blow it out slowly as I try to let Cole Swindell sing me sweet nothings in the form of "She Had Me At Heads Carolina."

But just like my musings, it's cut short when my father's name flashes across the dashboard. Sighing, I accept the call and wait only a second before his voice comes over the speakers.

"Well, I guess you didn't wait till tomorrow to hit the road," he says, his voice full of tender amusement.

"I was too excited to wait. Besides, the drive isn't that far," I say even though it's definitely the farthest I've ever driven on my own. The thought makes me frown.

"I wish you would stay at the house."

"Honestly, Dad, there are few things I'd like to do less than stay there."

He sighs, and while I wish I could spare his feelings, I won't take it back. The house I grew up in wasn't a home. It was a showpiece and nothing more.

"It was worth a try," he says with a chuckle. "I need you to do me a favor while you're there."

"What's that?"

"I need you to go to our place and get a burger—one with bacon and grilled onions and that sauce they won't let me buy by the gallon—and then send me a picture so I can live vicariously through you."

"Dad." I laugh but my heart still warms at the way he says *our place*. Boots On Bar and Grill is a Blackstone Falls landmark, and my mother would rather wear clothes from a discount store than step foot inside.

So it was perfect. It became our little getaway when we just wanted to catch up for a while without my mother lurking and sucking every ounce of joy from the room. I'd been envious of the relationship Montana's sisters had with their mother—it's why I never let myself be close to any of them.

"Oh and the onion rings! Can't forget those." He sighs wistfully like he's been dreaming about the beer-battered veggies. "You know I can't get away with stuff like that when your mother is around." His tone is still light as he says the words, but all I can feel is the sadness.

For him.

For me.

For the things I still don't understand.

"Well, it's certainly a hardship," I say, taking his lead and putting as much enthusiasm as I can manage into the words, "but I'll do it for you."

"That's my girl." A beat passes and then another as those three words hang between us. My whole life I wished he would choose me over her, but he didn't, and even now those three words feel hollow.

"Is it all right if I hop in the pool this week? You said no one is at the house until Saturday, right?"

He clears his throat, and I can see in my mind the way his face falls at my lack of acknowledgment.

"It is. Sundown Realty manages the house and property. I let them know to expect you in and out of there this week." Pausing, he adds, "I think Montana does some work for them. I know he's been to the house to handle some repairs on an on-call basis maybe."

"He didn't mention it," I say while my mind processes that interesting development. A sly grin spreads across my face as an idea starts to take root, making my heart beat a little faster. It's not foolproof, but I'm feeling good about my odds.

"He's done well out there with the farm."

Even though he can't see me, I narrow my eyes. "Careful, Dad, that almost sounded like you're being nice to my best friend."

A heavy sigh fills the line. "I've never *not* liked Montana but...it's complicated. I probably owe him an apology," he admits, and I snort because he *definitely* owes Montana an apology. "I'm not proud of all the choices I've made in my life, Ellison, and given the chance, I'm sure I'd change a few —but life isn't black-and-white and the choices sure as hell aren't easy."

It's too heavy of a conversation for the last leg of my drive, and I need a little boost to get me to the county line.

"We can talk about it later, Dad. I'll text you when I get home, okay?"

"It's always been home, huh?"

"Always."

"Drive safe, El, I love you."

"I will. Love you too, Dad."

Disconnecting the call, I let all of the unrest go as I scroll through my playlists until I find "Keep Up" by RaeLynn, shimmying a little in my seat as her voice echoes through the car.

This is exactly what I need to get me home.

My spirit sings with each passing mile, and by the time I pass the sign welcoming me to Blackstone Falls, I have enough bravado to take a gamble. If it pays off, it might just be the best welcome home present a girl could ask for.

6

MONTANA

"Dammit, cat!" I grunt as the black-and-white ball of fur flies past me off the porch and out into the yard, nearly knocking me off my feet in the process.

"Was that Buttons?" Grandad asks as he steps out of the screen door and peers down at a bowl of untouched food and water.

Sighing, I say, "Grandad, it's been almost two *years* since Buttons ran away. I don't think that was her."

"It was her, all right."

The conviction in my grandfather's voice makes my heart squeeze. He loved that cat, and while I'd heard plenty of miracle stories about pets returning to their homes after long absences, I couldn't imagine this being one of them.

"Grandad," I say gently, but he harumphs and holds up his hand.

"It was her. You'll see." My eyes move to where Celeste is drying a dish just inside the house. She gives me a sad smile before turning back toward the kitchen. I drag my palm down my face as I try and figure out how to prepare for the impending emotional crash.

My mind drifts to Vetted Paws, the local animal shelter over in Clementine Creek. They're primarily a dog rescue, but I'm sure if I give them a call they can find me a cat for Grandad so he stops hanging his heart on the hope that Buttons has magically returned.

"You'll see," he repeats before heading inside, the slight slap of the screen door echoing around me as I pray for patience. Losing that damn cat had been hard enough, but having to endure it a second time would just be cruel.

Taking a breath, I go inside, leaving my boots on the mat in the entryway. The house smells like brisket and corn-bread, and my mouth waters as I stalk toward the stove and drop a kiss on Celeste's cheek.

She smiles and I nod before taking off down the hall toward my room. I need a shower, and I need to wash this day away if I have any chance of being ready for Ellison's arrival in town.

My best friend coming home shouldn't be a big deal.

But she's not just my best friend. She's my person and the kind of girl that drives you crazy but still makes you want to claim her forever.

My lips twitch as I strip off my shirt and toss it into the hamper with the rest of my clothes. Flipping on the shower, I wait as the water warms to something reasonable, my gaze jumping to my reflection in the mirror. Looking around, I flex my abs *once* but it has nothing to do with Ellison coming home.

Absolutely nothing.

Tattoos cover my shoulders, wrapping around one bicep and onto my back. They're pieces of me that Ellison wasn't here for, which is both sad and exhilarating. I want her to get to know me again.

I want her to *want* to get to know me again.

To trace the ink on my skin with her fingers, her mouth, and her tongue and ask me what they mean as she reacquaints herself with my body.

My dick bumping the sink has me jerking back a step and chuckling as I turn for the shower. I tried hard over the years not to let my mind conjure images of Ellison and me together—because even though we'd been young, that one night together had been incredible. It was cliché and a little awkward and absolutely perfect.

That memory does nothing to help keep my dick in check as the hot spray washes over me, my muscles practically groaning in relief. I've pushed myself harder every day in the fields this week in anticipation of her arrival.

Idle hands would only get me into trouble, and I have no doubt Ellison will bring plenty of that to my doorstep.

My lips twitch as I lather myself up with the soap that Bea makes, and I'm not ashamed to say I *like* how it makes my body feel. This one is green tea and something woodsy I can't remember. It's smooth and silky against my skin and does nothing to ease how hard I am right now.

It's not even a choice when my hand wraps firmly around my dick and I pump it once, holding my fist at the head for a few seconds before sliding down to the base and doing it again. It's torture because I want it to be her. I want her legs wrapped around my waist as I drive into her over and over, her tits bouncing as she screams my name.

Fuck.

The rhythm and pressure and the fucking *fantasy* have me on the verge of coming in no time. Pressing my lips together, I swallow the litany of curses that want to escape as I paint the tile with my release.

I shouldn't be surprised that the only orgasm to knock

me on my ass recently is by my own hand to thoughts of being inside my best friend.

That should probably be a red flag, but it has my lips lifting on one side instead. She'd take it as a compliment and undoubtedly razz me about jerking off to her. But honestly, who could blame me?

She's her own yin and yang. The buttoned-up socialite with the fancy hair and designer clothes and the wild, cutoff-shorts goddess that only I got to see. My dick twitches at the way her hair would fall in loose waves around her shoulder, and I have to slam the water to cold to clear my mind.

Cleaning off the shower wall, I finish washing before tipping my head back under the water and taking a steadying breath. Despite my bravado, Ellison coming home has my belly swooping with nerves rather than butterflies.

Sure we're still *us,* but we're also *us* plus ten years. Talkin' on the phone and doing video calls and texting since Nan passed isn't the same as having her here with me. It's not seein' her smile when I make a joke or watching the way her eyelids fall closed on a sigh when she takes a bite of birthday cake ice cream because she was never allowed to have it at home.

We're not kids anymore, and part of me worries that she's romanticized a version of me that doesn't exist anymore. Lovin' her has always been easy, and I know that miles and years have no bearing on that—*but what if she doesn't like the man I've become?*

I'm not the completely carefree kid that ran headfirst into danger and supported each and every one of her reckless ideas. She needed someone to catch her when she fell or when things went south, and I'd been proud to be that guy.

And for the last however many years she'd given that job to some asshat named Blake, who hadn't had a single objection to our rekindled relationship. Something about it didn't sit right with me. He's lucky they're over, and chances are I'll never have to be in the same room as him.

Turning off the water, I dry myself haphazardly before wiping my fist against the mirror to clear the steam.

I need a plan.

And I need a plan before Ellison gets home because I know the moment I see her, every ounce of restraint I possess is gonna fly right out the window, and I can't let that happen. I need her to see the life I've made here.

The life we can make together.

"Montana! Supper!" Celeste's voice cuts through the musings running through my head, but it's just as well. All I need is a good meal and some sleep and everything will be right as rain in the morning.

7

MONTANA

My dreams of a quiet night were dashed about ten minutes before I was ready to excuse myself from the kitchen. I'd cleared the table while Celeste put the left-overs away. She'd huffed at me when I'd taken up the spot in front of the sink, pouring soap onto the sponge and scrubbing the dishes before rinsing them and placing them in the drying rack.

I'd had one foot down the hall when an alert came through on my phone. The motion-activated lights had triggered the camera on one of our unoccupied properties, but the culprit had remained out of sight.

If it was any other house I might have let it go and called the sheriff, but it wasn't just any other house. It's Ellison's childhood home and with her coming in tomorrow, I couldn't let it go. Leaving Grandad at the table, I thanked Celeste for dinner before shoving my feet back in my boots. And thank the Lord I threw on jeans after my shower.

My truck roars to life, "She's So Mean" by Matchbox Twenty blaring through the speakers. I might smile, because it's one of Ellison's favorite songs, if I wasn't so pissed about having to deal with the disturbance at her house.

Killing the lights on my truck, I slam it into park and climb out, closing the door as quietly as I can.

I hear the splashing before I even round the side of the house. There was a time when I'd be the one jumpin' into pools that didn't belong to me for no other reason than I felt like it.

Well, almost no other reason.

I missed those days.

Missed her.

My footsteps are silent as I walk across the grass and unlatch the gate, opening it and my mouth at the same time. "Listen, you gotta get out of here. If you leave willingly, I won't have to call the sheriff. I don't want to be a hard-ass, but this is private property and—"

The burst of feminine laughter has my chest tightening and my dick coming to life as I scan the pool for the source.

Son of a...

"I mean your ass is really hard, but would you *really* call the sheriff on me, Max?"

No. Way.

There's only one person on the planet who calls me Max.

Ellison Fucking Mills.

My lips twitch as my eyes lock on my very sexy and very naked best friend as she treads water in the deep end, thankfully cast in shadows.

"Eddie, where the fuck are your clothes?" I ask even though it's pointless. To this day, no one believed me that the girl in this pool, with her angelic smile and sweet-as-pie personality, was the cause of ninety percent of the trouble I got into growing up.

She looks down at her chest, and I have to work really hard not to do the same. "You've seen my boobs, Max." Her grin is wolfish. "Done a lot more than that if memory serves me correctly."

"You know," I say calmly even as I try and fight a smile, "most people just come over and say *hello* when they haven't seen someone in, like, ten years. You know—knock on the door, offer a casserole..."

"Where's the fun in that?" she asks. "Also you know *damn well* it hasn't been ten years." Taking a mouthful of water, she spits it in my direction.

"Eddie..." I warn but there's no heat behind my words. Not anger at least. Ellison's always made my blood run hotter than apple pie in a truck bed, and aside from takin' each other's virginities on the last night before she left for college, I'd never gotten the chance to touch her.

Not the way I wanted to.

"You could come in—the water is divine. What do you keep it set at?"

"I'm not swimming."

"Why not?" She pouts and I narrow my eyes, because she's baiting me and damn if I don't love it.

"You're naked."

"You afraid I'll see your *penis?*" she mock whispers, and I can't help throwing my head back and laughing.

"I know you've seen my penis."

"It was pretty spectacular. Nice shape—aesthetically pleasing." She points at my dick, her finger making a circle in the air as she talks. "Not all penises are created equally I'll have you know, but luckily, you got a prize-winning member, sir."

"Oh my Lord, would you please stop talking?" I beg as I drag my palms down my face and will myself to calm down.

There's no point trying to hide the fact that she's making me hard—my dick is shameless and she knows it.

It's also easier to ignore the idea that she's seen enough guys naked to rate me against them.

"You used to be a lot harder to fluster, Max."

There it is again—*Max*.

A nickname born from spite instead of adoration. We'd been seven or eight and she was mad I still called her *Eddie*. It hadn't been my intention, but when her family had moved in next to mine—still a country mile away—a couple of years before, I'd been unable to say Ellison. My missing two front teeth had made it impossible to say the l's in her name and so I'd started calling her Eddie.

It stuck, but she hated I'd given her a boy's name and retaliated by changin' mine. It was hardly punishment back then. I knew a pretty girl when I saw one, and Ellison Mills was the prettiest.

Still is.

"I wasn't expecting you till tomorrow. Thought I had time to mentally prepare for your arrival."

She smirks. "It's because I'm so fun, right?"

"Somethin' like that."

"Oh, that reminds me, can I stay with you tonight? My rental isn't ready until tomorrow."

"Because you weren't supposed to be here till tomorrow," I say with my head cocked to the side. I'd checked and rechecked the date like a madman—not that she'd know that.

Technically I could let her in. It was my property after all. Well, Sundown Realty's property but that was semantics.

Hell, I was sure she could stay here at her parents' house, but selfishly, I liked the idea of her stayin' with me tonight. It'd be just like old times except one of us wouldn't have to sneak down the road and into the other's window. We must have done it a hundred times, and I smile at the memory and the fact that we'll be neighbors again.

"You know you never have to ask to stay."

"It's just one of the many things I love about you." She swims closer, biting her lip and turning enough for the porch light to reflect off the tiny diamond stud in her nose. "Know what else I love about you?" she asks as she nears, and my gaze only locks on her tits below the water for a second before I meet her eyes.

Her Cheshire-cat grin is back, but I just shrug because they're really great tits.

And she knows it.

"What's that?" I finally manage.

"You're always willing to give everyone the shirt off your back." Her eyes widen innocently and I know the drill.

Sighing, I reach behind my head and pull my T-shirt off and hold it toward the pool as I look away. "I can't believe you didn't bring clothes."

"I did bring clothes," she sasses back, "but why would I make them wet when I can just wear yours?"

It's hard to argue with that logic.

Especially when water splashes and then falls onto the concrete patio, her wet feet barely making any sound over the blood pounding in my ears. I don't even need to look to imagine how fucking insane her body is as rivulets slide over every delicious line of her.

She plucks the cotton shirt from my outstretched hand, and I'm momentarily relieved. Part of me thought she'd hug me from behind—press her wet, naked breasts to my back just to fuck with me.

I'm such a sucker for this woman, but *God, I missed her.*

"You can look now, scaredy-cat," she taunts, and I roll my eyes as I turn to see her gathering a pile of clothes from the lounger. My shirt is plastered to her, her nipples poking at the fabric, and I groan.

She preens.

"You're gonna give me an ulcer."

"Oh please."

"How'd you know I'd be the one to respond tonight?" I ask, both curious and pissed at the thought of anyone else finding her naked and wet in the pool.

Shrugging, she says, "I didn't. But my dad said that you've responded to some of the on-call issues and I liked my odds." Popping up on her toes, she places a kiss to my cheek, her eyes sincere when she says, "I missed you, Max."

I'm sure this wasn't what her father intended when he shared that little snippet of information. That's a road I definitely don't need to go down tonight. Especially with how all over the place I am seein' Ellison. Grabbing her hand, I twine my fingers with hers as I lead her out the gate. "I missed you too, Eddie."

I missed you every damn day.

The words play on repeat in my mind, but even I know they're better left unsaid.

At least for now.

"Why aren't you stayin' here?" I ask as we walk out to the driveway.

She scrunches up her face like she ate something sour, and I hold up my hands in surrender.

"It's like you don't know me at all," she grumbles, and while it's meant to be teasing, the words are a sucker punch to the gut. She pushes my shoulder, and my skin tingles under the simple touch. "Oh, stop. You know that's not what

I meant. This isn't home; it never has been." She waves up at the monstrosity, and then she adds wistfully, "Besides, I'm hoping Grandad will make me breakfast in the morning."

"Glad to know I rank so high."

"Don't be so dramatic. You know as well as I do that he makes the best breakfast," she says as she shimmies into her cutoff shorts, forgoing her bra and panties and tying my shirt on the side, exposing her flat, tanned stomach.

"That shirt will never be the same," I lament while nodding at the knot that's undeniably gonna stretch out the fabric.

She looks down then back up at me. "Who said you were getting it back?"

So fucking bossy.

Her lips curve up into a sinful little smirk, and I want to back her up against my truck and kiss the hell out of her. She must know what I'm thinkin' because she takes a step toward me, forcing me to take one back.

She's been home for thirty seconds, and it's way too early to let my dick start running this show.

"You leavin' your car here or following me back?" I ask, watching as she pulls a bag from her back seat.

"And miss out on being your passenger princess?" She scoffs and I chuckle as I grab her hand and pull her to the other side of the truck.

Opening the door, I let myself watch her ass as she climbs up onto the running board and swings herself into her seat. I smile, caging her in with my forearms on the roof of the truck and her door as I wait for her to buckle her seatbelt.

"What?" she asks, and it's no doubt because I have a goofy smile splitting my cheeks.

"Just missed you is all."

Reaching out, she pats my cheek, her fingers dancing along the stubble. "I missed you too."

Straightening to my full height so I don't do anything stupid, I clear my throat and go for as casual as I can manage. "Well then, let's get you home before Grandad goes to bed."

8

MONTANA

The short ride back to the farm is anything but quiet. Ellison tells me about her trip and how it made no sense to wait another day to make the drive. I'm not complaining, but my pep talk after my shower really didn't prepare me for tonight.

Her long, tanned legs taunt me from the passenger seat, and all I want to do is rest my palm on her smooth skin and inch my way up to the hot slice of heaven between her thighs.

Kip Moore singin' "Somethin' Bout A Truck" is doing absolutely nothing to stop me from spiraling to things I have no business thinking about tonight when Ellison sighs. My head whips toward her as the truck rocks to a stop.

Her expression is wistful as she stares up at the light-blue farmhouse with the big wraparound porch and rocking chairs moving gently in the night breeze.

"It's just like I remembered," she says softly, and I wonder what she must be feeling. She'd cut herself off from not just me but *this* for so long.

"You ready to go inside?" I ask as I scan the partially

darkened windows. Grandad isn't usually in bed yet, but stranger things have happened.

Like catching Ellison skinny-dipping in her parents' pool.

Oblivious to the visual I've conjured of her soaking wet, she nods and pushes her door open while I reach into the backseat and grab her bag.

Her body is vibrating as she waits for me to meet her on the porch, a smile spread wide across her pretty lips.

"You don't have to knock." I chuckle and she sticks her tongue out at me as I turn the handle and push the door open.

"Oh, it smells so good in here," Ellison whispers as she kicks off her sandals and puts them next to my boots.

"Probably have some leftovers in the fridge."

"Woulda been easier tryin' to sneak in through the window," a low voice says from the direction of the darkened living room. "Y'all used to be much better at it back then."

Ellison startles and then throws her head back and laughs as I drop her bag and turn on the light.

"Hi Grandad," Ellison says from behind me, just wearing my T-shirt and the cutoff shorts she'd put on. But I know her bra and panties are still gloriously—and now awkwardly—absent.

My grandfather eases out of his chair with a grunt and a groan as she practically shoves me out of the way to get to him.

"Hiya doin', Dolly?" he says, his voice tired but still so full of life, the term of endearment he's always reserved for her making my chest squeeze.

"Boy did I miss you," Ellison says as she places a smacking kiss on his cheek then wraps her arms around him. She holds him tight, and I watch as they just stand there in the darkened room. This moment feels big—like she was coming home for *us* and not just herself.

Eddie had only asked me once to go to college with her. I'd declined and not because my grades were poor—they weren't. I could have gone, but my life is here on this land. It's not something most people understand but she did.

"See you still got that damn thing in your nose," Grandad complains, but it's teasing, and she grins as he taps his finger against the diamond stud.

"I just know how much you like it."

"Some things never change," he grumbles but puts his arm around her shoulders and leads her back into the kitchen. "Miss Celeste made cookies this afternoon."

"The thumbprint ones?" I ask as I grab the tea kettle and fill it with water. I'd tried getting one of those electric kettles, but Grandad had pitched a fit so I'd put it in one of the rentals.

"With blackberry jam," he confirms, and I barely suppress the moan that wants to escape.

"Is she in tomorrow?" Ellison asks as she swipes a cookie off the plate and takes a bite. "Oh my gosh, who is this baking angel from heaven?"

Grandad narrows his eyes at me as I pull mugs from the cabinet and shrug. He can be mad all he wants, but he knows she's the only thing keepin' him here full-time.

"My grandson thinks I need a babysitter," he says pointedly, causing Ellison to freeze midbite as her gaze ping-pongs between us.

"Your *grandson* thinks he needs help keepin' you outta trouble," I reply and watch as he meets my gaze and shoves an entire cookie into his mouth. I don't add that I need Celeste to help make sure Grandad takes his pills on time and listens to the doctor more than once in a blue moon.

I am barely keeping myself alive most days, and now I have the added responsibility of keeping Grandad alive too. It's a lot of pressure, but I'm doin' everything I can to make sure he sticks around. My grandfather easily could have passed away after Nan did. They'd been together almost their entire lives, and I wasn't sure he knew how to live without her.

Selfishly, I wasn't ready to let him go, and if suffocating him with love and attention and getting someone to tag team my efforts keeps him here, then so be it.

"I had my hip replaced, boy. Stop makin' it like I'm old and frail."

I snort because the man had been a menace postsurgery, insisting he help milk the cows and that he was fine to tinker around the farm. He smirks and shakes his head, but I'm thankful that it breaks the tension.

"So who is this mystery woman who keeps you boys in line?"

"Celeste Hadley," I say as I pour hot water into each mug. "There were five or six traveling nurses before Celeste, but Grandad chased them off."

He harumphs but doesn't correct me. Celeste had been our last-ditch effort. She'd put him in his place before she'd even sat down and impressed the hell out of both of us.

"That sounds nothing like you, Grandad," Ellison says with doe eyes and the fakest surprised expression you ever saw.

He looks at her with amusement dancing in his dark blue eyes and pats her hand.

"She lives in the cottage," I continue. "When I need to go

anywhere for the farm and whatnot she stays here in the guest room."

Ellison eyes me for a moment before turning her attention to Grandad. "Well, I'm glad you have someone here who loves you enough to fuss over you because these cookies are life-changing." Placing her hand over his, she squeezes it, her voice completely sincere as she says, "Don't break my heart, okay?"

"Of course not, Dolly." Leaning over, he places a kiss on her temple without releasing her hand. "When you're old you get to complain—that's all. Montana works hard so that I can stay on our land. I won't do anything to jeopardize that."

"Good," Ellison says, and I know she's swallowing down just as much emotion as I am. I know he means it but it's nice—reassuring—to know he understands what's at stake if I can't keep him safe here. Accepting the mug of chamomile and lavender tea, she launches into story after story of her kindergartners' shenanigans until we're laughin' so hard we're crying.

How long has it been since I had a night like this?

Not for the first time tonight, this thought has played through my mind. So much of my childhood and teenage years were wrapped up in the gorgeous brunette sitting across from me at this very table. My grandparents had treated her like their own, and while my sisters were out chasing boys and spending days at the lake, Ellison was here with me on the farm.

Grandad had taken great pride in teaching her about the land and the animals. On the days we worked until the sunset, he'd be waiting on the porch with three glass bottles of cola. It was a special treat, and I'll always remember the way that first sip felt when it passed my lips.

It's a memory I haven't thought about in years but one of my favorites.

We talk well into the morning hours, and when Grandad yawns again, I break up our little reunion party and help him to bed. He's lighter—we both are—than we have been in a long time, and it's all because of the girl currently walking toward my room.

The one with long tanned legs, no bra, and wearin' my shirt.

The one about to be platonically sleeping in my bed.

Dammit all to hell.

9

ELLISON

"Did he get settled all right?" I ask as Montana comes into the bedroom and closes the door quietly behind him.

"Yeah, I left a note for Celeste in the morning to let him sleep if he's not up at his usual time."

I bite my lip, suddenly guilty for throwing off his routine. "That's okay with all his medications?"

"Eddie, he's fine," Montana says as he drops his jeans to the floor and pulls on a pair of mesh shorts. "And stop starin' at my ass," he scolds without looking at me.

"Can't be helped."

And I'm not lying.

Montana has always been the absolute man of my dreams with his shaggy hair, shit-eating grin, and the most gorgeous brown eyes I'd ever seen in real life. His body has changed from a boy's to a man's in the years we've been apart, and every part of me has taken notice.

He was everything I'd never been allowed to have, and while we could have dated in secret, it never sat right with me. Montana was someone that deserved to be flaunted around for the world to see.

He'd been severely underestimated his entire life both in mind and spirit, and I loved him with everything I had.

I still do.

But I hadn't been willing to subject him to the kind of scrutiny that would have come from my parents. Not back then. We were kids, and Montana didn't deserve their ignorance, and he didn't deserve to be cut down by them at every turn.

So, I'd made a deal—an olive branch of sorts.

I promised my parents that Montana and I would be *just friends* and in exchange, they would leave him alone. It wasn't a perfect plan, but it was the only way my newly teenaged heart knew how to protect him.

It was also the only secret I ever kept from my best friend, and while I hated it, I couldn't regret it. It had worked and I'd kept him safe—I'd just thought he'd take the leap with me after we'd graduated.

I'd wholeheartedly believed that turning eighteen and having a freshly printed diploma would suddenly erase any and all obstacles.

It didn't.

And Montana hadn't followed me either—hadn't chased after me. It was something that still bothered me. It wasn't that he'd stayed in Blackstone Falls or even that he'd told me long-distance would never work. Montana hadn't been honest with me, but I never knew why. I'd made plenty of mistakes too and we needed to hash it out.

Just not tonight.

Because tonight made me happier than I had been in a long time.

Singing along to "Hell Yeah" by Little Big Town, my car

had barely crossed the county line before my heart had stuttered in my chest in anticipation. I was finally home. And an act of rebellion felt like the perfect way to make it official.

Without a lot of time to think about it, skinny-dipping had been the obvious choice. I'd taken a chance that Montana would be the one to investigate my evening swim, and the look on his face alone had been worth it.

It had been exhilarating.

But not quite as exhilarating as being in his bed—even if it's just to sleep. I've probably riled him up enough for one night, but tomorrow is a brand-new day.

Entranced, I watch as he pulls a shirt over his head, then pout as it covers the tattoos on his perfectly sculpted torso. The man has been shirtless all night; seems ridiculous to put it on now.

"What's the face for?" he asks as he climbs into bed next to me.

"I like you better shirtless." I say the words because they're obvious—but it's only a half answer and Montana knows it. Shrugging one shoulder I add, "I just missed being here. Missed you and Grandad, but it was hard coming back here too." I look up and see confusion marring his handsome face. "I've missed so much, but it was just easier to stay away rather than breaking my heart every time I would've had to leave Blackstone Falls."

Wrapping his big arms around me, Montana pulls us down the bed and maneuvers us until our heads are on the pillows and our legs are tangled together.

Like this.

I missed *this* so much.

"I hated you bein' gone. I understood some of it but not all of it."

We could have been together. You could have come with me. We've wasted so much time.

The words are loud in my head, but it's too late to start that conversation now.

"Not tonight," I whisper, and he holds me tighter, his throat bobbing his only tell to how he really feels.

When I received my acceptance letter to college, I knew before I even asked that Montana would never leave the farm. I just wanted a life with him—a life free from my parents to be with the boy who made my heart beat faster than any trust-fund kid they introduced me to.

I had to believe, deep down, that my parents had my best interests in mind when they paraded me around, but it wasn't easy. So much of my life had been scripted, and the only people who knew the real me were Montana, Grandad, and Nan.

Even his parents and sisters thought I was the quiet, mild-mannered girl who would uphold my societal standing by marrying for power instead of love.

I couldn't blame them—it's what I'd been raised to do.

Montana had been my wild card, and I'd held on to him with a death grip. I'd rebelled at every turn, and Montana had been my fall guy.

And he'd kept me safe.

Kept my secrets.

"Am I still your best friend, Max?" The question is so quiet it can barely be heard over the hum of the air conditioner.

"You'll always be my best friend, Eddie," he says with that knowing smile I remembered he only ever used with me—usually when he was exasperated by something I'd done.

But it had been mine.

Was it still *just mine?*

"Who was your best friend while I was gone?" I press and he chuckles, the sound lighting me up inside.

"Not really how it works."

"What do you mean?"

"It's not like I'm callin' someone up from the minors to play in the big leagues."

"Well, your first problem is thinking you're the big leagues, Montana Greene," I tease and then yelp when he pinches my side, making me squirm against his hard body.

It's a punishment I'll gladly endure.

"Why would I need to replace you when I knew it was just a matter of time until you came back?"

"I just want to make sure I don't have to set anyone straight thinkin' they get what's mine."

"Uh-huh. Who was *your* new best friend?"

"You know I'm not good at that," I say quietly and brace myself for the words that are inevitably coming.

Montana swallows, and I let my eyelids flutter close for the briefest second. "You did have a friend though, right?"

"I had some people I was friendly with," I say on a heavy sigh. "But you know how that world is, Max. I traded one fancy prison for another."

His arms grip me tighter, and I release a shuddery breath because it's over, and I don't want to dwell on the time we've been apart.

"Remember that time we tried to make Grandad a pumpkin pie because it's his favorite?"

Montana's chest rumbles with laughter, his eyes crinkling in the corners as he nods. "We almost nailed that one."

"Almost." I grin. "Except we forgot the salt."

"Actually I think *you* forgot the salt," he says pointedly and I lift one shoulder.

"Semantics."

"Nan swooped in after everyone took that first bite sayin' she must have mixed up the pies when she put them on the counter." We'd seen Nan trying to hide the pie she'd made earlier in the day when we'd declared we'd be tryin' to bake one.

"That woman was a lifesaver, and you know damn well she never forgot to put salt in." On a laugh I add, "But really, how could such a small amount make such a difference?"

"No idea, but to this day I'm a little gun-shy when I see one."

My eyes widen and my mouth curls up on one side before I can stop myself, and Montana notices because before I can blink, his fingers are digging into my sides as a peal of laughter is ripped from my lungs.

"Don't you even think about it," he demands as I squirm in his grasp, and even though I promise not to show up with a bunch of pumpkin pies—it's an empty one. There's no way I'm letting this little nugget of information go to waste.

"Okay!" I giggle breathlessly as he finally relents and rolls onto his back, pulling me with him. Propping my chin on his chest as I pant, I don't miss the way the sheet tents where his cock is more than a little excited to see me. I file that away too and say, "I promise no pumpkin pies."

He sighs but his lips twitch. "I have a better chance of winning the lottery than you not showin' up with five hundred pumpkin pies."

"Guess you should stock up on whipped cream then," I say teasingly but don't miss the way his eyes are absolutely molten in the moonlight. It's just a flash, but I know what I saw, and it's almost cruel that I have to sleep next to this man without having him inside me.

"Time to sleep before you get us in trouble," he says, his voice gruff and delicious to my ears.

"But trouble with you is my favorite kind."

His head shakes the slightest amount as he wraps his arms tighter around me.

"Goodnight, Eddie. Welcome home." He drops a kiss on the top of my head and I settle in, my cheek pressed to his chest and my leg draped over his. I try not to think about the way his big muscular thigh is sandwiched between mine and pressed firmly against my core.

Swallowing down a decade's worth of longing and a healthy dose of lust, I squeeze him tight and whisper, "Night, Max, see you in the morning," before sleep overtakes me.

10

ELLISON

"Y̶ou're lucky you're so cute all curled up in my sheets. Otherwise I'd be makin' you get up to help me this morning." Montana's voice is quiet but I don't miss the humor in it—I can only imagine what I look like right now, but I don't care.

"Just tell me I'm pretty," I say into the mattress. His chuckle, low and gravelly, floats between us like the riff of my favorite song.

"You're always pretty, Eddie."

"Liar," I retort as I stretch and turn to face him in the still darkened room. His sheets smell like wood and sunshine and *him*. It's the kind of smell that I want to bottle up and carry with me forever.

"Swear it," he says, holding up his hands, a smile teasing his lips. "Even that time your mother convinced you to get a spray tan before junior prom, and you didn't listen to the lady and went swimming as soon as you got home."

I snort remembering my mother's look of abject horror when I came out all streaky. "Took me a whole week before I managed to return to my natural skin tone."

We share a secret smile because he knows I did it on purpose. My mother had booked me a date with the son of one of her high society friends. He had grabby hands, and my objections had fallen on deaf ears leading up to the dance.

Montana and I had spent that evening watching a movie at his house while Grandad and Nan fussed over us. Nan made us get dressed up a week later, once I was back to normal, so she could document the occasion. That picture had lived on her fridge for a long time.

Pausing in the doorway, Montana looks back and smiles at me like maybe he's remembering it too. "If you hustle, you might be able to convince Grandad to make you breakfast."

"With bacon?"

"Maybe." He laughs but I'm already trying to untangle myself from the sheets.

"And French toast?"

"I dunno, but I'd hurry..." Montana disappears from the doorway, and I snatch up some clothes from my bag and head into the bathroom to change. I don't have anywhere to be today, and it feels so good.

Splashing some cold water on my face, I can't help but smile at the reflection staring back at me. Her face isn't contoured within an inch of her life, she's not wearing some death-trap spandex, and she definitely doesn't have to report back to her parents about the *connections* she made at some overpriced gala dinner.

She looks *happy*.

To be fair, any woman who got to curl up in Montana Greene's arms would probably look pretty happy. But it's not any woman.

It's me.

A whistle sounds from down the hall again, and I spit

my toothpaste into the sink before checking my reflection once more. Tucking everything into my bag, I make my way into the kitchen and find Grandad at the stove. He points to a cup of coffee without turning to look at me.

"Coffee's there, Dolly."

"How did you know I was here?" I ask as Hermie bulldozes into me the only way a puppy can, his tongue licking at my hand as I scrunch his face and coo sweet nothings.

"Stop givin' him a complex," Grandad grumbles, and I cover Hermie's ears.

"He didn't mean that. You're the goodest boy, aren't you? Yes you are," I say in the most obnoxious baby voice I can manage.

Grandad harrumphs, and I laugh as a gray-haired woman comes into the kitchen, an apron with chickens printed on the red-and-white fabric tied around her waist.

"Let me guess—nothing you're making is on your doctor's recommended meal list," she says with a familiarity that makes my chest ache—because I don't know her.

I missed this part of their lives.

"Oh, good morning, sweetheart. How are you?" Her smile is warm and falls somewhere between Montana's mama and his Nan. "I'm Celeste and I watch over these hellions."

"Hi Celeste," I say, giving her a shy wave. "I'm Ellison." Her eyes widen and she hustles around the table to wrap me in a hug.

"*The* Ellison?" she asks when she pulls away. Her hands rest on my shoulders and she holds me at arm's length as she takes me in before a smile spreads across her kind face.

"Oh Lord, you've seen her picture. You know who the girl is," Grandad bemoans over the bacon sizzling in the pan.

"Just for that, I'm makin' that tofu stir-fry you love so much for dinner. Balance out your attitude that you seem to be serving with breakfast this morning."

My eyes widen and my lips part as I stare at her. Celeste winks as she takes my hand and leads me to the table to sit.

"Now tell me all about yourself," she says as Grandad places a cup of coffee in front of her without a word.

Their dynamic is unexpected—with him being more than a decade her senior—but I sort of love it.

"Oh, umm, Montana and I were best friends growing up, and my parents and I used to live next door. They rent the place now."

"Damn kids were sneaking in and out of their houses a couple times a week," Grandad says as he places two eggs sunny-side up in front of me with grape jelly and buttered toast and three slices of perfectly cooked bacon.

It's stupid but my eyes well with tears because I haven't sat at this table for breakfast in years, yet he remembered. My parents couldn't be bothered to remember my birthday without consulting their calendar, but this man who has always just loved me like his own remembers how I like my eggs. Pushing back from the table, I wipe the tears away and then wrap my arms tight around Grandad's neck.

He still smells like aftershave, and I appreciate the fact that he doesn't tell me *it's just breakfast* because we both know it's not.

"Missed you, kid." I nod against his shoulder as I inhale again just because I can. He squeezes me tight then eases me back toward the table. "Go eat before it gets cold."

Celeste's eyes twinkle as I take my seat and shove a piece of bacon into my mouth. Grandad places a plate in front of her, and she thanks him before he settles in himself with a plate far more reasonable than I expected.

"Is that...fruit?" I ask with my coffee cup halfway to my lips. Celeste smirks and Grandad points his fork at me.

"Mind your business."

I giggle and he hides his amusement by taking a bite of his wheat toast.

"So, Ellison, what's on your agenda today? I'm making a roast for supper"—she eyes Grandad who tries to hide his smile behind his black coffee—"and we'd love to have you join us."

Giving her a watery smile, I nod and then dive into my plans for the day to distract myself from the way my heart squeezes in my chest.

Celeste tells me about her career as a traveling nurse, flying all over the country and the world. She has me near tears recounting some of her more colorful memories, and even Grandad cracks the occasional smile. Her big heart took her all over the place before she literally threw a dart at a map and headed for Blackstone Falls.

The story is almost unbelievable, but as I look at her in this space, I know it's more than just a coincidence that brought her here. Some might call it divine intervention, and I have no doubt Nan pulled some strings to make sure the love of her life was safe.

Cherished.

And maybe even loved.

Looks like I might not be the only one falling in love around here.

ELLISON: Do you know where Sundown Realty is?

ELLISON: Seriously, this town isn't THAT big

> MONTANA: It's a new storefront. I think
> Archer's girl is there

> MONTANA: Hold on I'll send you the
> address

A COUPLE MINUTES later my phone dings with an incoming text, and I pull my car onto the road. It's a short drive, but I still turn "Matchmaker" by Erin Kinsey down because apparently I'm *that years old* now and need it quiet to see better.

Double-checking the address Montana gave me, I turn into the gravel lot in front of a small cottage that's in the midst of getting some upgrades. The dark-stained-wood exterior is decorated with two crisply painted white windows and shutters flanking a maroon farmhouse door. The window boxes are empty, and the front planters have seen better days, but all in all it looks like someone is working hard to make this place shine.

Putting my car in park, I kill the engine and pull my sunglasses on before stepping out into the heat.

"Oh my gosh, are you Ellison Mills?" My head whips up at the sound of a very enthusiastic feminine voice.

"Yes?" I say cautiously as I step around the front of my car.

"Eeeee!" The woman squeals and then lunges at me, wrapping me in a hug and rocking us back and forth. She's covered in dirt, her blonde hair pulled back with a bandanna, and wearing the biggest smile I've ever seen directed at me.

Montana notwithstanding.

I'm speechless. Completely and totally speechless and so much so that I've forgotten my manners. And now we're firmly in the *nervous laugh* portion of this interaction.

Me—not her.

"This is seriously so great. Montana has told me *so* much about you!" She beams as she pulls away, completely unaffected by my internal freak-out. I know her name—Montana told me her name—and yet in this moment I have absolutely no idea what it is.

My mother would be appalled. The thought makes me smile.

"Would you believe I can't for the life of me remember your name?" I ask sheepishly because this hasn't happened before. My life revolved around making other people feel important, and that meant being able to recall names and information about any given person in a room.

"I'm Bea, and I think I can let it slide just this once considering we've never officially met." She grins and I relax just the littlest bit.

"You're an angel," I say and she shakes her head.

"Hardly." She snorts as she turns for the door. "Come on inside. I was just about to take a break anyway."

"Oh, um, okay, I just—" I stutter because I wasn't prepared for this level of social interaction. She's bubbly and adorable, and I kind of want to put her in my pocket.

"It's fine, you'll get used to me," she says with an unaffected flick of her wrist, and I snort, the awkwardness of the moment suddenly gone.

"I can see how this tactic worked on Archer."

"You mean how I just inserted myself into his orbit until he couldn't ignore me?" She grins as she walks over to a small fridge and takes out two sparkling waters. "To be honest, he did a lot of the work. He was shy—no surprise there—but the man sent me poems asking me out until I said yes."

My eyes widen and so does her smile as I process that piece of information. Truthfully, I didn't think he had it in him, but I couldn't be happier that they were able to make it work.

"Impressive."

"Right?" She sighs dreamily as she leans against the wall and takes a sip of her drink. "He's supportive and kind and," —she fans her face—"surprising if you know what I mean."

"It seems like he was just waiting for the perfect girl to come around."

She blushes and tips the can at me. "Thank you for saying that. It's weird being happy, isn't it?"

"I'm hoping to find out," I admit, and her smile turns sympathetic but it's kind and not condescending like I'm used to.

"You will." Her phone beeps and she pulls it out to look at it. "Archer is all about the little things." She taps something out and then puts the device back in her pocket. "Like right now, he's trying to find me goats because he knows how much I want to source local goat milk for my soaps."

"You make soaps?"

"I do. Plus lotions and lip balms. I'm Bea's Bubbles and Balms," she says with a flourish before launching into the details of what she does and how she makes everything before adding, "And while that's *the dream* it's not quite enough yet to do full-time, so for now I'll be the go-between for Sundown Realty."

"Well, that's freaking adorable and also really amazing," I say and I mean it. She's like walking sunshine, and I find that I can't help feeling invested in this woman and her quest for local goat milk here in Tennessee.

"And after all that, Archer doesn't have goats?"

"He doesn't, and unfortunately, we are not able to house them on his property."

"What about at Montana's?"

Bea pulls her bottom lip between her teeth and shakes her head. "Montana was *very* clear that he does not want goats."

"Oh my gosh, he's so dramatic. It was almost twenty years ago," I say, rolling my eyes as I imagine him pitching a fit over even being asked. "Tell Archer that Montana will house the goats, and y'all can just let me know when they're en route so I can have everything ready."

"Are you sure?"

Am I? Not really.

But this is exactly the kind of thing Montana would expect from me, and who am I to disappoint him?

"Totally sure."

"He's going to be pissed, isn't he?" She laughs and I shrug.

"Probably. But we have a special kind of relationship."

"Does it involve being naked?" she deadpans and now it's my turn to laugh.

"Not yet, but maybe if I'm lucky."

Raising her can, she says, "May the goats provide you the excuse to indulge in mutually beneficial apology orgasms."

"I'll cheers to that."

"So, not that I don't love the company but..."

"Oh, right. I just need to grab the keys for the house I'm renting. I got the email confirmation that it was ready but had a really hard time finding this place. I had to ask Montana for the address."

She eyes me for a second, and I have the oddest feeling she's assessing me—I just don't know why. She works here and I need the keys to my rental. It should be pretty straightforward, right?

"Of course." Bea nods and spins on her heels, moving stacks of papers on the desk and growling for a minute before letting out an enthusiastic *whoop* and turning toward me. "Here you go," she singsongs as she hands me an envelope. "That place is the cutest. You're going to love it."

Her smile is so bright and disarming that I hear myself say, "I can't wait."

11

ELLISON

My excitement over my new place lasted exactly three hours before the loneliness set in. I've lived alone most of my adult life, but after one night at Montana's house, I am already homesick. He'd asked if I wanted him to stay my first night here but I'd declined—foolishly. Now I'm on night two, and it doesn't seem to be any better.

I wanted to prove that I could do this. I could move home, rent a house, and not use my best friend as an emotional crutch. Things with Montana had always been complicated, and honestly, I hadn't taken the time to look ahead to the now. I'd been so stuck in the past—on the things that held us back—that I'd never truly thought about what I wanted.

I hadn't allowed myself the freedom to dream. But being here in Blackstone Falls, the possibilities are endless. Unfortunately, I'm going to need some more sleep before I start making forever-and-ever-amen kind of decisions.

Adjusting my pillow again, I roll toward the opposite wall, the clock on the side table taunting me as it continues to count the minutes I can't sleep. Resigned, I admit that while I don't miss the hustle and bustle of Savannah, I'm also not going to reacclimate to the near silence of Blackstone Falls overnight.

Sleeping with Montana had been a dream, and I didn't wake once all night. For all the shit I gave him—and planned to give him—he was everything good and wonderful in my life.

He also seems to be the key to sleep.

Huffing out a groan, I throw the covers back and climb out of bed. I'd done this so many times growing up, but instead of the teenage girl sneaking out of her house, I'm the grown woman casually strolling over to my best friend's house in the middle of the night.

I frown as I throw a sweatshirt on and pack clothes for the morning. At this rate, I'll be living with Montana in no time. The thought makes me smile as I look around the rental that feels nothing like me.

Arguably, I haven't been here long enough to give up on the charming cottage. On the other hand, there's a sexy cowboy sleeping just across the lawn with strong arms and rock-hard abs I want wrapped and pressed against me.

I lock the door and then walk down to my car and climb in. Starting it, I don't bother turning the headlights on. I'm not trying to wake Grandad, and the moon is bright enough I can see just fine on the short drive.

Thinking of Grandad has a smile pulling at my lips. He'd *known*. Montana and I thought we'd gotten away with sneaking back and forth between our houses, but he knew. And that meant that someone else probably knew too.

Turning into their driveway, I park farther from the house than I normally would and grab my bag from the passenger seat before stepping out of the car. Pausing, I close my eyes and listen to the sounds that made up the soundtrack of my childhood. Somehow, standing in front of Montana's house, the quiet doesn't feel as suffocating as it did at the cottage.

Shaking my head, I push the thoughts away. I need *more* sleep—not less—and that kind of runaway train was bound to keep me tossing and turning.

Hot guy or not.

Skirting around the porch, I walk the length of the house until I find Montana's first floor window. This had been his room growing up, but after his parents moved to Florida and he took over the farm, he took over the entire upstairs.

He said he'd moved back down to the first floor after Grandad's surgery, and that kind heart of his had a storm of butterflies taking up residence in my belly. Those flutters might have caused *flutters* elsewhere, and I grin as I pick up a small stone and toss it against the glass.

It clinks quietly so I wait.

And wait.

Annoyed, I grab two more from the ground and toss them in quick succession. This time, muffled cursing can be heard just before Montana pulls open the curtains and yanks up the window.

"You have a key, Ellison," he grunts, causing me to put my hand on my hip with a dose of the dramatic flair he loves.

"Excuse me for bein' sentimental and trying to climb through your window." He stares at me, unblinking and deliciously rumpled. "Oh, don't be like that, Max. I didn't want to wake the dog."

"Go use your key," Montana huffs before closing the window *and* the curtain, leaving me standing outside with my mouth hanging open. A laugh threatens to escape and I press my lips together to keep from waking anyone, animals included, as I walk back to the front door that I do in fact have a key for.

Lucky for me, I don't have to use it because even though he's annoyed at me, my best friend is standing there rubbing sleep from his eyes, wearing nothing but black boxer briefs and a *will you hurry your ass up and get inside* expression.

Sashaying past him, I press a kiss to his cheek and make my way down the hall as he closes and locks the door. His footsteps are heavy on the floor behind me, and my body heats at his proximity and the anticipation of being in his arms.

It doesn't matter how annoyed he is with me. Montana Greene is the God's honest definition of a cuddler. Collapsing face down on the bed, he groans, his voice muffled by the pillow. "For fuck's sake, Eddie, why aren't you in bed?"

"I just need to hang my clothes for tomorrow."

He mumbles something that sounds an awful lot like *I swear to God, woman* which I choose to ignore even if my lips twitch.

But any kind of retort is lost when I turn around and see the man laid out before me. The muscles of his back ripple as his chest rises and falls, his legs thick and strong from years of manual labor—but his *ass* is a thing of perfection.

The only time we'd been naked together had been the night we'd lost our virginities to each other. It had been incredible but it hadn't been *wild.* There'd been an appropriate amount of fumbling and figuring out how to move together to both get off.

I'd been too focused on memorizing every second he had his hands and mouth on me to think about sinking my fingernails into his ass to move him faster—harder. And regretfully, I hadn't appreciated how absolutely bitable it really is.

"Stop staring at my ass and get in bed."

"I missed out all those years ago because you, sir, have an exceptional backside."

"You can look at it all you want tomorrow, but I need to be up in three hours." He picks his head up and squints at me. "Seriously, why aren't you moving?"

I grin and then launch myself onto the bed close enough that he bounces a little. He growls and then turns on his side before pulling me down and locking my back against his front and tucking his massive paw at my hip.

"Isn't this better?" I ask as I snuggle down into the covers and exhale the stress of the day.

"It's great. Can we not start this game at one in the mornin' next time?"

"Promise," I whisper as he buries his face in my hair and relaxes against me. I've always adored his ability to pass out almost instantly while my racing thoughts usually keep me up half the night.

But that's why I'm here. That's why I threw a rock at his window and forced him to get up while the rest of the world sleeps. I've only ever felt safe in his arms, and right now that's all I need.

12

MONTANA

Blackstone Falls or the O.K. Cow-ral?
By Arden James

Earlier this week, neighbors in Blackstone Falls all gathered together to help round up a couple of cows that took a walkabout around town. Several reports stated that a small herd had escaped from the east pasture of Jamison Downey's farm and visited several local establishments in the heart of town. Cow sightings kept the sheriff's department busy as each one was rounded up for their return trip home...

I snort into my coffee as I scroll the article from the *Blackstone Gazette's* newest reporter. The paper had been around longer than Grandad, and while it covered more than just Blackstone Falls, we couldn't help rubbing it in the faces of the surrounding counties that the paper carried our name.

An incoming message scrolls across the top of the screen, and I swipe to answer, knowing my cousin will likely be halfway to a heart attack by now.

.   .   .

ARCHER: A reporter stopped by

MONTANA: Okay…

ARCHER: Looking for contact information on Sundown Realty

MONTANA: I'm not seeing the problem. Do they need a rental?

ARCHER: No, she wants to interview the owners

MONTANA: Just give her the email. We'll respond that we're happy to be part of the community but unfortunately cannot give an interview at this time

ARCHER: Why are you so calm about this?

MONTANA: Why are you so worked up?

MONTANA: If it's Arden James she's been going around to all the local businesses and doing little write-ups. It's not a big deal

ARCHER: But what if she starts poking around?

ARCHER: Something feels off—she looks really familiar

MONTANA: Is she from here? I don't recognize her name other than what I've seen recently

MONTANA: Did you read her article about Jamison's cows gettin' loose?

ARCHER: Yeah, hilarious if I hadn't been there pullin' one of 'em out of Miss June's rose bushes

MONTANA: Sorry I missed it (laughing emoji)

ARCHER: She said she's not from here

MONTANA: Miss June? I'm pretty sure she's never crossed the county line

ARCHER: Not Miss June—Arden James

MONTANA: Did you talk to her?

ARCHER: God, no. Bea was with me.

MONTANA: And what did Bea tell her?

ARCHER: That she would pass Arden's information on to the owners

MONTANA: See? I knew your girl would kick ass for us

ARCHER: So, you're not worried?

MONTANA: Not even a little

ARCHER: Well at least one of us isn't

MONTANA: All about the balance, man

. . .

SPEAKING OF BALANCE, I needed to find some and quick. Ellison had found her way into my bed the last three nights. Hell, in the two weeks she'd been home, it would be easier to count the days she slept at her place than mine. I loved it and I hated it all at the same time.

There'd been no lead-up to it—no discussion about co-sleeping or boundaries—and while we hadn't crossed any lines physically, I'd woken up with my dick hard and nestled against her ass every morning. She'd make a joke and we'd laugh, but the tension was undeniable.

Still, it felt too soon to ask her to jump into something with me right now. We hadn't talked about the end of her relationship with the guy in Savannah or any details about him at all. Ellison didn't seem heartbroken, but the girl also knew how to bottle that shit up like no one else I'd ever met. Not to mention, she was reacclimating to being back in Blackstone Falls and figuring out how to stand on her own without the watchful eye of her parents. I knew better than most the pressure she'd had to endure growing up, but I hadn't been privy to most of her life once she left for college.

And especially not after what happened.

Pocketing my phone, I take off for the barn. I know Ellison is around here somewhere, and it's as good a place as any to start. My boots are quiet as I move across the packed dirt on autopilot. I've made this trip a thousand times in my life already, and no doubt I'll make it a few thousand more. It's familiar, and right now I need it to help settle my soul.

I have a list a mile long of things I need to get done before it's harvest time for the cotton. We've been slowly moving toward all-natural pesticides and antifungal applications in the last few years, and the results have already been substantial. It is too soon to tell what the weather will bring us in the next couple of months, but if the projections are correct, we'll be looking at our best yield in at least five years.

It's a big deal, and I need to be focused on every single piece to make sure it all goes as planned.

My thoughts are interrupted by a soft voice as it filters out through the barn, and I slow my steps as I approach so I don't startle her.

"You're such a sweet girl, aren't you," Ellison coos at Sadie. The rich brown coat of the Tennessee Walking Horse looks darker in her stall, but her face is sweet and her eyes are kind. She's always been one of my favorites—Ellison's too—and she's been with us a long time.

"She missed you," I say as the horse pushes her snout into Ellison's hand, and I watch as the stress drains from her shoulders as they reconnect like old friends.

"Do you think she remembers me?" she asks quietly and nothing like the bold and brave woman I know.

"It's not even a question, Eddie."

As if confirming my statement, Sadie nudges Ellison's hand again, and she smiles as she presses her forehead against the horse's. It's sweet and powerful and I can't help but feel like I'm interrupting.

"Can I take her out?" Ellison asks as I turn to exit the barn.

"Of course. I can grab Marist and we'll head over and check out the fields. I need to go have a look anyway."

"Sounds great," she says with a smile that lights me up from the inside out.

We work in silence, each getting our respective horses saddled up and ready to ride. Marist is excited, his black coat shining in the sun as I lead him out of the barn. He's younger than Sadie, but unlike our sweet girl, Marist is a rescue we took in a few years ago.

"Ready?" I ask as Ellison comes up on the side of me looking like a dream on the back of Sadie.

"Oh, my goodness, such a handsome boy!" She coos the words at Marist, and even though it's obvious, I can't help myself.

"Thank you."

"Uh-huh." I'm surprised she stays upright with how hard she rolls her eyes. "Let's go, Max, my girl wants to run."

"Then lead the way."

13

ELLISON

My phone rings with the theme song for Cruella DeVil and I cringe just like every person in the movie when the villain comes on screen. Every cell in my body begs me to ignore it, but if I do, it will only be worse when she calls back.

I don't need worse, so I swipe accept and press the speaker button.

"Hello, Mother."

"For a moment there I thought you were going to make me leave a message." She sniffs and I roll my eyes. Sheri Ann Mills might live by the rule *the higher the hair the closer to Jesus,* but there isn't much holy about my mother.

"I was in the other room and heard it ring," I lie easily, knowing she doesn't believe me for a second.

"I still don't know why you didn't stay at the house. It's ridiculous to stay in something so...menial when you can stay at home."

My childhood home itself is stunning, but it's beautiful in the way a magazine spread makes a house look and not because it's warm and inviting. It has been through extensive renovations over the years, wiping away any traces of simpler or happier times.

"I don't need all that space. Besides, the cottage is closer to the school."

"And that boy."

My fist tightens around my water bottle as I try one of those deep breathing exercises I learned when I went to those three yoga classes back in Savannah. It's no use, and my good mood from the night before starts to wane.

"Montana isn't a boy, Mother, and he's *still* my best friend. I don't know why you dislike him so much, but we're not kids, and if you don't have anything nice to say about him you can keep it to yourself."

She huffs indignantly like we've never had this conversation before.

"Well, let me know when you're free, and I'll make a reservation for you and Dustin at the country club."

"Did you not hear me before I left Savannah?" I say, my voice rising with every word. "I will *never* go out with him. I don't care that you think it was a misunderstanding. He tried to put his hand up my skirt after I told him to stop. He deserved more than a punch to the face."

"You broke his *nose*, Ellison." She breathes disapprovingly like I was the one who'd gone too far.

It's probably a good thing she can't see the smile spread wide across my lips right now. Montana had wanted to murder Dustin, but once I wrestled his keys from his hands and told him how I'd thrown a punch just like he'd shown me, Montana had settled down.

"And he deserved so much more."

My mother is silent, and I have to pull the phone away to make sure the call hasn't dropped because this is a first.

"Then I'm sure I can find someone more suitable for dinner."

"No, no dinner. No lunches, no trips to the country club, Mother. I am happy not fitting into your world, so please stop forcing me into it." My phone buzzes with an incoming text and it could be one of those scam "your package couldn't be delivered" things, but it doesn't matter because I'm latching onto it like my life depends on it. "Oh I'm getting another call. We'll talk soon; tell Dad I said hi!"

I click the end button before she has a chance to respond and don't feel the least bit bad about it. I played their game for too long, and I'd lost so much of myself. I wouldn't let it happen again.

Blowing out a breath, I look down at the screen and smile at the one good thing I left back in Savannah.

BLAKE: Did you make it home all right?

ELLISON: Yes, and all settled in. How are things back in Savannah?

BLAKE: I have the flu

ELLISON: Oh gosh, I'm so sorry. I hope you feel better!

BLAKE: I don't have the flu. I'm just telling my mother that so she stops trying to set me up on dinner dates with her friends' daughters

BLAKE: I even called in a favor and got a doctor's note and took off a few days from work

ELLISON: That's a hell of a cover-up. You know you can't keep that up forever.

BLAKE: I don't need it to last forever—just like ten or fifteen years

ELLISON: I just told my mother off

BLAKE: (head explosion emoji)

BLAKE: How did that go?

ELLISON: About as effective as you'd expect.

BLAKE: So not very

ELLISON: Correct. She tried to set up dinner at the club with Dustin

BLAKE: The guy you punched in the face?

ELLISON: One and the same

BLAKE: Well I hope she respects your boundaries

ELLISON: We both know the odds of that are as likely as your fifteen-year flu

BLAKE: It would be a medical miracle

I SNORT and type out a goodbye message before tossing my phone onto the counter. Blake Reynolds might be the only real friend I made in Savannah, although our friendship was born out of necessity rather than anything else.

We'd met my senior year of college, bonding over our mutual disdain for overpriced dinners and pompous assholes who thought they walked on water. Our parents had been thrilled at our apparent fondness for each other, pushing us together whenever they could.

He'd been pining over a girl he couldn't be with, and I'd been harboring the hope that Montana would come to Savannah like a knight in shining armor and whisk me back to Blackstone Falls. It hadn't happened, and Blake and I seemed to be at an impasse in our lives romantically, so the solution seemed obvious, at least to me.

After one too many drinks at a fundraiser, I asked Blake to be my stand-in boyfriend. He laughed. I hadn't.

And the more we talked about it, both drunk and sober, the more it started to make sense to him too.

In the beginning, we tried to see if we could do it for real —if we had enough chemistry to make an actual life together—but it just wasn't there. We were friends with sometimes benefits who then had to dodge questions about marriage and children and a million other things we didn't have answers to. It wasn't a perfect setup, but it worked, and I think Blake thought it was a charade we could keep going forever.

But after I came back to Blackstone Falls for Nan's funeral, I knew my time in Savannah was limited—and Blake did too.

He hadn't talked me out of it or made me feel guilty for needing to leave. He was perfect in every way men in that world weren't.

He just wasn't meant for me.

Five minutes back in my hometown and I knew my

heart would only ever beat for one man. A tall man with dark hair and brown eyes, who saw every one of my imperfections and loved me harder because of them.

And while I want to hurdle over any and all reservations and obstacles, I know I still need some time to come to grips with this new chapter in my life—find some balance maybe.

And besides, if years couldn't lessen this pull toward Montana then nothing would.

14

MONTANA

"Sold" by John Michael Montgomery plays from the speaker of Ellison's phone beside her on the lounger of her parents' pool. Her pretty face is pointed toward the sun, and even though sunglasses cover her eyes, the quirk of her lips is enough to tell me she remembers this song as well as I do.

Growing up, I'd thought that song was all I needed to know about wooing a girl, and I practiced my slick dance moves on Ellison. She'd rolled her eyes and told me I was bein' ridiculous, but really she was mad the girl in the song had blonde hair and hers was a rich dark brown.

She hasn't spotted me yet and I make up my mind on the spot—kicking my shoes off and dropping my keys and phone softly in the grass. Ellison's head lolls to the side, and her smile widens as I join in on the next chorus, shimmying and reviving some of the rusty dance moves I'd retired in our youth.

Ellison laughs, her breasts bouncing in the hot-pink bikini top, and I can barely focus with the way her sun-kissed legs look with one knee bent and the other stretched out toward me. She's hot as hell, and just because I know she'll love it, I change the words to brown hair, brown eyes and really belt it out.

She claps along, whistling and catcalling me before falling sideways in a fit of giggles in the lounge chair.

"What do you think? Did I live up to the original?"

"I mean," she says when she's gained some composure, "it's hard to match perfection, but your enthusiasm is noted."

I snort as she swipes at the corners of her eyes. Offering her my hand, I pray she's too distracted to see through my intentions. When her soft palm slides against mine, I don't wait. Rushing forward, I use her momentum and drop my shoulder, hoisting her up and off the lounger before she can react.

Ellison squeals and latches on to me like a spider monkey, her hands grabbing at me as I take two steps toward the pool and launch us into the deep end.

She lets out a colorful string of curses before we hit the cool water, both of us weightless for a split second before going under. I love the initial drop below the surface, the displacement of water that leaves you suspended before forcing you up again. Bubbles surround us, and I grunt as Ellison's foot not so accidentally makes contact with my stomach, but it's so worth it.

I'm just about to tell her that, but instead of sucking in a lung full of air when I surface, I suck in the wave she splashes at me. Coughing and sputtering, I can't help but laugh, the denim of my jeans plastered to my legs and no longer as fun as when I first had this idea.

"Really proud of yourself, aren't you, Max?" Ellison asks, her dark ponytail stuck to the side of her head.

"A little."

"Well good, because my sunglasses are currently in a relationship with Davy Jones's Locker." I follow her gaze, shamelessly taking a perusal of her body in the water before locating said item gently swaying along the bottom.

"Don't worry, Eddie, I'll—"

"Oh no," she says, her expression mischievous as we both tread water, "lose the shirt and pants, good sir." She points at the diving board and I roll my lips inward. "And make it good, because you know how much I like to judge your *technique.*"

I try not to react to the suggestive lilt she puts on the word technique, but it's impossible as I pull myself out of the pool and strip out of my shirt. The fabric lands in a wet *plop* on the patio next to me, making Ellison pump her fist in the air while yelling *take it off* and other things that have heat creeping up my neck.

My jeans are heavy and rough against my skin, and the friction as I push them over my dick has me swallowing a groan and then a chuckle as Ellison motions for me to turn around—the girl is really after the full show today.

And dammit if I don't want to give it to her.

"You getting a commission for wearing those boxer briefs?"

"Shut up, Eddie," I say on a laugh as I toss my jeans and socks next to my shirt before stalking toward the diving board. This is a game we've played a hundred times before —minus the sexual tension and innuendos of course. My need to constantly try and impress Ellison was only matched by her drive to make sure she could nail every trick, jump, and flip I did too.

Girl always did know how to keep me humble.

"Let's see it! Double backflip with a triple tuck!" she yells like she has any idea what that would actually look like, but

I nod seriously before stepping onto the board and blowing out a breath. Locating the glasses at the bottom, I lock eyes with Ellison before jumping on the end of the board.

She throws her head back and laughs the minute I tuck my arms around my legs, cannonballing into the water. It's the last thing I hear as I break the surface of the water, and this time, I let myself drop as far as I can before kicking my legs and swimming down. My fingers wrap around one of the lenses, and it's enough of a hold for me to shift toward Ellison before kicking up like a rocket. I emerge from the water like a breaching whale and she yelps, no doubt in surprise, before clapping and cheering.

"Bravo!"

It's ridiculous.

Childish.

But it's the most fun I've had in a long time and that's saying something.

"Your protective eyewear, ma'am," I say as I gently place her sunglasses on her gorgeous face.

"Why thank you," she replies, and even through the darkened lens I can feel the heat in her gaze, and it no doubt mirrors my own. The urge to reach out and pull her body against mine is almost unbearable, but we have plans.

Because of course we do.

"We need to, uh…" I start and then have to clear my throat when she reaches out and her calf brushes against my thigh. Fuck. "We need to dry off and head over to Mason's for game night."

"Game night," she deadpans before pushing her sunglasses onto the top of her head and narrowing her eyes at me. "You're serious."

"Yeah, and he's really excited."

"Okay, well, I can just see you when you come home."

"Nope, you're coming."

"What? Why? I don't even know him."

"I've told you about Mason and his brother, Bodhi."

"Foster brothers, right?"

I nod. "Came down here and have been working for Case and Otto Thayer doing landscaping..."

"That's all great but it doesn't explain why I have to go." She pouts and it's as frustrating as it is adorable.

Worrying my bottom lip with my teeth, I try and figure out how to accurately describe Mason but then shrug and go with, "You'll understand when you meet him. Guy is... hard to say no to."

"That's never been a problem for me."

Tell me about it.

I swallow the words and swim to the side of the pool, wiggling my ass for her benefit before pulling myself onto the patio.

"Let's go, Eddie, the guys want to see you."

Her steps falter as she grabs the towel she left lying on the lounger, her head whipping to me so fast that water droplets fan out in an arc off her hair.

"Guys? As in plural?"

"What? Yeah, for game night. Mason and Bodhi live together so..."

"You're not sellin' this, Max."

Rolling my eyes, I grab my wet clothes off the ground and hold them in my fist, already resigned to the fact that I'm driving home in my boxers.

Wouldn't be the first time.

Won't be the last.

"It's not a big deal. It's Archer and Bea—you met her already—Jensen and then Mason and Bodhi."

"Oooh, the sheriff, huh?"

"Hey now," I start with my hands on my hips, but she just giggles and shakes her head.

"Fine, I'll go to your game night but don't expect me to have fun." My lips twitch but I nod solemnly.

"Course not."

"Well, let's go so I can shower and get dressed." She motions down her still damp body. "Someone threw me in the pool, and I don't want to be *wet* for game night."

Making no effort to hide her perusal of my body, Ellison grabs her things and then saunters out the side gate, leaving me to catch up in a hurry.

Whistling, I take my time because Ellison Mills is a hell of a view.

15

ELLISON

Montana can't stop lookin' at me as we take the ATV back through the fields to the house Mason and Bodhi are renting, and it's got nothing to do with the fact he thinks I look pretty tonight.

Which he already told me.

No, this is because he knows I'm nervous. Because despite my upbringing and my practiced bravado, I really hate social gatherings and meeting new people. Events of any kind have me donning my mask before I even step foot through the door.

It's engrained.

Reaching over, Montana takes my hand and squeezes. "It's not like that, Eddie."

I'm sure he's right, but a part of me imagined we'd just live in this little bubble, and we'd never have to socialize with anyone but each other and one or two others here and there.

The idea is completely unrealistic, but it didn't stop me from wishing it were true. Growing up in Blackstone Falls, I didn't fit in. People mistook my standoffish demeanor for being stuck-up or prudish when it couldn't be further from the truth. I desperately wanted friends who didn't care about my net worth or how I could help advance them to the next level using my family's connections.

It was lonely—so damn lonely—and after a while I was thankful that the invitations stopped. I hated pretending, but people here just didn't understand what my childhood was like.

What my life was like.

But not anymore.

I squeeze Montana's hand back, acknowledging that I did hear him even if it sent me spiraling. But tonight, for him, I need to try. He missed out on a lot growing up too, and I selfishly loved that he picked me over the field parties and tractor pulls down by the lake. Sure, he dragged me out sometimes, but Montana was the guy all the guys wanted to be and all the girls wanted to be with.

But for some reason he traded all of that for me.

Parking outside the cabin, I can't help the smile that crosses my face. Montana's mama had paid us twenty bucks to clean this place when some of their family surprised them from out of town and needed the cabin in a hurry. It wasn't anything crazy—just changing the linens, mopping the floors, and cleaning the bathrooms—but Mrs. Greene had been so thankful, and I'd been filled with a sort of pride I'd never experienced.

I'd *earned* my share of the money and it felt *good.*

My own mother had been properly horrified when I'd come home proud as a peacock to tell her what I'd done. My father had come to my rescue, mollifying her before pulling me aside and explaining that, like our special father-daughter dates at Boots On Bar and Grill, some things are better left unsaid.

"You ready?" Montana asks, startling me from the memory and bringing me back to the present.

"Sure I can't convince you to go home?" I ask, biting my bottom lip and giving him a wide-eyed expression. "I'll even show you my boobs," I add for good measure.

His eyes drop to my chest as his mouth opens and closes before his gaze returns to mine. Turning, he jumps out of the ATV, a slew of curses leaving his kissable lips before he ducks his head and glares at me. "You got me all riled up. Now let's go."

"I could take care of that for you back at the—"

"Out!" he barks, and I chuckle as I grab the tote at my feet that holds the buffalo chicken dip and crackers I whipped together. Montana said it was overkill, but it'd be a cold day in hell that I'd show up empty-handed.

The outside of the house is worn but tidy, the lap siding enduring years of Tennessee summers and just as many winters. Bright flowers line the window boxes, and a doormat sits perfectly in line with the dark blue door.

We're halfway to the porch when said door flies open, revealing a guy much younger than Montana and me. His shaggy brown hair peeks out of his backward baseball hat, but I can't get over how wide his smile is.

"You guys are the first ones here. Is this her? Oh man, this is so exciting." He says everything without taking a breath before he's bounding down the steps and wrapping me in a hug.

"Oh...um..." My eyes meet Montana's and he shrugs, a smile playing on his lips.

"Sorry, sorry should have asked first," the guy says, releasing me from the embrace. "I should probably be used to that considering my brother is one grumpy SOB, but the Thayers are huggers. They're over in Clementine Creek, but

I'm sure you know that. I forget where I am sometimes. I'm Mason by the way. Can I take that bag from you?"

I gape at him, my mouth opening and closing not unlike Montana's had moments ago, but this time for an entirely different reason.

"Sure," I say finally as my brain works through the menagerie of things I haven't fully processed yet and relinquish the dip to our host.

"Mason, this is my best friend, Ellison. Ellison, this is Mason Amato. I told you that he and his brother run a crew for Case and Otto Thayer at Twinscapes doing landscaping."

Mason beams with pride, and my heart warms at the sight. It's the way he stands straighter and his shoulders roll back the slightest bit that tells me he's proud but humble. Hardworking. I may not know him but I've spent my whole life reading people, and Mason Amato is one of the good ones.

"It's really nice to meet you."

Mason takes my hand, his boyish smile back in place. "You too. Now come on, I'll introduce you to my brother." Climbing the porch steps, Mason leads us inside, placing my bag on the counter before motioning around the space. "Make yourselves at home."

The formerly dark walls have been painted lighter shades of tan and light green for the living room and kitchen respectively. It's clean and lived in but not quite a home. There are few personal touches outside of the ones Montana's mama would have added—decorative pillows and a soft blanket on the couch and white plates with ornate blue designs displayed above the kitchen cabinets.

It's the home of a person detached from the space.

It's exactly how my apartment was in Savannah. I'd been

there for several years but my heart and my home had been here in Blackstone Falls, and I never felt the need to make that apartment *my own.*

I'm just about to ask Mason how long they'd been here when a guy emerges from the hallway, his piercing dark eyes jumping from Montana to me in a flash.

"Bodhi, this is Ellison," Mason says with a smile, and I offer one of my own.

"It's nice to meet you." He nods, his blond hair cut neatly on his head. He's bigger than Mason, a little older it seems, and not nearly as friendly.

"Don't worry," Mason says conspiratorially. "He'll warm up to you, then he's just a big teddy bear." Bodhi grunts and mumbles something I can't hear as Montana snickers beside me.

"Sorry we're late," Bea says as she bursts through the screen door, Archer blushing furiously on her heels.

"No, you're not," Montana says with a wink but Bea just shrugs, completely unaffected by the implication.

"You still beat Jensen," Mason adds helpfully as he passes out drinks and plates as Bodhi pulls a couple of boxes of pizza and wings from the counter and places them on the kitchen table.

"Who beat me?" Jensen Kade asks as he steps inside with a box of something from The Poppy Seed, the bakery in Clementine Creek.

"Everyone," Mason says with a chuckle, but I'm a little in awe of the way Jensen grew up. He is a few years older than I am, and I haven't seen him much—or at all—since leaving here almost a decade ago.

"You're drooling," Montana whispers, my head whipping toward him because *no I most certainly am not* but I touch my hand to my lips all the same just to be sure. My best friend laughs and I want to be mad but I can't because *wow*.

"Hey, Ellison, welcome home," he says with a smile and a nod.

"Thanks, it's good to be back," I say, finally having found my manners. The guy who had always been good-looking grew up *hot* with a chiseled jawline, stunning cerulean eyes, and a dimple that is too much to take. Not to mention the way his muscles test the integrity of his shirt, leading me to believe he makes that sheriff's uniform look damn good.

I must still be staring because in the next second, Montana's palm is sliding down my back, and he's not shy about the way he grabs a handful of my ass.

"Watch it," he murmurs just low enough for me to hear, and the thrill of excitement that shoots up my spine has me blinking up at him as my lips part the slightest bit.

"Or what, Max? Are you jealous?" My words are a whisper, but his hand grips me tighter, tension and desire radiating between us like some kind of force field. All I want is to push myself flush against his body and see how long it takes him to snap.

His eyes are blazing, the flecks of gold in them utterly molten as he stares down at me. "You'd like that, wouldn't you?"

My retort is on the tip of my tongue as I squeeze my thighs together because *gah this is so freaking hot* when Mason's chuckle sounds around us.

"Everyone grab some food before the games start, and uh, there's an open bedroom back there if you guys need to sort yourselves out."

Laughter erupts around us as I try to pull back from Montana, my face heating at practically trying to dry hump him in the middle of this party.

But he doesn't let me go.

Instead, he stares into my soul, the promise of *more* plain in his gaze and *oh my, yes please.*

"All right, Casanova, Imma steal your girl before you guys accidentally burn this place to the ground with all those fuck-me vibes about to ignite," Bea says as she, quite literally, wedges herself between us with a saccharine smile at Montana and a wink at me.

Properly chastised, he steps back with a shake of his head like he's trying to right himself after realizing the room had been spinning.

"I need a drink," I tell Bea, and she snorts as she leads me toward the fridge.

"Dang girl, after that little show I need a cigarette and I don't even smoke!"

You and me both.

16

MONTANA

The evening is substantially less eventful after Bea steals Ellison from me for what I can only assume is girl talk. They giggle and whisper, talking animatedly as I continue to sneak glances at the girl who shouldn't have me completely in knots but does anyway. The guys don't try to hide their amusement at me becoming completely unhinged at my best friend ogling Jensen. Even Bodhi snickers at my expense, and the guy barely reacts to anything.

But I'd lost any sort of reason as I'd watched her stare at him. Hell, I'm man enough to admit that our resident law enforcement officer is good-looking with his big muscles and movie-star appeal. Still, I wasn't this guy. If the Lord above had been standing in the kitchen with us, I would have only been able to see Ellison. She'd been right to call me out for being jealous because *jealous* was an understatement.

Mason had jokingly offered a bedroom for us to "*sort yourselves out*" and had my feet not been rooted to the floor I would have hauled her over my shoulder, stalked down the hall, and fucked her into the mattress until she promised never to look at the sheriff like that again.

"You're up, Montana," Archer says, motioning to the few remaining numbers in the muffin tins on the counter and handing me a Ping-Pong ball. So far, the prizes tonight had ranged from cash to candy, nips of alcohol, glasses with the nose and mustache on them, and a dozen other ridiculous things.

It had started after Mason had watched a couple of family challenge videos like this on social media and thought it looked like fun. The guy was impossible to say no to, and honestly, there was no reason we couldn't humor him with a monthly game night.

And really, it was so much more than that.

Mason and Bodhi had settled more into Blackstone Falls over the couple of years they'd been here. But while Bodhi always seemed ready to bolt with one foot out the door, Mason was trying like hell to belong in our small town. He wanted permanence—stability—and I'd do anything to help him. Plus I liked hanging out with these guys.

And Bea.

And now, Ellison.

She'd been tentative at first, but after a couple of rounds, she'd joined in with the trash talking and storytelling. She fit here, and aside from me wanting to bury myself inside her until this manic feeling subsided, I liked her in this space.

"Quit stalling and take your shot, old man," Mason heckles from across the counter, and I snicker as I line up my shot and send the ball bouncing down the granite countertop.

I fist pump when it lands in the one labeled 13 and saunter to the table to claim my prize, snatching up the matching cup. "Old man, my ass," I gloat as I snap the five-dollar bill between my fingers for everyone to see.

There's only a handful of numbers left, but they're spread out between the two muffin tins, and the more Jensen continues landing in the empty spaces, the more colorful his cursing becomes. Guy might be in charge of keeping the peace around here, but he's off duty and all bets are off at this point.

Bea nails her next turn and the one after that too, earning her a not-so-sweet kiss from Archer and a bunch of hoots and hollers from the rest of us. Jensen misses every shot, and the game is finally put to rest when Ellison and Bodhi land the last two numbers.

"Game was rigged," Jensen grumbles, and it has Mason's normal smile growing impossibly wider.

"Oh, come on, Sheriff. You had fun," Bea says with a wink as she wraps her arms around Archer's waist. She rests her head on his sternum, because that's as high as she reaches, but I don't miss the way his arm automatically goes around her, pulling her tight against him. It's not that I'd never noticed their small displays of affection, but somehow with Ellison in the room, I'm more aware of the possibility I could have that too.

That I want that.

That I've never wanted anything as badly as to be able to claim Ellison in a crowded room and not just because I lost my shit earlier over her looking at Jensen.

I want her to be mine and I want to be hers and I want every damn thing that goes along with it.

I just need to figure out how to do it.

The round of goodbyes takes forever even though it's probably no different than normal. I can't even appreciate how well tonight went because all I can think about is the way I need her pressed against me, her body hot and needy and begging for *me.*

"You all right, Max?" she asks as we make our way down the porch steps and toward the ATV, but all I can do is nod because if I open my mouth, I'm going to say something I can't take back like *I want to fuck you until you only ever think of me.*

I'd like to think I'm more of a gentleman than that, but dammit, right now I don't want to be.

Ellison slides onto the bench seat next to me, and I have to look away as her dress rides up her tanned thighs. My hands grip the steering wheel, the leather creaking at the force of my grip, and I don't have to see her face to know that her eyes are wide and her kissable fucking lips are parted.

She may think she knows what she's doing, but she has no fucking clue. Hell, most of the time I don't have a clue. But right now, as we drive back to the house with only the sounds of the Tennessee night around us, I know exactly what I want.

And I don't want to wait.

The barn casts a shadow over us, and as soon as I've thrown the ATV in park, my hand is around the back of her neck, pulling her toward me. My lips crash against hers, and Ellison doesn't even hesitate for a second before she's pushing her tongue into my mouth and her breasts are pressed against me.

"I hated seein' you look at him like that," I growl and turn my body so more of me is touching more of her. But it's not enough.

"Like what?" she huffs as she manages to wedge herself between my chest and the steering wheel as she straddles my lap.

"Like you wanted him," I grit out as she rocks her hips against me, and I move my hands up to cup her breasts. They're fuller than when we were eighteen, and I have half a mind to rip the dress apart just to see them spill out into the moonlight.

"You should see how I look at you." She moans the words as my fingers tweak and pull at her nipples, fondling her as she gasps and writhes against me. *You should see how I look at you.* I have no idea what to do with that, but right now all that matters is her.

"Right now I want to see how you look coming all over my fingers."

"Do it." The words are a command as her teeth nip at my earlobe. My groan is low and pained as I maneuver us until I'm standing and she's spread out on the bench seat. The hood would be preferable, but it's too damn hot after racing back here.

She leans back on her elbows, and I want to strip her down and fuck her senseless right here and then take her inside and do it again. But for now, I settle for dragging her panties down her legs and shoving them into the pocket of my jeans and pushing the hem of her dress all the way up until she's completely exposed to me.

I stare at her, completely transfixed by the absolute beauty before me.

"Montana, please." Her plea has my gaze snapping to hers, her chest heaving and her lips parted, but it's the way she said my name—my real name—that has my mouth crashing against hers as I tease my thumb against her clit.

Ellison gasps into my mouth and I kiss her harder, one hand braced on the seat next to her and the other between her legs as her hands fist in my hair. I slip one finger inside her and then another, her back arching into me in the most spectacular way as she bucks her hips, desperate for release.

"I need more," she pants as I kiss down her neck and over the valley of her breasts before crooking my fingers and sucking her nipple through the fabric of her dress. She screams my name, the sound echoing in the otherwise quiet night, and I can't help but chuckle as she pulses and flutters around me.

She's beautiful like this—flushed and sated in the moonlight and well on her way to bein' mine.

"God, I needed that," she says as she sits up and reaches for my belt buckle, "and now I need—"

My cell phone rings in my back pocket, the sound shrill compared to the seductive lilt of Ellison's voice, but I know who's calling—it's the only ringtone that's different because it has to be. My hand wraps around her wrist as I pull the device out. "What's wrong?"

17

ELLISON

"We have to go," is the only thing Montana says after hanging up the phone and reaching for my hand.

I could hear Celeste's panicked voice over the line, and instead of me screaming Montana's name as he made me come harder than I ever have in my life, sirens fill the air as we race across the lawn to the house.

My panties are still in his pocket, my thighs slick with my release, but it doesn't matter. The only thing that matters is getting to Grandad.

He promised me.

The ambulance pulls up before we reach the house, two guys I recognize from town jumping out and racing up the porch just as we're rounding the corner. My heart drops to the floor as we burst into the living room.

One of the guys is talking to Grandad and Celeste as the other hustles back outside to grab the stretcher. Grandad looks pale, and for the first time in a long time he just… complies. He accepts the oxygen mask and doesn't argue as Celeste describes the last couple of hours. He's loaded onto the stretcher, and Montana squeezes my hand harder.

Guilt settles in my stomach like a lead balloon. While Montana and I had been playing games and fooling around, Grandad had been in trouble. He'd needed us and we weren't here.

Is this my fault? If Montana had been home, he would have gotten help faster.

I see Montana's head nod slowly in my periphery, but I can't make out the words that Celeste is saying.

"Hey, are y'all ready to head to the hospital?" Jensen says as he walks in through the open door. "I already called Mason and Bodhi. They'll stay here and watch the dog. Can you drive?" He directs the question at Montana who nods, and maybe it's because his presence is so imposing or that subconsciously I can recognize that he's not just standing here as Montana's friend but as Sheriff Kade, but it's enough to bring me back to the present.

"You're here. How did you—" My voice is raspy, and I'm not entirely sure I'm making sense.

"Heard the call come in on the radio and was in my car before the transmission was even finished." His smile is reassuring like he has everything under control, and maybe he does; I just know I'm relieved to see him.

"You wanna change?" Montana asks and I nod, thankful for a minute to gather myself. I push up on my toes and kiss his cheek before racing toward the bedroom.

I don't even bother closing the door before my dress is in a pile on the floor and I'm pulling on panties, jeans, and a T-shirt and grabbing one of Montana's flannels. I know the hospital will be cold, but I throw my hair into a messy bun anyway and hustle back to the living room. No one has moved, and I thread my fingers with Montana's like I'm the one holding him up and not the other way around.

Pressing a kiss to my forehead, he leads me out behind

Celeste and Jensen, helping me into the truck before we take off for the hospital. It's silent except for the low hum of "This Heart" by Corey Kent mixed with the sound of the tires on the asphalt.

I want to say something but *he's gonna be fine* feels empty when I don't know if he is. I don't know what's wrong and I don't know how to fix it; I just know I'd give anything to make him okay.

"He's going to be fine," Montana says quietly but firmly as we park in a spot close to the emergency room entrance.

My head whips to him as my lips part. "I'm supposed to be sayin' that to you."

He nods and rolls his lips inward as he stares out the windshield, making it feel like he's a million miles from here.

"Grandad sees a cardiologist, has an appointment next week to talk about getting a couple stents put in. I think that's probably what we're lookin' at."

"Do you need me to call anyone? Your parents or your sisters? I can do that so you can focus on Grandad."

Like I've broken a spell, I watch as his lips turn up ever so slightly on one side, his head turning slowly to look at me.

"Thanks for bein' here, Eddie." I nod frantically because I need that reassurance more than he could ever know. "Celeste called my parents, and I'll text my sisters when we know more."

"Of course, that makes sense. Are you ready to go in? Do you need a minute?"

"No, I'm ready," he says with a half smile before leaning across the cab and placing a soft kiss on my lips. "Thank you."

"Always."

IT WAS WELL into the early-morning hours when we finally got cleared to go back and see Grandad. Montana had been right about the stents, and even just seeing him postsurgery, he looked like himself again—said he felt better too.

It was good news. *Great news.*

And I'd lost it.

No one pointed out the tears streaming down my cheeks as I stood frozen in the doorway. I was blindsided by my reaction, but what was worse was I couldn't stop it. It wasn't until Grandad held out his hand toward me, beckoning me to him, that I felt my heartbeat start to slow.

He was the second Greene man in the room to offer me comfort, and I accepted it, shamelessly tracing the freckles and scars on his hand with my fingers. His nurse had kicked us out not long after, and I'd felt every muscle in my body the entire drive home.

Mason and Bodhi had gone back to their place, saying they'd take care of the morning chores so Montana could rest. Archer and Bea had texted us while we were at the hospital to say they'd dropped off muffins, a breakfast casserole, and a couple of pints of fruit for breakfast.

As everyone rallied around Grandad, my heart was damn near ready to burst. It's not that I didn't know how people in Blackstone Falls treated their neighbors, but I'd never been a part of it.

People had been more likely to bless my mother's heart than bring her a casserole. She'd alienated us from this town and the wonderful people in it. No one had been unkind to me, but I never felt like I fit in anywhere.

Except with Montana.

But maybe that was my fault too. I'd feared rejection so I

stopped putting myself out there at all. It wasn't something I could fix overnight, but I could make the effort now that I'd claimed Blackstone Falls as home.

But that would have to wait till morning.

The exhaustion was too great as I let Montana lead me to his bedroom and straight into the shower. I was thankful, the smell of antiseptic lingering even though we were no longer at the hospital. I needed to wash it away just like the fear that still clung to my skin.

Montana must have felt it too. He was quiet, his hands gentle as he rinsed the shampoo from my hair, the intimacy of it so much more than anything I'd ever experienced.

We'd dried off and thrown on some clothes before crawling into bed. He'd wrapped himself so tight around me it was hard to breathe, but just like the shower, I needed it as much as he did. And with only a few hours until the sun was due to rise, I drifted off, exhaustion mixing with a flicker of hope that everything would turn out all right.

18

ELLISON

They kept Grandad another night at the hospital. He'd been less than thrilled, but I'd been relieved. While my emotions ran freely rampant the entirety of the incident, Montana had been stoic—hyperfocused and anything but fine. I spent any and all available time trying to get him to talk about how he was feeling, but he still hadn't cracked.

It's been three days since Grandad came home, the man letting us fuss over him for exactly one day before declaring we were driving him crazier than a wet dog in a truck bed. I couldn't blame him, honestly.

Between Montana, Celeste, and me, not to mention half the town, Grandad had grown tired of all the attention, even threatening to never make me breakfast again—*the horror*. I'd taken that threat to heart and changed my focus to my best friend which turned out to be worse than dealing with Grandad on the days he was feeling particularly ornery.

Instead of letting it out, Montana had bottled up every single feeling and locked them down tight. He was moody and distant, working late and distracted when he was home.

I'd never seen him like this, and the fact that he'd become this person I didn't recognize in the years I'd been gone gnawed at me.

Montana had taken on the responsibility of the farm and his grandfather's care, and it had changed him. He hadn't just grown up; he'd forgotten how to live—how to ask for help. Jensen had led the charge the night Grandad had been rushed to the hospital, making arrangements and taking the guesswork out of Montana's hands.

I was thankful because I didn't think Montana would have done it himself. Lord knows I'd been zero help that night. He wanted people to see the happy-go-lucky guy instead of the man compartmentalizing every single fear and pressure to not only keep his family's business afloat but also manage the health of a man who meant the world to him.

It was unfathomable to think someone could shoulder all that alone. I helped out where I could, Celeste and I doing our best to make the house as stress-free as possible, but after a couple of days I needed to shake things up. Montana had practically turned into a zombie, and while Celeste had her reservations, I knew I needed to help him reset.

My way.

After having run errands all day, I've tucked myself away to get ready. Looking around, I worry my bottom lip with my teeth, pushing away the doubt and sending up a little prayer when I hear the front door close followed by boots hitting the floor.

Taking one last deep breath, I position myself on the bed and wait. The paperback in my hand is more of a prop as I hear Montana's footsteps heavy on the hardwood. The closer they get, the faster my heart races and the harder it is to hide my smile.

"What the hell is that?" he asks without preamble as soon as he opens the bedroom door, his gaze locked on the giant framed picture of a cow behind me above his bed. "And that?" His gaze ping-pongs around the room to the obnoxious knickknacks I bought today for this exact reaction. "Jesus, Eddie, I was only gone a couple hours and you rearranged the whole damn place!"

It's an exaggeration—kind of—but I watch with glee as his chest rises and falls faster with each new thing he notices.

The Christmas card of him in his boxers.

A hideous blanket I found in the bargain bin draped across the end of the bed.

His and hers robes hanging on the bathroom door.

"I just thought it was time to take our relationship to the next level," I say sweetly.

"You what? What level? You're moving in? I mean it's fine, but dammit, Eddie, I think there should have been a conversation first."

Batting my eyelashes, I lean one hand on the mattress and use the other one to push my boobs up in the low neck of my tank top. Montana's gaze drops immediately to where I'm one heaving breath away from a nipple slip before looking up, his face flaming and his jaw clenching.

"You want to talk? I love talking."

"You're in my bed and you're in my space and fuck if you don't look good there, but I'm not playin' house with you."

I pout because I know how much he hates it. And how much he can't resist it either. "So you're saying you need a commitment before I can move the rest of my stuff in?"

"I'm saying that I have a lot of shit goin' on right now and a case of blue balls that I may never recover from with you sleeping in my bed every night. But seriously, what the hell is all this?"

"You could have had me literally every single night since I got here—that's on *you* not me." Throwing the paperback onto the bed, I stand and watch as he takes in the smallest pair of boyshorts I own as I snag leggings from the drawer I shoved them in—he doesn't miss that either. "It's okay, Max. I don't want to stress you out if you're not ready for a commitment. I can go sleep at my place." I add with a shrug, "It's no big deal."

"It's no big deal," he mutters under his breath as he scrubs his hands over his face. "It's no big deal? Fuck, Ellison, of course it's a big deal." He waves his hands around, his voice rising as color crawls up his neck.

"Why?" I demand, and his nostrils flare as emotions flash through his gaze.

Come on, Max.

"Because—" The word is harsh, his breathing audible as he stares at me.

And I wait.

But it doesn't take long, the fight draining from him as his body sags onto the end of the bed, his head in his hands. My heart breaks for him even as relief floods my veins.

Finally.

Stepping up between his legs, I gently drag my nails along his scalp and watch the way his muscles bunch and flex, the tension visible as he exhales through his mouth over and over. It feels like hours have passed when his arms finally come around my waist, his head turning to the side so he can rest his cheek on my stomach.

I wrap my arms around him and just hold him the way

I'm sure no one has since the day I left here. I should have been here for him—really here—and not just the sporadic, meaningless text messages that we'd exchanged before Nan passed.

"I can take the picture down if you hate it," I say because I'm drowning in the heaviness of this moment.

His shoulders shake with silent laughter, the movement vibrating through me before he throws his head back and laughs. It's rich and full and so damn beautiful my eyes well with tears I have to blink away as a smile stretches across my face.

"Come here, you," he says as he pulls me onto the bed. I yelp, bracing my hands on his chest before he rolls me onto my back and presses his lips to mine.

It's sweet and exploratory, and I relish in the decadence of this uninterrupted moment.

"Are you okay?" I ask when he rests his forehead against mine as I draw little circles on the small of his back.

"I would say all this was overkill but..." He sits up enough to meet my gaze. It's open and vulnerable and I wish I could just hide us away somewhere for a while. "I needed it."

"I know."

"I really hate that blanket," he says as his tongue peeks out to wet his lips, and I can't resist leaning up to nip at the bottom one.

"That's why I picked it." My grin is full of mischief as I add, "Matches your eyes."

He snorts. "No it doesn't."

It really doesn't, but that's not important right now because my best friend is smiling, and I'll do anything to make sure he keeps it up.

"Why don't we go take a shower and then we can negotiate which of these gorgeous additions to your bedroom get to stay?"

He opens his mouth and then closes it, his lips turning up into a sinful smirk. "You're on, Eddie. Let's go."

19

MONTANA

It had been a week since Ellison dumped all her yard sale finds into my bedroom. The negotiating process had been *intense* and fun as hell.

And exactly what I needed.

At the end of the day, it was all trivial, but I appreciate her for forcing me back to the present.

Grandad had scared the hell out of me. The notion that I truly am alone here if anything should happen crippled me in a way I hadn't prepared for. He'd always been ageless to me, and I'd pushed all the evidence to the contrary from my mind.

Even with Ellison in my arms most nights, sleep hadn't come easy. We needed to have a come-to-Jesus conversation about what's going on between us. We'd just jumped back into our old routine like years didn't separate the then and now. We both deserve answers and a whole lot of truth that's gonna hurt like hell.

Maybe.

Probably.

Foolishly, I'd thought Ellison returning home would

make things easier, but so far, she'd mostly just had me tied up in knots.

Fatigue settles over me as I pull up to the Kettle and Kiln looking for my third cup of coffee before heading over to Sundown Realty. I need to check on Bea's progress and see what kind of manual labor needs to be done. The woman has proven herself a hundred times over, and I need to make sure Archer and I do our part too.

Opening the pressed-tin door, I step back and hold it wider as a woman walks toward me juggling a messenger bag, a coffee, and a pastry box. I want to ask her if she needs help, but she rights herself just before the threshold and looks up at me and smiles.

Her auburn hair is loose around her shoulders, and glasses frame her pretty face. She looks familiar.

Oddly familiar.

But I can't place her. The glare of the sun reflects off her dark frames, and she says a quick *thank you* before hurrying to her car.

Brows furrowed, I make my way inside and meet Karina's narrowed gaze.

"Don't you have a girlfriend?" she asks accusingly with a hand on her hip, and I hold up my hands in surrender. I also don't correct her that Ellison had kind of dodged that label conversation.

"She just looks familiar is all. Like she reminds me of someone, not that I've met her before."

"Uh-huh," Karina says, unconvinced as she continues to watch me.

"Do you know her?"

"Sure, that's Arden James," she replies, pointing to a framed article on the wall. "She came in here a couple of weeks back and talked to Nicolette and me about opening the Kettle and Kiln—sweet girl."

Arden James, the new reporter for the *Blackstone Gazette*. I'd read her last article this morning about the pros and cons of changing the stop sign to a yield at the turnoff for Cedar Lake, the lake that sits on the Clementine Creek-Blackstone Falls line.

It was a fairly riveting collection of testimonies, and I found myself heavily invested in the debate. The thought makes me smile, because if that's not a small-town problem I don't know what is.

"Maybe I saw her picture in the paper then." I nod, my curiosity sated, and turn my full attention back to Karina. "Can I just get a coffee?"

Her eyebrows are somewhere in her hairline as she stares at me. I try for a smile but it's half-hearted and tired.

"Oh honey." She makes my drink without another word, all the while throwing sympathetic glances over her shoulder. "Should I make a cup for myself and you can tell me—"

The shrill sound of my phone ringing cuts her off, and I pull it from my pocket. I mouth *one minute* before answering.

"Hey, Jensen, what's going on?"

"You're never gonna believe this..."

"I JUST WANT TO CLARIFY," I say, pinching the bridge of my nose between my thumb and forefinger and honestly afraid of what I'll find when I open my eyes. "You took Grandad around town and terrorized the good people of Blackstone Falls with..."

"Baked goods," she adds not so helpfully. "And little plastic cows."

"Baked goods," I repeat even though I've heard this story no less than ten times, "and little plastic cows—"

She drops one into my hand, the black-and-white miniature no bigger than a nickel. It's cute, and I can only imagine the look on everyone's face as they discovered these things behind plants, hidden in sugar bowls, and generally just not where they belong.

Not that there's a *right spot* for a bunch of tiny plastic cows—but still. After hanging up with Jensen, my phone hadn't stopped ringing with people callin' to say they saw Ellison and Grandad all over town.

"I mean the article about Jamison's cows was hilarious, and we thought that'd be the best way to honor them." Ellison says this like it should be obvious and I'm boring her. It also means she and Grandad *planned* this. Pretty sure you can't get these things in bulk around here.

"Blasting country music from the car while wearing," I continue while ignoring her, "matching Hawaiian shirts." Her grin is wide, and the mischief in her eyes almost has me cracking. But I don't. I can't.

"Technically," she says rocking side to side, "I'm wearing a dress and it has pockets! Isn't that fun? And Grandad looks so cute."

My first reaction to seeing my grandfather was to laugh because in my entire lifetime I'd never seen him wear anything with quite so many *colors*. It was comical, sure, but unease still weighed me down like a lead blanket.

Sobering, I run a hand through my hair. "Ellison, you took Grandad with you, causin' a ruckus—"

"Delivering banana bread and other baked goods is

hardly *a ruckus,* Max. Lighten up a little—seriously, this is like the *least* crazy thing I've ever done."

"He was *just* in the hospital and—"

"And he's fine. I hear you, Max, I do. But I drove, made sure he wasn't carrying anything too heavy, and made sure he took plenty of breaks. I kept him hydrated—old man had to stop and pee every ten minutes."

"Yeah, I know. Sheriff Kade called to ask if Grandad could please stop peeing on the fence posts around town." I glare at her and she grins.

"What else then? His heart? Montana, he's fine, and you keepin' him cooped up all day every day isn't helping any. He's doin' great—his doctor said so. We both needed to get out, so we ran around town and had some fun."

"But he still needs to take it easy."

"And he did," she says, not backing down. "You think I would let anything happen to the man who has shown me more love and affection than my own parents?"

"No," I say firmly even though a part of me still felt like it had been reckless. "I just wanted to make sure he was safe."

"And you don't trust me to do that?" she asks, her voice going up slightly at the end, hurt clear in her tone.

"Ellison..." I groan and look up toward the sky. "That's not what I meant."

"That's what it sounded like."

My head falls forward to meet her gaze, a storm brewing in the umber depths. But that's not what I want. I never want to fight with her. Taking a step forward, I reach for her hands, lacing our fingers together.

She lets me but only barely.

"I didn't mean it to sound like you didn't care or that you were unsafe—but it's just me here, you know? My parents and sisters are gone and it's a lot. I didn't realize how much until I saw the ambulance outside the house."

"You have people who care about you, Montana. Jensen and Celeste, Mason and Bodhi, Archer and Bea—they all rallied for you. For Grandad. You've created a family here all on your own, and you need to let them help."

"It's not that easy."

"But you'd do it for them," she says with a small squeeze of my hand, and I sigh because I know she's right.

"I will...try."

Her expression softens just the littlest bit. "Good. And you should know Grandad had a really great day." She smiles but it doesn't quite meet her eyes. "You should go in and talk to him about it."

"Are...you coming?" I ask slowly, but she shakes her head.

"I think we could all just use a night alone. I have orientation tomorrow for school anyway, so it makes sense that I sleep at home."

Home.

I want to yell that the rental is *not* her home. I may own the damn thing, but it doesn't make it mine, and being in it a handful of days sure as hell doesn't make it hers. I want her here, in this house with me. I want it to be ours.

But I need to slow down this runaway train before she takes off for the hills. Swallowing down my frustration, I breathe out a sigh. "If that's what you want." A night apart would probably be good for us, but it doesn't make me hate it any less.

Walking her to her car, I kiss her offered cheek and close the door once she's settled. Exhaustion hits me like a tidal wave as I watch her drive down the road and away from me. It's the kind that makes me want to drop my ass onto the dirt and wait for the sun to dip below the horizon before ever attempting to move.

It's a fantasy for another day.

Dragging myself up the porch steps, I catch a glimpse of black fur darting around the house. That cat is gonna cause nothing but heartache, and I've already got that in spades. Scrubbing a hand over my face, I head inside to find Grandad and figure out how the hell I'm going to manage this new whiskered complication in my life.

20

ELLISON

It's early as I sit in the parking lot of Blackstone Falls Elementary and stare at the brick building that I attended, once upon a time. I barely slept last night, and it had everything to do with being alone in the cottage, returning stilted texts with Montana.

"Country Boy's Dream Girl" by Ella Langley plays on the radio and I'd smile, because this song is amazing, if I weren't still caught up in yesterday. Last night, I'd been the one who needed space, but leaving didn't make it hurt any less.

I'd gotten too comfortable being in Montana's house—in his bed. We hadn't set up any real rules or anything—just jumped into things as if adding sex and physical intimacy would be no big deal.

I'd be lying if I said my body doesn't crave him. But I need to slow things down before we end up drivin' toward a cliff in a truck with no brakes.

My phone vibrates in my purse, and I narrow my eyes at it before hauling the bag into my lap, growling as I try to find the damn thing. My mother would be appalled at the contents of my favorite knockoff—lipstick, Chapstick, receipts, snacks, wrappers, gum that I can't remember buying, mascara, a phone charger, and a dozen other random things.

Mentally, I add *clean out purse* to my to-do list before the actual school year starts as I snag the device in the bottom corner. And like I conjured him with my inner musings, Montana's name appears on the screen.

MONTANA: Good luck today, Eddie. You're gonna do great and they're definitely gonna love you.

ELLISON: Thanks, I'm only a little nervous. Everything go okay last night?

MONTANA: Grandad had a few choice things to say to me about how I acted

ELLISON: He knows it's because you love him so much

ELLISON: You feel big things, Max, and I adore that about you.

MONTANA: Yeah well it didn't stop him from telling me I was acting like a jackass

I SNORT, because there's no way Grandad called him a jackass.

> ELLISON: Did he actually say that?

> MONTANA: That was the gist

Glancing at the clock, I type out one last message.

> ELLISON: Jackass or not, I love you

> MONTANA: I love you more

> MONTANA: You're going to impress the hell out of them today

Smiling, I send a heart emoji before turning off my car, grabbing my blazer from the passenger seat, and opening my door. It's sweltering today, and sweat gathers at the nape of my neck before I'm fully upright.

Moving quickly, I make my way across the parking lot without breaking into an all-out run. The shadow cast by the gymnasium offers little relief but I'll take it. Stepping up to the door, I try not to focus on my reflection as I press the intercom and wait to be let inside.

Signing in, I smile at the woman behind the desk and take a seat in the offered chair. The school, from what I can see, is the same but *different* than I remember.

Colorful walls and murals make my heart sing—it's a drastic change from the sterile environment we'd had in Savannah. I'm so distracted, I barely notice the sound of the buzzer as the receptionist lets someone else inside. He repeats the same process before turning toward me. He's handsome with dark hair swept across his forehead and olive-green eyes.

"I'm Calvin Spence," he says with a rehearsed smile as he offers me his hand, and while his expression is practiced, I can still feel the warmth in his gaze as we shake.

"Ellison Mills."

"Oh good! Y'all already met," Mrs. Erikson says as she buzzes past and motions for us to follow. "I'm Regina Erikson but please call me Reggie." She's dressed in a fitted bright-pink dress with matching fringe at the bottom and black high heels. It's Barbie meets *The Great Gatsby's* Daisy of elementary school principals but somehow she pulls it off flawlessly. Her blonde hair is tied into a sophisticated knot at the top of her head, and her makeup is fresh and understated.

She looks...natural, which shouldn't be a big deal but is considering the majority of women I've encountered over the years have had at least *one* procedure to speak of. Not that they would admit it of course.

Deny.

Deny.

Deny.

Age is but a number unless you're in certain circles and then age is the only thing keeping you relevant in the conversation.

"Can I just say,"—Reggie beams at us from across the desk in her office with more enthusiasm than I'm ready for —"that we are all *so* excited to have you with us this school year!"

She's remarkably younger and much warmer than my last principal, but that's probably not saying much considering I'd been locked into a contract with a private school in Savannah after graduation. Courtesy of my mother.

There wasn't much I missed from there aside from the kids and this really cute boutique called Halcyon. Word on the street was that the owner, Ellie, had opened a second location in Tennessee, but I'd been too focused on the move home to look into it.

Mentally adding that to my to-do list under cleaning out my purse, I smile as Reggie continues to talk before giving us a tour of the school and showing us to our respective classrooms. Calvin is slotted to replace the beloved art teacher and waves as he ducks inside his room, leaving Reggie and me in the hall.

"Your resume is very impressive, Ellison," she says as we pause in front of another room. "I realize you grew up here, but this is going to be very different from what you're used to."

"I'm looking forward to the change. Working in Savannah, while rewarding, stifled a lot of the creativity I'd hoped to bring to my students," I say honestly. "I feel like this is exactly where I need to be at this point in my career."

Her smile is understanding and warm as she motions to the doorway in front of us. "Then by all means."

My heels click on the tile as I cross the threshold, and I'm struck by the brightness in the room. The white walls are covered with colorful posters, tiny desks and chairs are organized neatly, and bookshelves cover the entire wall under the windows.

"Please let us know if there's anything you need. Our budget isn't huge, but we have a little set aside to get you and your students settled for the start of the year."

Thanking her, I smile as she excuses herself back to her office, leaving me to hunt my way around the room.

I love it.

And it's amazing how comfortable I already feel in here, personal touches aside. This space is exactly what a kindergarten room should be. In Savannah, the day was regimented and not in a casual *keep the kids on task way* but in the way that forces kids to grow up far quicker than they deserve.

"Please tell me you're ready to get a drink," Calvin says from behind me with a pointed look. I'm surprised to see how much time has passed when I glance at the clock on the wall.

"If you insist," I say, surprising myself.

"I do, and you can call me Cal. I always get nervous and introduce myself as Calvin, but literally no one calls me that."

I laugh as we walk down the hall and out into the parking lot. "Where do you want to go, Cal not Calvin?"

"Cute," he says drawing out the words and making it clear he does *not* think my teasing is cute. "How about Boots on Bar and Grill? I'll drive—I'm still getting used to this town." He narrows his eyes. "Which one are you dating again? I really don't feel like fighting off a boyfriend today."

I laugh as I follow him to a silver Prius. "This tracks," I say, nodding toward the car.

"I'd be mad if it wasn't true."

Climbing in, I click my seatbelt into place before answering his question. "I don't have a boyfriend," I say but that doesn't totally feel right, "but Montana Greene is my best friend and we're…"

"Involved?" he offers with a smirk.

"Yeah, I mean, we're not *not* involved but there's no label," I say lifting my shoulder and letting it drop. We'd kind of brushed over that the other night. "I'm honestly not sure what we're doing."

"I bet it's fun whatever it is. That man is climbable."

I snort but still feel my cheeks heat because he's not wrong. Montana is everything I've ever wanted, and now that we've started something, I'm keenly aware of what's at stake. "What about you?"

"Currently unattached and looking to decompress after my last job. My sister Hannah is married to Case Thayer and they're settling down—and it felt like it was time to do the same and—"

I gasp, the back of my hand making contact with his bicep. "No way! She's the one who owns that cute little bookstore in Clementine Creek, right?"

"Ow," he whines, rubbing a palm over his arm while keeping the other hand on the wheel. "I thought people were supposed to be nicer in the south."

"That's a common misconception," I say with a sly grin, mostly to cover the surprise I'm feeling at being so comfortable with someone I just met.

It's...unsettling.

And nice.

"Apparently."

Pulling into the parking lot of Boots On Bar and Grill, Cal turns off the ignition and we both get out of the car and head up the walkway. He holds the door, and I thank him before grabbing a high top off to the side. It's still early, and we have the place mostly to ourselves.

Jude Rhodes is behind the bar, and I give him a small wave which he returns even though I'm not entirely sure he remembers me. Not sure it matters.

Everyone who walks in is a neighbor and friend, and Mr. Rhodes always makes you feel right at home. He has run this place for as long as I've been alive, with Jude and his brother popping in from time to time to work busing tables or filling orders in the kitchen.

Mr. Rhodes would stop by our table to shake my father's hand and ask how the food was, catching up on a whole lot of nothing during the times we could sneak away. Besides being with Montana, being here was some of the happiest times of my childhood.

Cal looks around like he's never seen anything like it and maybe he hasn't. It's not quite a dive bar but just barely. T-shirts folded and pinned in tight squares line the ceiling. It'd started out as kind of a game—Mr. Rhodes thought it would be fun to tell people if they brought shirts from other bars, he'd let them put them on the ceiling.

The rule was you had to have a good story and everyone in the place had to vote on its potential ceiling status. Once the ceiling was full, the same rule applied, but if your shirt was accepted you got to take your pick and swap with one already on the ceiling. It was the ultimate victory.

I'd been here a couple of time to witness the ritual with Dad. The energy of the bar and the animated cheering of the patrons has the corner of my lips curving up, even if the memory is bittersweet.

I order a mojito and Cal orders a beer before he squeezes his eyes shut and pinches the bridge of his nose. My heart immediately hurts for him because I recognize the move—I've done it countless times trying to push off a headache.

"Are you all right?" I ask as the waitress places our drinks on the table. We thank her, and I order the pretzel bites in hopes that some carbs will give my new friend the boost he needs.

"I'm" —his gaze meets mine and I raise a single eyebrow

at the lie he's about to tell— "tired." Cal sighs and plays with the condensation on his glass. "Today was great, and I'm excited to be here." He worries his bottom lip with his teeth and I wait. "It's hard to adjust to everything being so *normal.*"

There's a lot Cal isn't saying, that much is obvious, but what he *is* saying hits me hard.

"On the plus side, we're doing this together. I haven't lived here in a long time, and my situation has definitely changed so—I get it. At least some of it. Did you follow your sister here?"

Nodding, he takes a sip from his drink before rolling his eyes. "My parents are free spirits, and Hannah and I grew up mostly on the road. We went all across the country and around the world looking for adventures. My parents couldn't be tethered to one place for long—they still can't. But that was hard on my sister and me. We craved stability disguised as the next big thing."

"That sounds exhausting."

"It is. We grew up chasing the idea that we weren't made for normal everyday constraints but the life of a wanderer..." he trails off and I wait for him to gather himself. "Our aunt and uncle own the bar in Clementine Creek, Tap and Table, and when Hannah came to help out she never left. Hell, she's even married—never thought I'd see the day."

"Clementine Creek will do that to you. Plus, I've heard the Thayers are great."

He chuckles before sobering. "They are, but I wouldn't be here without her." Looking up at my confusion, he adds, "She made it possible to break the cycle—to set down roots. It was the right choice for her, and being here, I know it's the right choice for me *but* it's hard to slow down no matter how bad you want it." Cal scrunches his nose and my lips twitch. "That makes me sound really entitled and whiny."

"Can I ask where you were before this?"

His fingers absentmindedly play with the condensation on the glass again as he says, "I spent a few years working with an organization like Teachers Without Borders in refugee camps overseas. It was really rewarding and also incredibly challenging—sometimes terrifying."

"I'm sure that's an experience that stays with you... becomes a part of you."

"I'm not sure I know how to stay in one place."

"Do you want to?" At his hesitation I continue, "You're allowed to feel what you feel and roots aren't for everyone, but I think it might be too soon?"

"I don't know how to be uncomfortable."

I blink at him because I definitely cannot relate. I'm almost always uncomfortable regardless of whether or not I can hide it.

At my blank stare he adds, "Anytime I've ever gotten this feeling, I've just moved on. No ties meant I didn't have to stay. But I want to be here with my sister—make up for lost time—I just don't know how to get over this feeling."

He rubs at his chest as I mull over what he said and take a chance. "What if you took a little vacation?"

"Seriously?"

"Why not? We still have a little bit before the school year starts and there's plenty of places around here you could go to for a couple days." Swallowing hard, I give him a little more of my own truth. "I think we're both trying too hard to live up to the *idea* of it right now instead of accepting that change takes time."

"Wow," he says a little breathlessly, and I know it's at least partially for effect because his expression is amused, "you're really smart."

I stick my tongue out at him and he chuckles.

"What? I'm not great with the friend thing, but I have good ideas sometimes."

Tilting his head to the side, he stares at me. "You're not great at the friend thing? You seem pretty great to me, although I might not be the resident expert on long-lasting relationships."

Now it's my turn to deflect, choosing to study the mint leaves in my drink for a minute longer before finally saying, "I grew up here but we never *fit* here. My parents are pretty influential in certain circles. I learned at a young age what it meant to attend functions and events to keep up appearances instead of working the land and being a part of the community."

"I hate that for you."

I shrug. "It was a long time ago." I pause, frowning. "I mean I guess not that long ago. I moved to Savannah, Georgia, for school after I left here. My parents were going to travel and then move closer to Nashville, but a few months after I left they bought a house not far from my campus, and I retreated into myself like I was still under their thumb. I'd moved to a different state and I still couldn't get away from them."

"What happened after you graduated?"

"I took a job teaching at a private school in the city. My mother had a hand in that too," I say bitterly, "but when Montana's grandmother passed away a few years ago, I came back for the funeral. No matter the time and distance between us, it wasn't something I could miss." He nods, but I get the impression he has no idea how to process that kind of connection. "Montana and I rekindled our friendship, and I waited out my contract before moving here for good."

"Why didn't you do the long-distance thing? People do that all the time, right?"

It was a loaded question if I'd ever heard one, and I shove a pretzel bite in my mouth to buy me a minute of reprieve. It's delicious, the texture perfect, and complements the tang of the honey mustard I dunked it in.

"Being away from Montana was complicated. We *still* have a lot of things we need to work out. We would never have been good at being apart, and it was easier for me to keep the distance—physical and emotional—for the duration of my contract. We used that time to rebuild our friendship." I leave out the other complication because it's not worth muddying the waters.

"Have you told him any of this?"

"Some of it. But I—we—just dove into things like we hadn't been apart for a long time. We jumped ahead ten spaces, and now we're reeling with how to make new us be old us while adding adult problems and intimacy."

Cal lets out a low whistle before chuckling as I take a massive gulp of my drink.

"I feel like this is heavy for a trial friendship outing."

Snorting, Cal throws a balled-up napkin at me. "You should have thought about that before you went and invited me for drinks. I'm a done deal."

I narrow my eyes. "You invited me."

He waves his hand in a flourish. "Semantics." His smile widens and so does mine.

"So, what about you?" I ask, leaning forward and batting my lashes. "Dating? Attached? Need help swiping on some apps?"

"You truly are selfless," he deadpans.

"It's one of my best qualities."

Shaking his head, Cal fiddles with a paracord bracelet on his wrist before meeting my gaze. There's humor still in his, but it feels forced now.

"Uh, not dating or attached and probably focusing on me for a while." He rolls his eyes like that is truly a hardship —but he's not wrong. Self-reflection can be a bitch. "My sister already tried to play matchmaker with me and this guy, Tanner. Have you met him?"

"I don't think so."

"He's a transplant. Was married to one of the Thayer wives and now co-owns Vetted Paws with the scary guy."

"Hank?" I ask, trying to sort through the brothers in my head.

"No, I met Hank—I think his wife is scarier honestly."

"That sounds nice."

"Sure," he drawls. "No, this guy married the sister— Rhea, maybe? Starts with a "S" I think."

"Oh, Sorren! I remember him being super hot but not scary," I say because even though I didn't interact much with them, that whole group was well known even in Blackstone Falls.

"Definitely scary," he confirms, and I roll my eyes at his dramatics.

"So, what happened with Tanner?"

"He's gorgeous, don't get me wrong, but he's not ready to date anyone and honestly neither am I. He's gotta work through his own stuff, and God knows I have enough anxiety for everyone, so we're probably doing our friends and family a favor on this one."

My heart hurts for my new friend.

"You're allowed to be happy *and* adjusting. You're allowed to be all the things." He raises an eyebrow in challenge, causing me to scoff. "We're talking about you not me."

"Hmm..."

Pointing a pretzel bite at him, I narrow my eyes. "I'm serious."

"Me too." He finishes his beer and places the empty glass on the table. "Besides, I'm devoting all my energy to this relationship,"—he motions between us and I snort—"so I can't possibly take on anything else right now."

"I *am* a lot of work."

"From your mouth to God's ears, sweetheart."

We only last a second longer before we dissolve into giggles. Moving back here has been so much more than I could have imagined. Without the constant weight and expectation of my parents, it's like I'm finally able to breathe.

If I put myself out there, the only person they have to judge is *me*.

I've never had that before.

Tears cloud my vision at the realization. Cal's hand covers mine and he squeezes it. He doesn't ask, and I get the feeling he doesn't need to because he can feel it. He knows what this is without me having to say a word.

I hate this for us.

But maybe, together, we can finally show the world the people we were always meant to be. It's cheesy but I don't care. I won't live in the shadows of my past because the future is bright and beautiful and I fucking deserve to be happy.

We both do.

Clearing my throat, I motion to the menu. "Do you want food? I think this day calls for food, and I have to send my dad a picture of a burger anyway."

"That's not weird at all."

"It's a long story," I say with a wry smile as he snatches his menu up and looks at me over the laminated edge.

"Lucky for me, we've got time."

21

MONTANA

"**A**re you sure this isn't overkill?" Archer asks, wiping the sweat from his brow as he hangs the strand of fairy lights from the porch ceiling.

"May I remind you that I took care of the entire cleanup of your Valentine's Day date with Bea?" I pause and smirk. "Also that I got her number for you..."

He grumbles something under his breath but otherwise doesn't comment. My cousin wooed his girlfriend via text before she agreed to go on a date with him. And because of how shy he generally is, he'd set up an intimate date in the high school gymnasium where they first ran into each other.

The privacy had helped take the social pressure off so he could be himself, and it worked because they've been together ever since.

I am happy for him and I want that—with Ellison—and it is time to do it right. I'd never gotten to date her, and that was a problem I planned to rectify. We'd gone out plenty of times but never with the intention that it was anything other than two friends enjoying each other's company.

If the time since she's been home has told us anything, it

is that we need to slow down and enjoy getting to know each other again.

Romantically.

Looking around, I take in the inflatable farm animals in the yard and the battery-powered votives in the grass that spell out *Date me?* and smile. Between the lights and the hanging baskets we'd hung with the bright-pink and white flowers, the space is both playful and intentional.

I want Ellison to know we can still be *us* but that we can be something more—everything more—because she's my end game and I want to be hers too.

I just need to remind myself that I need to date her before I marry her.

"You know she's gonna say yes," Archer says from beside me after folding up the ladder and placing it in the back of the truck.

"I know," I say, running my hand through my hair. "It's just weird. I've known her for so long, and having her back feels like no time has passed—which is great—but time *has* passed. A lot of time and we keep brushing over it."

"I don't think there's any right or wrong way to date your best friend. But also, you probably should take anything I say on relationships with a grain of salt considering Bea is my only reference."

"Just because she's your only relationship doesn't mean you can't offer advice. Y'all have something special, and I'm happy for you."

He blushes as he dips his head. "Thanks. It's too soon but I just want to marry her." His words echo my thoughts from a moment ago.

My head whips to his, and I can't wipe the smile off my face. "Well, when the time is right, I'm here to help construct an epic proposal."

"I appreciate it." Archer looks down at his watch and then holds out his hand. "I gotta head out. Good luck with Ellison."

I take his hand and pull him in for a half hug before he gets in his truck and takes off for home.

With nothing else to do, I take a seat on the porch steps and wait for my girl.

ELLISON

AFTER SAYING GOODBYE TO CAL, I take the long way home and cruise the backroads for a while. I let my fingers dance in the breeze, the windows down ruining my perfectly styled hair from this morning, but it is so worth it.

I have a job I'm actually looking forward to, a classroom I can't wait to decorate and...I made a friend. All my life I've been accepted or tolerated because of the people I was with like Montana or my parents or Blake.

But never just because of *me*.

I have hope that one day I can be real friends with Bea and the guys, but right now they're still Montana's friends.

Cal, on the other hand, has no real ties to our little corner of Tennessee. His brave face for the world mimics my own in so many ways, and it feels good to have someone else understand—a sort of kinship. Blake understood the ins and outs of my parents' and his parents' world and we were close but that wasn't *me*.

Not the real me anyway.

The lyrics of "Double Down" by Chris Young float around me as my car follows the road back to my cottage. I feel more settled than I have in a while, not just happy to be back but like I can breathe a little easier—like being here is the right choice.

Turning down the driveway, I let my car slow and take a couple of deep breaths as I roll along, careful not to kick up too much dirt as I go. Montana said he'd be here when I get home, but as I approach the house, I can't help the way a laugh bursts from my lips as I stare in disbelief at the transformation.

Large inflatable cows and goats and other farm animals litter the yard, my eyes taking everything in before landing on Montana. His big body unfolds as he stands from the porch steps, and I throw my car into park before grabbing my purse and getting out.

My smile is wide, but my steps falter as my gaze snags on the candles set out in front of the inflatables.

Date me?

"I realized," Montana says slowly in that southern drawl I love so much, forcing my gaze to his, "that I've never taken you out on a date."

"We've gone out before," I say with a frown.

"Nothing that was real and intentional." Taking a step closer, he laces his fingers with mine, pulling me to face him. "I want to take you on a date. One where you fuss over what you're gonna wear, and I take the truck to get washed before knockin' on your door with flowers, wearin' my good jeans to pick you up."

My lips part because while I've gone out on countless dates, no one has ever made my heart race in my chest like the man before me. "That sounds nice," I manage and he grins, "but I think you still need to ask me."

"Ellison,"—he says my name with reverence and the air pulses with the intensity of this moment—"will you go out with me?"

"If I'm free," I say, using our joined hands to pull his chest flush against mine before popping up on my toes and brushing my lips against his, "definitely, yes."

"Tomorrow?" he asks, his lips curving up into a smile.

"Tomorrow."

22

MONTANA

As promised, I pulled out my good jeans and a button-down shirt, with the sleeves rolled halfway up my forearms. Just like the song, "I Like It, I Love It" by Tim McGraw, my truck is cleaner than I've ever seen it, and I picked up a bouquet of pretty, pink peonies because I want to do this right.

Ellison deserves the effort, and there's nothing I want more than to give that to her. So much of my growing up had been watching Grandad and Nan dancing in the kitchen or him pickin' her flowers from the garden.

One year, he'd planted an entire field of sunflowers so she could see them from the house. It had been an incredible undertaking, but her smile had been radiant. They'd come back on their own, the seeds making way for the following year. But we haven't touched that field since she passed—choosing to cut the flowers for her funeral service instead of letting them go to seed. It'd be too hard to see the blooms that next year when she wasn't here to enjoy them. I've debated having one of the guys just till the field but I can't bring myself to do that either.

Grandad had sown that field with love and devotion for the woman he'd cherished for more than half a century, a woman he mourned but still celebrated every day. I want that kind of love and I want it with Ellison.

Instead of making me nervous, it settles me in the best possible way. How lucky am I that I get to woo my best friend? I'd always tried to take care of Ellison growing up, and it wrecked me when we were apart. I hated not being privy to the intimate details of her life—the things that made her happy or sad, accomplishments and heartbreaks. It wasn't my place then but I'll never let that happen again.

We deserve our chance at happiness, and dammit, I am going to give it to her.

Taking a breath, I slow the truck as I pull down the driveway to her cottage. White oaks line each side, making it feel like some kind of fairy tale on this stretch of dirt and gravel. My heart races as I pull to a stop next to her car.

I've been here a hundred times before. I'd made sure everything was perfect before she moved in—combing through every inch of the tiny house and driving Archer crazy in the process. Part of me wants to tell her tonight about Sundown Realty, but the other part knows I need to wait.

Tonight is about reconnecting and enjoying bein' able to show her off to the world.

Let everyone know she's mine.

Reaching over, I grab the flowers from the passenger seat before stepping out of the truck. My boots crunch across the gravel, the cadence in my steps steadying my nerves as I cross the porch to knock on the door.

Footsteps echo inside a moment before the door opens, and I damn near lose my breath. Ellison's smile is coy, *knowing,* and she has every right to be because I can't get enough of just looking at her. From her worn, tan cowboy boots, up her long legs to the flowy hem of her burnt-orange dress, up to the cinched waist and the V cut of the top that shows off enough of her breasts to have my mouth watering—Ellison is a fucking dream.

No, not a dream, a reality.

My reality.

"You look incredible," I finally manage, awe heavy in my tone. She blushes the slightest bit as my gaze finally locks on hers.

"So do you, Max."

"These are for you."

Her fingers brush against mine as she reaches for the bouquet and immediately brings them to her nose, her eyes falling closed as she inhales and then sighs, a smile playing on her lips.

"My favorite."

"I know." Wide brown eyes blink up at me full of surprise and adoration. *I remember so much more than that, Eddie.* "Why don't you put them in water and then we can go?"

"You haven't told me where we're going," she says over her shoulder as she turns back toward the kitchen and I follow. The space is pretty much the same as when she moved in, with white walls, black cabinets, light-gray granite countertops, and cherry-stained floors. It's beautiful but it's not Ellison, and I'm not sure if it's actually that the cottage doesn't fit her or if I'm just so fixated on how well she fits with *me*.

"We're going to The Backyard."

"What's that?"

"They do farm to table, like the Iron Cask, but it's more

laid-back. You can still get pasta and steak but there's also sliders and barbeque."

"Sounds perfect."

Her reassurance has my shoulders relaxing because aside from figuring out how to ask Ellison on a date, picking a restaurant was definitely the most stressful. I didn't want to take her somewhere fancy and have her think I was trying to impress her like one of the losers from her parents' country club, but I also didn't want to take her somewhere too casual and have her feel like this is less than the life-changing evening it is.

"Well, let's go then," I say before leading her out to the truck, my hand gently resting on her lower back. Getting the door, I help her into her seat, and just as I'm about to close it, she leans forward and cups my face. Her lips are soft against mine, sensual and exploratory as I brace one arm on the roof and lean into her.

Ellison tastes like mint and something fruity—something delicious—*she's* delicious. And I have to stop myself before I'm tempted to slide my hand up her thigh and under the hem of her dress.

Hell, I'm already tempted, especially with the light citrusy scent of her perfume invading my senses and driving me wild. She told me it's an oil, not a spray, because regular scents give her a headache.

And I get it, but whatever it is has me hard and fucking aching for her before we've even left the house.

Wrenching my mouth from hers, I have to blink several times to make her come into focus I'm so drunk on her taste. Ellison's cheeks are flushed, the pink coloring making my dick twitch as I try to catch my breath.

"That's a hell of a hello," I manage, and she gives me a wicked grin.

"You're a hell of a guy, Max."

Smirking, I give her a quick peck on the lips before closing her door and rounding the hood of the truck. The AC is cranked, and it's a good thing because I need to chill my ass out if I'm going to make it through dinner.

"Best Thing Since Backroads" by Jake Owen hums through the speakers as I travel the path I came before turning and heading toward the restaurant. Without thinking, I reach over and take Ellison's hand in mine and relish the way she links our fingers together where they rest on her thigh.

"Tell me more about yesterday," I say, giving her a smile. We'd talked a little while I cleaned up the candles and took down a couple of the farm animals but I want, *need*, more.

"Well, I told you I made a friend, Cal—he's Hannah's brother." I nod because Hannah had been so excited about her brother puttin' down roots here right along with her. "It was just so *nice* to talk to someone as *me*, you know?"

"I'm proud of you." The words almost get lodged in my throat because I do know. Ellison has never been naturally outgoing. Any and all interactions she found herself in were almost always because of me or her parents.

"Thanks," she says shyly. "Me too."

We talk the rest of the way there about Cal and their classrooms and how she feels about being able to add some of the lessons she's passionate about to the curriculum. Ellison is lighter since she got home, her wings starting to spread after being forced to stay closed for so long. She's beautiful.

Resilient.

And I'll do everything in my power to help her soar.

23

ELLISON

M ontana listens the whole way to The Backyard, smiling and asking me questions, squeezing my hand, and is simply engaged in what I'm saying. Blake had always listened but it was different. I was barely keeping myself afloat, and he had supported me because he knew the intricacies of our world.

Dreams and ambitions were second to survival.

Frowning, I turn to Montana as we park, completely ignoring everything else but him. "Hey, I need to tell you something before we go in there."

Eyebrows crawling up his forehead, he turns in his seat and faces me, the hard set of his jaw the only thing that betrays the way he's bracing himself.

"I told you that Blake and I ended things—"

Montana holds up his free hand as the other one tightens its hold. "You don't need to tell me anything. I know you were with him for a while"—he swallows hard— "as long as you're not with him now, I mean."

"Blake and I were—*are*—friends." He blinks at me so I

continue. "We tried actually dating at first but realized it just wouldn't work between us."

"But you were with him for years."

A statement, not a question, because he's right.

"We were. As friends. It was easier for us to just continue the ruse—appease our parents and prevent any match-making that would require additional painful dinners at the country club or out in town."

"He was your fake boyfriend?"

I lift a shoulder and let it drop. "In a manner of speaking."

"Why didn't you tell me? All this time and I could've— *we* could've..." His voice trails off and he rubs his palm over his jaw as he looks away from me and out the windshield.

"I couldn't," I say quietly, and his head whips to face me, the intensity in his eyes making me question if I should have done this tonight. "I wouldn't have survived that, Montana. I was still locked into working at the school, not just a couple of months but *years.* It was hard enough seeing you after Nan's funeral and having to go back to Savannah. Being away from you was hard when we weren't talking, but it was so much harder after that." Wiping a lone tear from my cheek, I exhale a shuddery breath as I add, "I wouldn't have survived if we constantly had to say goodbye knowing the crash would always outweigh those pockets of happiness."

His eyelids squeeze shut, and I grip his hand harder, silently begging him to understand.

"I hate it," Montana whispers, and those three little words are full of so much hurt, my heart squeezes in my chest.

"I didn't know another way." It's my turn to stare out the windshield, taking in the adorable white painted brick building with peony bushes and a *Dogs Welcome* sign leading to the outdoor seating around the side. "I'm sorry I ruined things tonight."

"You didn't ruin tonight." His hand tugs on mine until I pull my gaze back to his. "It's just hard to hear that all that was going on—that you were so miserable you were fake dating someone just to make it through each day. I've never wanted that for you."

"And now it's over." Blinking away the tears, I reach over and cup his cheek with my palm. "I'm home and that part of my life is done. I just didn't want it hanging over us—me—tonight."

"Need to work on your timing," he murmurs, but a smile tugs at his lips as he turns his face to place a kiss on my palm.

"But you're not mad?"

"I'm...not mad."

"You're not happy either."

"Eddie," he says, swallowing hard, his Adam's apple bobbing in his throat, "you're gonna need to give me a minute to reconcile the fact that another man had years that could have been mine." I open my mouth to speak but he shakes his head. "Part of me gets it—I do—but the other part wants to break shit with my bare hands. Do you still talk to him?"

"We're still friends." His eyebrows climb up his forehead, so I add, "Only friends. He knows how I feel about you."

"He better—I don't care how much money he has; I'll still kick his ass all the way back to Savannah."

Launching myself at him over the center console, I crush my mouth against his, my body awkwardly contorted at this angle. No one has ever defended me so passionately, and his indignation on my behalf is the hottest thing I've ever seen.

Montana's hand tangles in my hair, his fingers fisting

the strands as he holds me in place and devours my mouth. It's both pleasure and punishment and I can't get enough. I'm just about to climb the rest of the way over and into his lap when he pulls back and rests his forehead against mine.

"Do you still want to do dinner?" I ask hopefully, but Montana shakes his head, the movement awkward with him still resting against me. "Takeout?" I try again, my voice kicking up an octave with the desperation pumping though my veins.

"Nah, I got something else in mind."

MONTANA TRADED his baseball hat tonight for a cowboy hat he had in the backseat of the truck after we parked in the grassy lot owned by Jake Booker and home to the Brew, Q 'n Boogie. I'd never been here, but Montana had told me about plenty of nights comin' down to support his friend and blow off some steam.

The field is packed, food trucks lining the perimeter, and I recognize a handful of people, but Montana just pulls me along to the end of the row to where a bright-blue truck sits, *The Backyard* scrawled in white letters along the side.

"See? Not all is lost," he says with a sheepish expression and the lift of one shoulder.

"I like this," I say, looking around and watching the people laugh and dance around us. It's refreshing, and while a crowd isn't normally my favorite, there's something comforting about the simplicity of it all. A field is just a field, but add in a stage and a place to dance and it's *home.*

"Yeah?" he asks, and I nod before wrapping my arm around his waist and resting my cheek against his chest. "I wasn't gonna be able to sit long enough to be polite back there."

He hitches his thumb toward the parking lot, and I roll my lips inward and take a steadying breath before turning my face up to meet his. "What's good here?"

Ten minutes and two containers of takeout later, we find ourselves at the picnic table on the far side of the field. Montana pulls a burger the size of his face out and takes a bite, sauce dotting the corner of his mouth. His smile is playful and he seems so young like this—like this is a place, with the music and chaos, that settles his nerves and calms his soul.

We should all be so lucky.

I open my own container and grab my fork and knife before dumping an unhealthy amount of syrup on top of my chicken and waffles. I'd had it in Savannah, but it wasn't the same, and one small bite confirms what I already knew— there's no place like Tennessee for comfort food.

For me at least.

We eat in silence, only commenting on the band or topics less likely to stir up any kind of trouble because I've already done enough of that for one night.

"I'm still gonna take you out on a real date," Montana says with a final wipe of his hands before discarding his napkin in the now empty container.

"What are you talking about? This is a real date." I look around like his logic will suddenly make sense.

"No, a real date where we eat inside with cloth napkins and I get to pull your chair out and you get to order a bottle of wine because I don't know the difference."

"This is a real date," I repeat because I'm still trying to process what he said while keeping my blood pressure in check. "I don't need cloth napkins and bottles of overpriced wine. I just need you and the way you look at me like I hung the moon and you couldn't fathom bein' anywhere else than here with me."

"Fine, but I still want to take you to a nice dinner."

"And that's great,"—I wave a hand toward the stage—"but this is great too."

We stare at each other, the band hitting the opening chords of "Sideways" by Dierks Bentley and it's exactly what we need. Ditching our trash, I can barely contain myself as I grab Montana's hand and find an open spot in the crowd. He chuckles but guides me with ease, moving us around flattened grass like we do this all the time.

Because we used to.

And now he's better.

Better than I remember.

Better than he was with me.

I push the thought away because it doesn't matter. I could spend the rest of my life comparing and wishing instead of living and *enjoying* the moment.

Montana's body is hard and unyielding as he spins me into him before pushing me out and spinning me until I might be sick. I laugh and he smiles as the song transitions into something slower and he brings me in close.

"You still got it, Eddie," he murmurs as the band croons the words to "Play it Again" by Luke Bryan.

"I hate that you're better," I say without thinking.

"Why?" he asks as his palm presses against my lower back, eliminating any and all distance between us. His length is hard against my belly, and when he knows I can feel him, he asks again.

"Because I don't like thinking about you spinning some other girl around or what happens after."

"And what do you think happens *after*?" His emphasis

on the last word sends a shiver racing down my spine. I want this man beyond reason, and even though I was the one asking for space, it's the last thing I want or need right now. At my silence, he continues, "There have been girls, Eddie. But this,"—he rocks his hips into me— "only you do this to me. Did I show them a good time? Yeah—I did because I'm a god damn gentleman, Eddie, but I get you out here for one fucking song and I want to strip you outta your clothes and bury myself inside you."

"Then why are we still here?"

"Because I wanted tonight to be perfect—show you what it can be like with *us*. Together."

"I already know we're perfect together, Max. That's never been a question." His heart hammers against my chest as he presses us tighter together.

"But we never got to do this—to be out here and let everyone know you're mine."

The song changes and so does the beat as the band jumps into a lively version of Russell Dickerson's hit, "MGNO."

Montana spins me out, his body controlling mine until I'm panting and turned on and pulled tight against his again. I can feel people watching us, but I can't make myself care when his eyes are absolutely blazing and his jaw is set like he's tryin' not to lose control.

There's no question who he belongs to—who *I* belong to.

But it's not enough. I want to see him snap, and I want him unhinged like he was before we'd gotten the call about Grandad. He'd been wild and I want that side of him back—to see what we could really be like if he'd just let go.

"Montana."

"We shouldn't do this tonight."

"Why not?"

"Because it's not the way I—"

"You what, Max? Wanted to lay me down on a bed of roses and make love to me all through the night?" His jaw clenches and his nostrils flare, his fingers digging into the small of my back. "Do you have any idea how bad I want this, Max? How desperate I am to feel you lose control?"

"You wanted to slow down—*we agreed* we'd slow down."

"And maybe we agreed for the wrong reasons. Maybe we've been trying too hard to fit into the past while still trying to lock down our future."

"Yeah?" he asks but it's more like a threat than a question.

"Yeah," I toss back with the same level of sass as I press my chest firmly against his, my nipples hard and pebbled and wanting. "I don't want to recreate our first time. I don't want someone else's version of what a perfect relationship looks like."

"So, what do you want?"

"You, Max. I want you."

24

MONTANA

"Are you sure this is what you want?" I ask between kisses as her hands dive under my shirt, her nails digging into my back as she pulls me flush against her.

Fuck, that feels good.

My hands grip her ass, and I rock her against my cock as I move her backward up her porch steps until her back collides with her front door. My hand fumbles with the knob before pushing it open and ushering her inside.

The door slams with the help of my boot, but I barely hear it over the blood pounding in my ears. Ellison's hands yank at the buttons of my shirt until I'm forced to pull it over my head and toss it to the side.

"Yeah, I'm definitely sure." She bites down on my lip before soothing the sting with her tongue, and I groan as my restraint slips a little more. Her eyes are appraising as they rake over me, my dick punching at my zipper with each second that passes.

"Dammit, Eddie, I want you so bad."

"Not before I have your cock in my mouth," she practically growls as she reaches for my belt with greedy hands.

"Not yet," I grit out.

I love seeing this side of her—wild and frantic—but I'll never last with those perfect pink lips wrapped around me, sucking and swallowing and punishing me in turn.

Fuck, I want it—but not yet.

My hands grip her ass and I spin us, pinning her to the wall. Her nails scrape against my scalp and I want to purr like a cat—lean into her touch and submit to her every demand.

"Bedroom," I manage on a groan as she rocks her hips against me, and I can't help it. Slamming my lips against hers, I sweep over every inch of her sassy mouth with my tongue.

"It's too far."

"Tell me what you want, Ellison, and I'll give it to you, but fuck, baby, I need you to tell me what we're doin' here." I need her to say it. I'm desperate for her words—the ones that will obliterate the line we'd maintained as best friends for most of our lives.

The one that says there's no going back.

She whimpers, her nails clawing into my shoulders as she tries with enthusiasm to get herself off as she's caged between me and the wall.

I have half a mind to let her, but all I can think about is seeing her spread wide for me, naked and wet and begging for me to devour her.

"You're wasting time and I need you. Please...can you just—"

Knock. Knock. Knock.

"Ellison?" The voice is deep and familiar, and I can't school my features fast enough as her hooded gaze meets mine. Her brows furrow—she's confused and I'm *pissed*.

You have got to be fucking kidding me.

Time stops as the knocking continues, my heart racing for an entirely different reason as her hand pats my chest, her body wriggling out of my grasp so she can stand on the floor. I have to steady her, but before I can say anything else, she's padding across the room to the front door before yanking it open.

"Dad?" Her tone is surprised and a little bit irritated, and I'm thankful for the latter. "What are you doing here?"

"Ellison, hi." His gaze travels to me, his smile faltering. "I didn't realize you had company."

Dragging my hand over my face, I count to five and try not to lose my shit on Ellison's father. *I didn't realize you had company*, my ass. He parked right next to my god damn truck.

The prick.

"Evening, Montana," he says coolly and I cross my arms over my bare chest, relishing the fact that his daughter couldn't wait to tear my shirt off.

"Mr. Mills."

Stepping into the house, he closes the door behind him as he stares at me, Ellison's gaze bouncing between us before turning on her father.

"What are you doing here? It's nine o'clock; you couldn't wait till tomorrow?"

"I need a place to stay and hoped you'd be willing to help your father out for the night."

"What do you mean? Your house is literally right there." She waves her hand in a direction not close to where her childhood home is. "That makes no sense."

Lips pressed into a thin line, I watch as he debates how much to tell her—how much he wants to tell her in front of *me*.

"It's a long story," he says finally as my hands clench into fists, my arms flexing as I try to maintain my composure.

But it's hard. It's so damn hard when this man damn near destroyed me without a second glance. He'd broken my heart and my spirit without an ounce of remorse. Even now, his expression gives nothing away like he's still looking down his nose at the same eighteen-year-old kid.

But I'm not that kid, and he's in for the surprise of his fucking life if he thinks I'm going to let him ruin us again.

"Max?" Ellison's voice cuts though my spiraling thoughts, bringing me back to the present—the look on her face telling me everything I need to know. Evan's lips twitch the slightest bit as I snatch my shirt off the floor and pull it over my head.

Ignoring him and the absolute rage inside, I stalk over to Ellison and cup her face in my hands before slanting my lips over hers, swallowing the gasp and moan that follow.

It's only seconds but it feels like a lifetime when I finally pull away, her cheeks flushed and her eyes glassy as they search mine.

"I'll see you tomorrow," I say loud enough for her father to hear. He doesn't say anything, but I don't miss the way he shifts from one foot to the other either.

"I can come over later and—"

Shaking my head, I drop a soft kiss to her mouth and another lingering one on her forehead. "Tomorrow." She huffs and I chuckle even though there's nothing funny about this moment. The tension is so thick you could cut it with a knife, and while I know I'll have to come to some sort of truce with Evan for Ellison's sake—today is not that day.

Heading for the door, I slow my steps and drop my voice so only he can hear. "I'm not going anywhere, so if you try anything—if you hurt her in any way—*I will ruin you.*"

His eyes widen the slightest bit, eyes that had held so much contempt the last time we spoke, while his mouth presses into a firm line.

But I won't back down.

Not this time.

Ellison is mine and I won't let him destroy us again.

Not again.

25

ELLISON

W atching Montana stomp down the porch steps has my heart taking up residence in my throat. I'm missing something—I can feel it. The tension in the room is so much heavier than just my father cockblocking us tonight.

And what did Montana say to him on the way out?

My father's expression had been heated but also *resigned.*

Time to get some answers.

"What are you doing here?"

Dragging his hands down his face, he blows out a heavy breath before meeting my gaze. He looks exhausted, and I can only imagine what that could possibly mean.

"I filed for divorce."

"You did?" I ask, genuinely surprised because I honestly didn't think he had it in him. He'd been miserable as long as I could remember with only pockets of happiness when he and I were together.

It never made sense to me that he would stay. He was wealthy in his own right, but he'd never been obsessed with being one of the social elite like my mother. But still, *he stayed*—stayed with her after I graduated from high school, moved to Savannah where I attended college, and stayed close after I got a job.

None of it made sense.

Dropping down into the armchair, he tilts his head back and looks at the ceiling. Without speaking, I move around the kitchen, pulling out glasses and a bottle of whiskey. I make us two drinks, mine on the rocks and his neat, before handing it to him and curling up on the couch.

"What happened?"

"What didn't?" he responds before taking a healthy sip, his focus on something behind me. "I don't want to speak ill of your mother."

"We are *way* past that," I say pointedly, his lips twitching upward even though he still looks haunted.

"I didn't realize the lengths she'd go to keep us together." He laughs but it's completely devoid of humor. "I'm going to lose almost everything to that woman. But you know what? None of it matters. As soon as the ink dries I'll be free, and even if I have to rent a studio apartment over Montana's garage—it's going to be worth it."

I can't help it; I laugh, because the idea that my father would have to rent an apartment from Montana is hilarious. But I don't truly know how much of that is true and how much is exaggerated for my benefit.

"Did you just ignore it all these years, or were you truly that blind to what a terrible person she is?"

His face contorts into a grimace, and I know that part of me doesn't want his answer. I need it—but that doesn't mean I want to know the lengths the woman that birthed me would go to keep up appearances.

"There was a lot of pressure on your mother and me to get married," he says quietly, staring at his glass. "She knew

I wasn't happy and we agreed to take some time apart." His smile is sad as he continues. "I met someone. I wasn't looking, but when I saw her, I couldn't look away. She was amazing, beautiful, and kind, and I had been mesmerized."

"What happened?" I ask as dread settles in my stomach.

"I didn't know if it would work out with this woman but I knew I wanted to find out—I wanted to try. So, I went to talk to your mother—she deserved a conversation at least—but when I got there she told me she was pregnant."

Even though I knew it was coming, I couldn't stop the way my eyes welled with tears as I tossed back the rest of my whiskey.

"People coparent all the time," I manage, desperately trying to reconcile that my father stayed with my mother simply because she was pregnant with me. I didn't have to ask if he'd gotten a DNA test—our resemblance has always been strong, our eyes especially, with the flecks of gold so stark against the rich brown.

He shakes his head. "Not back then and not in our world. She would have taken you from me, and I wouldn't have survived that."

"But then why stay once I turned eighteen? And why placate her all these years? You knew what she put me through—you knew I didn't belong and you just went along with it. Hell, sometimes I wondered if you cared at all. I mean, I know we've gotten better over the years, but it's not like it was all smooth sailing with us." My heart races and the words spill from my lips, each question ratcheting up my anger and hurt from years of being forced into a life that wasn't ever mine.

"Your grandparents established a trust for you that you'll have access to when you turn thirty-five." He swallows hard. "I'd been advised that one of the stipulations for you to receive it was that your mother and I had to remain married for that time as well—a punishment for me wanting to leave. As for the rest, I have no excuse. She made it excruciating at times, and it felt like the only way to get through it was to distance myself for a while. It wasn't fair to you and for that, Ellison, I am truly sorry."

"You said you'd *been advised*," I ask, my head tilting to the side as his expression darkens. "What does that mean?"

"It means it was never actually part of the agreement."

"You just blindly accepted the terms she put in front of you?"

"Try to understand how difficult it was for me. I'd had to tell the woman I was falling for that we couldn't be together, wrap my head around becoming a father with a woman I knew would make my life a living hell, and reconcile that I was now responsible for an innocent little girl whom I still am not worthy of." Tears glisten in his eyes and I have to blink back my own. "I just wanted to protect you, and I didn't want to be the reason you'd have to forfeit the money."

"I've never cared about the money. I still don't."

"I know. But your mother had been manipulative. If I'd been thinking more clearly, I would have known that your grandparents never would have put something like that in the conditions. They weren't loving, but they were decent people and they were thrilled to have a granddaughter."

My mother's parents had passed when I was young, too young to remember them. My father's parents had been much the same—it was why I'd so eagerly taken up a place at the table with Nan and Grandad.

I craved the affection and they'd given it freely.

"What about all the years you were barely there? All the times you *left* me with her."

"It wasn't by choice," he says quietly before meeting my gaze. "There were a couple of times I threatened to leave her, the contract be damned, but"—his voice breaks on the last word—"she would've taken you and no judge in the state of Tennessee would have changed that. So," he says tiredly, his shoulders sagging with the admission, "I had to keep my distance to keep you safe. I couldn't risk her leaving in the middle of the night—you would have been gone forever."

"What changed?" I ask, my mind reeling, "What changed now?"

"I was contacted by a...reporter," he says wryly, an odd inflection on *reporter*.

"Really? Isn't that confidential?"

"It wasn't about that specifically, but our conversation raised enough questions that I did some digging of my own."

"And?"

He sighs and the sound encompasses decades of a miserable life, not just the present. "And your mother is worse than we thought."

"Unlikely." He raises an eyebrow at me so I shrug. "I've known it for years; I just couldn't escape her."

"I'm sorry for that too."

"Honestly? I can't dwell on that anymore. I'm here and I'm happy and I want to build a life with the man I've loved since the day we met." My father blanches so I say, "I hope that you can find your happiness too."

His phone buzzes in quick succession and he pulls it out of his pocket, barely glancing at it before handing it to me.

SHERRI ANN: You better get back to
Savannah before people start talking, Evan.

SHERRI ANN: You'll be nothing without me.
I won't let you and Ellison ruin everything
I've worked for

SHERRI ANN: I've done everything for this
family and you had one job and you still
messed it up!

SHERRI ANN: I won't let you get away with
this. I will take every dime and you'll be left
with nothing. You disgust me—crawling
back to that godforsaken town.

SHERRI ANN: Answer me!

"Wow."

He snorts. "I have to survive the divorce first."

I nod, because that's no exaggeration.

26

MONTANA

MONTANA: Meet me in the field

ARCHER: Beer?

MONTANA: All of it

ARCHER: Oh boy…

JENSEN: I'll be there

MASON: Us too

JENSEN: Are you always gonna answer for him?

MASON: Probably. I think he has this group chat on silent

MONTANA: I'd be offended if I wasn't so pissed

> ARCHER: Plenty of time to be offended
> later, let's just get to the field

P ocketing my phone, I grab the beer in my fridge and trudge out to the barn I'd repainted last summer, the red-and-white paint still crisp in the lamp light. Sliding into the driver's seat of the ATV, I have to take a steadying breath as my thoughts immediately go to the night I had Ellison spread out on the seat as she screamed my name.

I'd gotten this damn thing for Grandad, but I'd never be able to look at it the same. I'd intended for him to cruise around in it, but he said he much preferred commandeering the tractor instead.

Because of course he did.

I could use any vehicle on hand here to pull the ATV out if he got it stuck—hell, *I* could probably heave it out of most situations without any help at all. But that wasn't my life and while I wasn't complaining, I wasn't *not* complaining either.

It starts up with a soft purr and I drive it out the back and onto the dirt path, cutting through the yard and disappearing farther away from my responsibilities.

And the way this night had gotten out of hand.

Hurt and anger course through my veins, the entire night on a loop inside my head. I'm exhausted from the highs and lows, but I'll be damned if this is the universe's way of telling me Ellison isn't the girl for me.

Because she's not just the girl for me.

She's the *only* girl for me.

Grumbling, I park next to the firepit and climb out, gathering some newspaper and lighter fluid from the seat beside me. My boots are silent on the crushed grass, the area well acquainted with my late-night visits.

Gathering some wood, I set everything up and light a match. The blaze is immediate, the accelerant doing its job enough that I'm already nursing my first beer when the sound of Archer's truck coming down the path disturbs the sanctuary of this space.

Doors open—not one but *two*—and I can only assume my cousin brought his girlfriend. I like Bea, and it's not that I don't want her here, but I'm not really looking for any words of wisdom from the female persuasion.

"You got a permit for this fire?" a husky male voice asks from behind me, and I chuckle as Jensen drops a folding chair next to me and sits with an audible sigh.

"No, Sheriff, I don't."

Cracking open a beer, he stares at the fire before shrugging. "I'm off duty."

"No need to worry. I filled up the water barrel before I came over," Archer says with a huff as he sets his chair down on the other side of Jensen. "You're welcome," he says pointedly as he leans up to look at me. I raise my beer and watch as his eyebrows follow the motion.

"Thanks," I say half-heartedly.

"Jesus, what happened to you?" he asks and I shake my head once.

"Fuck if I know." Turning to Jensen, I ask, "Why were you with Archer?"

I can't be sure in the light, but I'm almost positive he blushes. "Had to pick something up."

"He likes Bea's soap," Archer adds helpfully with a smirk.

"Is that a euphemism?" I ask, immediately causing both of them to scowl.

"No," Jensen says before squaring his shoulders. "I've been workin' so much with us being short-staffed, and I'm exhausted—barely got time to shower let alone sleep. Been using that soap she makes and it's nice, doesn't dry out my skin."

He takes a drink of his beer and I reach over and touch his arm. "Oh, that is nice," I say to get a rise out of him. It works, but I can't dodge the jab he throws at my bicep in retaliation. We laugh and he tells us about the shenanigans happening over in Clementine Creek including the good, bad, and absolutely ridiculous.

It feels good to laugh—even if just for a short while.

"You guys get started without us?" Mason says with a smile as he steps out of the shadows, grabbing chairs for himself and Bodhi from the back of Archer's truck.

The worn path between the properties is the perfect go-between and we use it often.

The first time they came upon the fire, it had been to make sure the field wasn't burning. After that, it was because this is where we all gather now—aside from game night.

At one point a variety of the Thayers would make a habit of stopping by, but it didn't happen as often with them all settling down, leaving the bachelor life in the rearview mirror.

"Montana is havin' a meltdown," Archer says before taking a sip of his beer.

I scowl at him then look back at the newcomers. "Just wanted to come out and enjoy the night."

Bodhi's lips twitch the slightest bit as he accepts a beer from Mason and settles into his chair. There's an ease to their relationship—a level of comfort and comradery that the rest of us will never breach. They may not be bonded by blood, but there's not a single person who can argue that they're not brothers.

"Uh-huh. So trouble in paradise then?" Mason asks with a cocky smile as he kicks his legs out in front of him, crossing one work boot over the other.

"No," I say at the same time Jensen and Archer say *yes*. The jerks. Looking back at the fire, I go for flippant. "Unless you got some words of wisdom for me, y'all can shut it."

"Isn't he supposed to be the nice one?" Jensen asks the group, causing a couple of snickers as the flames from the fire climb into the night sky.

"I *am* the nice one. Things just got complicated tonight."

"We're gonna need more than that," Jensen pries. Whether it's just his natural inclination to dig for information or that he's a gossipy fucker I'll never truly know, but tonight I can't fight it.

"I took her on a date, a real one, date went to shit—we pivoted—date got better. Went back to her place and her father showed up with an *it's complicated* story about him bein' back in Blackstone Falls."

"When you say you *went back to her place,* you mean..." Mason says with a grin and the one track mind of a guy in his early twenties while completely ignoring my glare. Bodhi sighs heavily next to him, and I appreciate the unspoken support.

Turning my attention to Archer, I watch as his eyes widen with recognition and sympathy. He's the only one who knows what happened, the one who helped me build an empire that would stand against the wrath of Ellison's father.

One I'd love to rub in his face.

"So obviously you and her father have a history," Jensen

says easily, "and what? He's back and you think he's going to keep you from her?"

Did I think that?

No, because I told him I wouldn't let it happen.

"It just feels like since we started tryin' to do this the right way, everything's just gone to hell in a handbasket in the last twenty-four hours."

"So go back to what you were doing before," Mason says matter-of-factly before taking a sip of his beer.

If only.

"I don't know if it's that easy," I admit.

"Did you ask?" Mason says with his eyebrows halfway up his forehead. "Seems like you're getting worked up a lot over nothing before you know it's something."

All eyes turn to look at him, but he only shrugs like it's the most obvious thing in the world. Kid may be a goofball most of the time, but he's seen more in his years on this earth than most will their whole lives.

"Just let me know if I need to bury any bodies," Bodhi says over the crackle of the fire, the faintest hint of a smile on his face.

"You've been hanging out too much with the Thayers." Jensen groans and we all chuckle although I have no idea if Bodhi's offer is legitimate or not.

"Man, I miss them," I say, happy to have the focus shifted from me. "They doin' okay? I can hardly keep track of what they got going on over there."

Archer snorts. "I don't know about the Thayers, but I heard our beloved sheriff had to do a wellness check on Miss Thelma and she answered the door wearing only—"

"Do *not* finish that sentence." Jensen shudders and I bark out a laugh as Bodhi's mouth falls open, and Mason giggles like it's the best thing he's ever heard. "It still gives me nightmares."

"And they say nothin' happens in a small town," I tease, and he glares at me because we both know Miss Thelma is hell on wheels on a good day. The spitfire of a woman dedicated her time—and wardrobe—to her cat, Louise, after her husband passed away. Now there isn't a shirt, skirt, or legging that doesn't have her beloved cat's face on it.

It was honestly impressive, and if that wasn't enough, she also made a county-famous Moscow Mule that could knock a grown man on his ass. I'd often wondered if there would ever be a spark between her and Grandad, but so far I hadn't flexed my geriatric matchmaking muscles.

Also, I wasn't entirely ready to accidentally walk in on Grandad gettin' busy. I wish I could say it had never happened, but that'd be a lie. No grandchild should ever be subjected to that kind of encounter. But he and Nan had been happy and I was happy for him for still bein' able to get it up.

But Lord have mercy I didn't need to bear witness to it.

Or hear it.

"Why are you makin' that face?" Jensen asks, but I shake my head.

"You don't want to know."

I'm not lying—but at the same time, I want what they had. To be old and wrinkly and still chasing her around the house, grabbing her ass and kissin' her breathless.

We have forever to get living and she needs to catch up.

"You'll have to let me know what that's like," Mason says quietly, his gaze fixed on the fire.

"What?"

"Getting to love someone your whole life."

You'll find it. The words are on the tip of my tongue, but I swallow them down because I don't know. I have no idea what he's been through and if his past will ever truly allow for a future.

But I can pray—and I do—for him and Bodhi to find peace and love and sanctuary in Blackstone Falls. It's been almost two years since they landed here, but I still wouldn't be surprised to find they'd fled in the middle of the night.

Mason gives me a boyish, aw-shucks grin and he looks every bit his twenty-three years. "Don't worry. It'll happen for me—for us," he says motioning to Bodhi. "We're just picking up somewhere in the middle, and I think it's nice knowing that people can love each other through all the stages of life."

Well shit.

Holding my beer out to him, his bottle clinks against mine, and he nods before turning back to the fire. His words resonate deep within me—the rightness so obvious now that they've been spoken by someone else.

Finishing my beer, I let the bottle drop into the grass below and look up at the stars.

I've loved Ellison my whole life, but I can't help thinking it's about time I let myself fall for her too.

27

ELLISON

I snuck out of the house before my father woke, desperately needing space and praying for some sort of clarity. The entire situation has left me unsettled both with my father and Montana, not to mention the texts from my mother. Exhaustion seeped from my pores as I shuffled around the kitchen before deciding I needed to get away.

Making sure to start the coffee pot, I text Cal, my first ever 9-1-1 friend text, and smile uncontrollably as he sends me several expletive responses one right after the other before asking what time we are meeting.

Apparently, he had no idea just how much fun being my friend would be.

With less growling, we agree on the Kettle and Kiln, and I breathe a sigh of relief when I pull into a spot at the front of the shop. The coffee shop hadn't been here when I was growing up, but I liked it immediately the first time I'd driven by.

Normally, I'd wait in my car, but my nervous energy has me pulling open the pressed-tin door before I can second-guess it.

The inside is bright and airy—inviting—and the sign behind the counter reads *You make 'em. We bake 'em* where a woman sporting a long braid smiles at me while stocking the front case with muffins.

"Morning!" she chirps, her blonde hair and pale skin at odds with the sun in Tennessee. "I don't think we've met. I'm Nicolette," she says, her stunning teal eyes sparkling as she offers me her hand.

"Ellison. It's nice to meet you," I say automatically as we shake. It's unusual; I can't think of another time outside of Blackstone Falls that anyone wanted to get to know me simply because I walked in the door.

"Are you with Montana Greene?" she asks, her lips curving up as her head cocks slightly to the side.

"Yes?" The single word is a question because despite the cluster that was last night, I *am* with Montana.

Her smile is both knowing and sympathetic as she presses her palms against the counter and grins. "He's in here all the time going on and on about you." She winks and I blush. "Y'all will have to come for my pottery class. Couple sessions can be *very* sensual." She winks again as Cal strides toward the counter, removing his sunglasses and tucking them into the collar of his shirt.

"I'd apologize for being late but I'm not sorry," he deadpans, and Nicolette snickers as I turn to face him, my eyebrow arched expectantly. "What? It's barely morning and she's"—he hitches his thumb toward Nicolette—"used to me."

"And here I thought we were friends," I tease.

"I got out of bed for you, didn't I?"

"Your sacrifice is noted," I say solemnly as I turn back toward Nicolette who doesn't bother to hide her smile.

"What can I get you two?"

After ordering the largest coffee I've ever seen, Cal and I settle into a little table in the corner. I pull my own mug close to me, letting the warmth seep into my hands even though I'm not cold.

"So..." Cal presses as he stares at me over the lip of his cup.

"So, my father is divorcing my mother, who is apparently more diabolical than even I realized, and he couldn't stay at their house in Blackstone Falls for whatever reason and him showing up at my place effectively cockblocked me when Montana and I were trying to rip each other's clothes off in my kitchen."

He blinks at me, his mouth falling open probably at the ridiculousness of that run-on sentence.

"I don't think I've had enough coffee to work through that," he says finally.

"Me either."

"What is bothering you the most?"

Taking a sip of my coffee, I think about his question—really think—and the answer is not easy to admit. "I feel like I can't have both of them in my life if I want to be happy. There's tension that I think goes beyond my parents not wanting me to date Montana in high school."

"Really?"

"I always thought my father didn't want us together, but after talking to him last night, I can't help but wonder if my mother put him up to it, you know? I mean, she never liked Montana either but...I don't know. None of it makes sense."

Nodding slowly, Cal puts his cup on the table. "I think that you've put too much pressure on making your return home the best thing that's ever happened to you. And that was before"—he makes a circle with his hand—"all of this happened. I'm not saying you don't deserve all the magic and excitement, but maybe look at what you actually want right *now*—what you can control. Do that and make everything else secondary." He shrugs. "You need to prioritize."

It sounds easy enough.

"You're right."

He sighs dreamily. "I never get tired of hearing that."

Rolling my eyes, I take a sip of my coffee, my mind already sifting through everything I'd been hung up on before settling firmly on Montana.

My father's presence had been so much more than a minor inconvenience. I'd wanted so desperately to cross that line with a tall, dark, and delicious cowboy. The flirting and the banter had been fun, but I craved the connection above all else.

The one that zipped through my veins and made me feel like we were tethered together. The thought is calming and I let it wash over me, calming my soul and the discontent that pulled me out of the house at such an ungodly hour.

My mother's drama can wait.

And so can my father.

"So what are you going to do?" Cal asks as he sits back and crosses his ankle over his knee.

"I'm going to get my father out of my house and settled, establish some boundaries with him, and then I'm going to find Montana and make sure he knows exactly where we stand."

"Well," he says, tipping his cup back and placing it on the table. "Let's get you another coffee; you have a hell of a day ahead."

Nodding, I smile and pull out my phone and type out a text.

ELLISON: I have a lot to take care of today, but I plan on being in your bed tonight

MONTANA: Are you sure?

MONTANA: I want to see you but I don't want it to be more stress.

ELLISON: I'll use my key if I have to but it's nonnegotiable

MONTANA: Fuck that's a relief

ELLISON: We need it

MONTANA: I need you

ELLISON: I'm yours.

28

MONTANA

It's dark out when my bedroom door creaks open and closes with a barely audible snick. I spent all day waiting for this moment, working harder in the fields to pass the time before stumbling back here too exhausted to keep my eyes open.

I think I was scared she wouldn't show, so I made sure I wouldn't miss her if she didn't. Heart pounding in my chest, I don't move, and I don't dare look at the clock because the only thing that matters is that she's *here*. Shadows move across Ellison in a sultry kind of dance, and I want so badly to reach out and trace every single one.

She pauses at the side of the bed, shimmying out of her shorts and pulling her shirt over her head, the lace barely visible on her bra and panties as she pulls the covers back. I swallow hard as she slides in next to me, the mattress barely registering her weight.

"I'm not sorry I woke you," she says quietly as she closes the distance between us, draping her leg over mine and leaning over me.

"You used your key."

"I told you I would."

My unspoken *I didn't believe you* hangs between us, her dark eyes searching mine before she dips her head and presses a gentle kiss against the column of my throat. Her breath is hot on my skin as she does it again.

And again.

My Adam's apple bobs as I release a shaky breath into the silence.

My hand moves from where it's resting on the mattress, up over her hip to draw small circles on her back, dipping barely under the lacy waistband of her panties but eliciting a shiver from her all the same. Her skin is soft and smooth, and it's like the blanket of darkness makes us a little bolder. There's no game to be played right now and nothing but the intentional shift of her body closer to mine to tell me what she needs.

"Montana?" Her voice is like the softest caress, forcing my gaze to meet hers. "I don't want anything between us. I want to feel all of you." Her gaze drops to my lips, and even with the shadows cast across her face, I don't miss the hunger as she waits for my response.

But I'm not ready for words just yet, my heart in my throat making it damn near impossible to speak.

I've never not used a condom—priding myself on always protecting the women I'd taken to bed before this, as well as myself.

But that was before.

And there'll be no one after this.

Trailing my palm up her spine, I relish the goose bumps that cover her skin. The way she reacts to a simple touch has my blood running hot in my veins.

"I've never done it without one."

Her smile is wicked as it slowly spreads across her face,

her hips rocking against my leg that's sandwiched between her thighs. I can feel her heat, the friction of the lace, and how absolutely soaked she is for me.

"But you'll do it for me..." She draws out the last word, making it not a question but a challenge.

"Yes," I rasp, the concession stealing what little breath I have from my lungs.

"I'm safe," she murmurs, pressing her covered tits against my chest, reassuring me with the statement and her body.

"Me too," I grunt as my hand moves to grip the back of her neck, holding her in place as I let go of every last reservation I've ever had about crossing this line.

It's intoxicating—feeling how taut her body is strung just waiting for me to give in to her, to give in to this glorious unknown that's always been between us. The one that we've waded in just far enough to taste but never enough to indulge.

Her body molds to mine as I guide her head down to meet my lips. Her fingers flex against my bare chest, and I know she wants to sink her nails into my skin—to feel grounded in my body as she comes apart.

"Do you want it as badly as I do?"

"Yes," I whisper against her lips as I pull her down the rest of the way until her mouth is hovering above mine. She doesn't fight my grasp and I know right now, in the darkness, she'll surrender to me—to everything I want and everything I have to give.

My tongue licks along her lower lip, and she trembles as a little gasp escapes her. "Max."

The plea in her voice slices through the last of my restraint as I crush my mouth to hers. Ellison moans, the sound reverberating between us as I slide my tongue into her mouth and roll her underneath me.

The movement traps my arm against the mattress, making me pull back long enough to unhook her bra and toss it across the room before covering her body with mine again.

There's no talking this time.

No smart-ass remarks or sassy comments or digs intended to rile me up beyond all reason.

Her breasts are full and round as they press against my chest, her nipples hard and aching for me as I rock my hips against her lace-covered pussy. She moans and I swallow the sound, her leg hooking over mine as she searches desperately for a way to be closer.

I love this side of her, and I hate how long it's been since she's been so exposed to me, both body and heart. There's no pretense here, just desire for all the things we haven't said aloud.

Pushing up, I dip my fingers below the waistband of her panties and pull them down her legs, throwing them onto the floor before discarding my boxer briefs. I have to stop myself from reaching for a condom. It shouldn't be this big of a deal but it is because it's *her*. I can't stop thinking about the way she so freely asked for what she wants, not only inviting me into her body but trusting me as I hover over her gorgeous body once again.

God damn, it's been so long.

So fucking long since I had her last.

Since I had her like *this*.

I want to slam into her and I want to make love to her and I want to taste every inch of her twice over before I let myself come.

I want so much more than just tonight.

As if sensing my inner musings, Ellison's slender fingers weave through my hair, gripping the strands as she pulls my face to her for a bruising kiss. I follow her lead, teasing her entrance only long enough to coat my dick with her wetness before rocking inside her.

She holds me tighter and kisses me harder with each thrust until she's pulled me down on top of her, my body covering every inch of hers.

"Ellison," I manage to rasp out as her mouth moves across my jaw to nip at the tendon in my neck. I don't know what this is—this desperation pouring off her in spades as we climb higher and higher toward the inevitable pleasure we're chasing.

I push her harder into the mattress, caging her in and pinning her down until she's writhing and moaning and clawing at my back.

"Please."

She begs me over and over to let her come, my body in complete agreement, sweat coating my brow as I rock and swivel my hips.

I'm torturing us both and I don't know why. Maybe it's to remind her who she belongs to even though we've never spoken the words out loud. Maybe I should have because there'll be a cold day in hell before she's anything but mine after tonight.

Hell, since she came back to Blackstone Falls. She gave us a second chance when we'd never even had a first.

Grunts and pants fill the air, my entire being content to consume her in this moment. But when Ellison's hands move to grip my ass, her nails digging into my flesh, I snap. I piston into her, the bed scraping against the floor as she forces me hard—*deeper*—inside her hot, wet heat.

She comes first on a silent scream, her head thrown back

as she clenches around me—wave after wave of her release strangling my dick until I'm coming too. I bury my face in her neck, sinking my teeth into her shoulder, and ride out the most incredible orgasm of my life.

Bright dots dance behind my eyelids, and I have to remember to breathe as I try to regain my composure, licking and kissing the marks I left on her delicate skin.

Ellison is limp beneath me, her fingertips trailing lazily up and down my spine. We don't talk—don't make a sound —and I wish we could stay like this forever. I could live right here inside her for the rest of my days.

29

ELLISON

"What I wouldn't give to crawl back into bed with you, wake you up right with my head between your legs." Montana's voice is quiet and husky, and I can't quite pinpoint his location in the room. Heat gathers in my core, his words so deliciously tempting in my sleepy state. Nuzzling my face into the soft cotton of the pillow, I stretch my arms in front of me while wiggling my front against the mattress, craving any kind of friction.

Smack.

"Ow!" I yelp as his palm comes down hard on my backside and *oh wow I definitely like it.*

"Stop shaking your ass at me when you know I can't do anything about it." He laughs as I roll onto my side and squint into the mostly darkened room.

"Come back to bed and you can do more than just spank me." I bite my bottom lip to keep from laughing as he growls and drags his hands down his face.

"Dammit, woman—do you know what it's like trying to herd cows with a hard-on?"

"Can't say that I do, Cowboy."

"Watch it, Eddie, or I'll end up tyin' you to the bed and punishing that mouth of yours."

His words send a shock of lust through my veins, and even though my smirk is firmly in place, I can't deny how wet I am at the implication.

"Promises, promises," I say with enough sass to maintain the charade.

He stalks across the room before coming back toward me, pausing at the edge of the bed, and I'm torn between ripping off the covers and offering myself to him or just hoping and praying he makes good on his threat.

"I'm not old enough for all the gray hairs you're giving me, and I haven't had you nearly enough to make up for it. Hell, you haven't even been inside the county line that long."

"Just a little closer and you can come inside all you want and—"

Montana slaps his hand over my mouth at the same time he places a kiss on my forehead. Taking a giant step away from the bed, he walks to the bedroom door, muttering and cursing as he goes.

"One of these days, the rest of the world will realize you're not as innocent as you claim to be," he says, but there's a fond expression on his face. He *likes me* like this and honestly, I like me like this too—that this can finally be us.

Sure, I'm really pushing his buttons before either one of us has even had caffeine, but I like that I can just be me when we're together. I can be sassy and carefree and a little bit daring, and none of it matters because Montana has always been there to catch me.

It's been a long time since I felt safe enough to be this bold—this reckless. Shamelessly flirting with Montana, tempting him, shouldn't feel this freeing but it does, like shedding another layer of the person I had to be in Savannah.

I missed this.

"I'm only wild with you."

"You keep sweet-talking me and I might never leave."

This time I do throw back the covers, and he groans as his eyes rake over every naked inch of me.

"That's the idea," I purr as he stalks back across the room and drops to his knees at the edge of the mattress. Strong, callused hands grip my ass, his fingers digging into my flesh as he drags me to him before wedging his broad shoulders between my thighs.

There's nothing sweet about the way he devours me. There's no hesitation as he nips and licks and sucks before sliding two fingers into me, curving them just enough that I have to suppress a scream as I come faster than I ever have in my life.

It shouldn't be this good.

He shouldn't be this good.

"God damn, you're sexy," he rumbles, his tongue still lazily dragging up and down my slit. "I could do this all day long."

"I thought you were going to be late," I breathe out with less teasing and more moaning as I walk the line of being too sensitive and desperately craving more.

"Good thing I know the boss," he says with a wicked gleam in his eyes as he pinches my clit between his teeth and stars burst behind my eyelids.

"Thank God for that."

MONTANA WAS DEFINITELY late to work.

Very late.

He'd gotten me off twice with his mouth before flipping me onto my hands and knees and pounding into me from behind. He'd been completely unhinged, pleasuring me as if he'd been waiting years to taste me and was making up for lost time.

And isn't that what we're doing?

Pulling myself out of bed, I smile as I walk to the shower, my muscles deliciously sore from last night but more accurately *this morning*. Montana had loved me thoroughly, teased me relentlessly, and absolutely obliterated all my senses.

It was the kind of thing you want to hold on to forever and pray it will always be this way. With the lengths we'd taken to get back here, I had to believe that it would—that *we* would make it.

Dressing quickly, I braid my hair and forgo any and all makeup, opting for a moisturizer with an SPF instead. I'll have to put a little more effort in once the school year starts, but for now, I'll enjoy the simplicity of this routine.

Stopping in the kitchen, I give Grandad a kiss on the cheek before pouring myself a cup of coffee and joining him at the table. The morning paper is spread out before him, and I shimmy out one of the pages he's already read, earning a judgmental eyebrow.

"I'm gonna need that back," he says pointedly.

"You already read this one."

"No,"—he taps the left side of the open paper—"I read this side, not this one." His finger moves to tap the right side and I grin.

"Well, I appreciate your willingness to share. I'll give it

back when you need it," I say with a sweet smile that has him chuckling and shaking his head.

I'm halfway through the article by Arden James on the benefits of small-town communities when Grandad's low rumble breaks the silence.

"Heard your father is back in town." He eyes me over the lip of his coffee cup, casually taking a sip as if he's talking about the weather.

"He is," I confirm even though it's redundant. "He's divorcing my mother and waiting for her to take everything not nailed down to the floor."

"That woman always was a piece of work." I snort because that's putting it mildly. Reaching over, he places his hand over mine. "How are you holding up, Dolly?"

The nickname warms my heart, and I can't remember a time it didn't bring a smile to my face. It's always just been mine. Grandad call Vienna and Aspen each something different, the sentiment making me feel like one of them.

"I'm...conflicted," I admit, playing with the corner of the paper with my free hand. "I'm happy he's finally leaving her. I'm sad that so many years of his life were wasted being in a loveless marriage. I'm angry he's here—creating tension with Montana when all I want to do is enjoy finally being together. My mother is awful, and I think Dad is still keeping a secret from me, and I just feel so damn tired."

"Want me to get some whiskey to add to your coffee?" he asks, and I appreciate the seriousness in his tone.

"No, I—"

My phone buzzes next to me, and I glance down at the screen, feeling the way my smile curves up on one side before stretching across my face.

BEA: Goats will be arriving at two!

BEA: That's still okay, right?

ELLISON: We're gonna find out

ELLISON: (gif of baby goat jumping around)

BEA: On a scale of one to Godzilla destroying Tokyo, how mad is he going to be?

ELLISON: I can't wait to find out

"I HAVE A BETTER IDEA," I say, looking up at Grandad. "How do you feel about goats?"

30

MONTANA

I hear the little fuckers before I even see them—my blood pressure skyrocketing with each *bah* and *blet* that comes from the pen behind the barn.

The one that's supposed to be empty.

"Eddie!" I bark, startling at least one of the horses, but it can't be helped. I do *not* do goats.

"Hey, Max!" Ellison says brightly as I push my way outside where no fewer than ten goats of varying sizes prance happily around the paddock. "Aren't they the cutest?"

Ellison holds a small one in her arms and nuzzles her face against the white fur, her mischievous gaze never leaving mine. Hermie sits at her feet, his tongue hanging out as his tail moves fast enough over the ground to create a little dust storm.

Traitor.

"Eddie," I say through clenched teeth because as hot as she is and as cute as the damn goat is—*I do not do goats.*

"I know you said you didn't want goats, but Bea is looking to expand her business, and it's silly for her to find somewhere to get goats' milk when you have plenty of room right here. Besides, Grandad loves milking the cows, so I'm sure he'll like the goats too—you know, really give him a challenge. Besides he's really taken with that one, wants to name it Patches, you know, to go with Buttons." She points at a little tan goat with white blotches, and I growl as I internally count to five with talk of cat- and goat-themed names.

"He's already seen them?! The man just got out of the hospital; he doesn't need a challenge. He just had stents up in his heart. Hell, him gettin' the tractor stuck is challenge enough." Pinching the bridge of my nose, I pray for patience and everything else I can think of.

"To be fair, I had no way of knowing when they'd arrive." She worries her bottom lip with her teeth, her eyes wide as she stares at me. "I can admit the timing could have been better with everything we have goin' on."

"You think?" I drag my hands down my face before staring up at the sky, the fight draining from me with a startling quickness. "Why does it have to be goats?"

Ellison squeals, and my lips twitch because I can't stay mad at her even though I'm still *pissed* at the prospect of having these ornery little shits here.

"Look! Maybe we can even do goat yoga!" Ellison beams as she holds the little animal out to me, and I sigh as I take it.

"You better be naked when I get done today."

"This morning wasn't enough?" she teases with her head tilted to the side.

"Never enough, but also that was before you brought home goats."

"They're Bea's goats."

"Yeah, like that makes a difference."

Her eyes sparkle as she pops up onto her toes and places a kiss on my cheek. "You can have anything you want."

"I want a lot of things..." I let the words trail off, a wicked smirk playing on my lips.

"I just bet you do."

"Hey, so you're cool about the goats?" Archer asks cautiously as he follows the same path I took out of the barn. Bea gives me a nervous smile, eyeing the goat in my arms.

"I'm paying him in sexual favors," Ellison says with a shrug as Bea nods and Archer's face flames.

"Your sacrifice is noted and much appreciated, but I need to know, what's your aversion to goats?" Bea says with far too much glee.

"There's no story; I just don't like them."

"There's definitely a story," Ellison stage-whispers, earning a glare from me and another beaming smile from Bea.

"We've just never gotten along and—"

"He's scared of them," Ellison says with a grin.

"I have a healthy respect for their personal space," I counter and she snorts. "Ellison bet me I wasn't faster than them in a foot race."

"Hoof race." Archer snickers and so do the girls.

"And that I couldn't run from one side of the paddock to the other before one caught up to me."

"And?" Bea asks, practically vibrating with anticipation at my obvious demise.

"I wasn't watching where I was goin' and one of 'em ended up blocking my path to the fence as the others kept racing toward me. I made a break for it, but one of the little fuckers bit me on the ass as my foot hit the bottom board of the fence."

"Ripped half the seat of his jeans right off," Ellison adds helpfully.

"Well, your experience is duly noted and your sacrifice appreciated," Bea replies solemnly a half second before both girls dissolve into giggles. It's adorable, and I can't help but smile as they move toward the fence and proceed to name all the goats things like Lavender, Apricot, Cornbread, and a half dozen other food-inspired items I'm bound to forget.

"You love her?" Archer asks quietly as his eyebrows climb into his hairline. Before Bea, we never would have had a conversation like this—funny just how much a woman can change your life.

"Feels a lot like falling," I say honestly as Hermie's big head nudges at my hand. I've loved Ellison Mills my whole life. I loved her as the girl next door and my best friend and the girl who was determined to give me a heart attack simply because it was a Tuesday and she needed to let loose.

I've loved her platonically.

Romantically.

I've been *in love* with her a while.

But I've never gotten the chance to fall for her.

"   r you," he says, his gaze locked on Bea. "I al   ju'd find this but me?" He chuckles softly. "I never thought I'd find it at all, let alone first."

"Of course you would have," I scoff, but he just shakes his head.

"Relationships come naturally to you—people and love; it's all the same. You make it easy, man. You make people feel seen and heard. You never gave up on me." Now it's my turn to scoff, but he just shakes his head as he says, "If you hadn't claimed me as family,"—he waves his hand around—"I wouldn't be here."

"You *are* family," I say not because he's blood but because to me he just *is*, "and you're bein' dramatic. How many people do you think would take me seriously about opening up a realty business in a small college town?"

"So you're callin' me a chump?" he asks, humor plain in his tone.

"Definitely."

He snorts. "My bank account says otherwise."

"Imagine if you'd let me *really* pick the name." I pause for effect. "I bet we could have tripled our income."

"Only because people would think we were running a brothel in Nowhere, Tennessee."

"Discretion is key I've been told."

"Yeah, well, I'm sure they would have been more than a little disappointed to learn the *Harness and Hoe* was not some underground sex club."

In reality, I'd had no intention of making our business sound like a southern brothel, but it had been a hell of a lot of fun getting Archer riled up over it. We'd settled on Sundown Realty as an ode to "Ain't Going Down Till The Sun Comes Up" by Garth Brooks.

The man is a legend, and I'd only had to sing one and a half verses before Archer gave in and Sundown Realty was born.

While the fields of cotton were profitable, it wasn't a sure bet. Weather, soil conditions, and a host of other factors played a role in our ability to keep the farm running year after year. We'd been lucky, keeping a hand in livestock to help supplement the need for more help as Grandad had stepped back from the heavy lifting. Archer's situation had been more dire than mine, having lost half his soybean crop the prior harvest.

We'd made a plan and taken a risk that would have put

us in a hole we never would have been able to crawl out of... but it worked.

And until recently, we'd managed to keep our ownership of the multimillion-dollar company under wraps. Some days I still couldn't believe that we'd pulled it off—kept pulling it off and continued to grow despite being two guys who'd never had the heart to leave the land they'd inherited.

"I think the real miracle is that you were able to deliver that line hardly blushing at all."

Archer rolls his eyes. "I sent you the listing with all the properties available from here to Nashville. More than a few that would work for us."

"I'll take a look tonight and we can set it up," I finish as Bea and Ellison turn back to join us.

"I really do appreciate this, Montana," Bea says as she rests her hand on my forearm. "And whatever soaps, lotions, you name it—they're yours."

"It's..." I look at Ellison out of the corner of my eye. "It's fine. Grandad likes that lavender one you make."

"Of course." She nods as she settles against Archer's side, his arm coming around her with an ease I've only ever seen when he's with her. "We need to stop at your house before we go to mine tonight."

"Wait," Ellison says as she stares at them. "I thought y'all lived together?"

This time, it's Bea whose cheeks heat. "Not yet," she says with a smile. "I was engaged before I moved here and it didn't end well, and while Archer is *nothing* like my ex, we've been taking it slow."

Ellison gives me the side-eye. "Are we doin' it wrong, Max?" she asks, but the smile stretching across her face tells me there's no way she thinks we're doing it wrong.

Especially after last night.

Thank God.

But now all I'm thinking about is *doing it* and, *fuck,* the fact that she already promised to be naked when I got home.

And now I'm half-hard just thinkin' about it.

"I think you make your own rules, Eddie."

She grins. "But how come you don't want to stay at my place?"

"For starters, you moved half your shit into my bedroom your third day here—not to mention that damn Christmas card that keeps reappearing no matter how many times I throw it out."

"Christmas card?" Bea asks quietly.

"It's hilarious; I'll show you later," Archer says with a snicker.

I narrow my gaze at him before turning my attention back to Ellison. "Besides, I'm not really up for a repeat of your father cockblocking us anytime soon."

Bea's eyes widen, and Ellison raises a shoulder and then lets it drop. "Agreed. Especially because you made me use my key instead of crawling through your window the next night." Bea's gaze bounces between us like she can't quite tell if we're joking. We're not. "On the plus side, Dad hasn't come back to the cottage unannounced after that incident."

"It's been like thirty-six hours," I grumble as Archer looks wearily at me.

"I saw him talking to Arden James at the coffee shop. That's weird, right?" he asks, and something niggles in the back of my mind. Evan Mills is still on my shit list, so I can't distinguish which thoughts are rational as they race through my head.

"She reached out to me wanting to do a piece on the farm and our experimental pesticide success."

My gaze slides to Ellison who frowns. "He said that a

reporter reached out to him—it's what got the ball rolling on him filing for divorce. Could it be a coincidence?"

"I dunno, Eddie."

"I feel like you and I should talk—over coffee or wine, your choice," Bea says as her head tilts to the side, her attention ping-ponging between us. My girl smiles widely and nods her gratitude at the reprieve evident.

"Look, Max, my second friend! I've made *two friends* since I've been back!" I chuckle even though my heart hurts for her. She's making it a joke, but underneath I know she's truly excited about the prospect of having people other than me in her corner—people who are invested in her and not just because of me.

For all her bravado, she's still just a girl who's never been able to take anyone at face value. There were always ulterior motives and backhanded compliments just this side of *bless your heart.*

I'd never blessed anyone's heart, but the people Mr. and Mrs. Mills exposed their daughter to made me want to wipe out every other word in my vocabulary but those three.

"I'm proud of you, Eddie," I say, throwing her a wink.

"Me too."

"Am I chopped liver?" Archer asks, and even though he's trying to look affronted, he misses the mark and just comes off looking confused.

With a smile on her face, Ellison walks over and wraps Archer in a tight hug. "I love seein' you all grown up."

"We're basically the same age. You know that, right?"

She sighs and then pulls away. "Yeah, but you made it." He stares at her, his Adam's apple bobbing. "And it gives me hope that I will too."

31

MONTANA

The days have flown by since Ellison surprised me with the goat invasion, and I am only slightly less annoyed than I was the day of their arrival. I've done my best to avoid them—even the cute little ones that hopped and pranced around like they were in some barnyard parkour event.

But mostly, I've been workin' from sunup to sundown with no end in sight.

Ellison has been much the same, busy with lesson plans and getting her classroom ready, and I am so damn proud of her. She's had dinner with her father a couple of times but thankfully hasn't asked me to join them. I need to talk to the Mills patriarch one-on-one but I'm not ready, and every time I think about it, I'm unable to curb my anger.

Part of me knows it is slightly misplaced. The stress of the farm and Grandad and her father's unexpected arrival in Blackstone Falls have all contributed to my reaction. It is easier to lash out at the man who has done so much to derail my future—*our future*—than deal with the impending breakdown I can feel on the horizon.

"You keep doin' that and you're gonna wear a hole in my floor," Grandad says without looking up from the newspaper in his hand, startling me out of my spiraling thoughts.

And just in time too.

"Sorry," I mumble as I pour more coffee into my cup for no other reason than to have something to keep myself still for a couple of seconds.

"You should take the day off."

"What?" I ask, confusion furrowing my brow.

"A day off. Take Ellison to the lake or go for a drive and get away from here for a while. She starts school soon, and harvest season is right around the corner. It's only gonna get busier."

I open my mouth but then close it just as quickly. Things with Ellison have been the only thing going *right* since we threw out all the rules and started bein' us again. We've spent every available moment together—from early-morning coffees and dinners with Grandad and Celeste to a couple of evening rides with Sadie and Marist before falling into bed together at the end of each day. Life with Ellison has been nothing short of amazing, but Grandad was right —we've only had pockets of time and it would only get worse.

"I think you're right," I admit as I pull my phone out.

"That happens more often than y'all give an old man credit for." He harumphs and I can't help but snicker as I type out a message.

MONTANA: Let's go to the falls

ELLISON: When?

MONTANA: Right now

> ELLISON: I need like an hour. Are you sure you can take today off?

MONTANA: Grandad is insisting

> ELLISON: Tell him he's my favorite

MONTANA: I thought I was your favorite (crying emoji)

> ELLISON: If you'd suggested taking me to the falls then you'd be my favorite (kiss face emoji)

MONTANA: Fine. I'll grab lunch and pick you up in an hour

> ELLISON: XOXO

"Ellison says you're her favorite."

"See? A little effort goes a long way," he says with a smirk, and I roll my eyes.

"Yeah, yeah." Dropping a kiss on the top of his head, I squeeze his shoulder. "Love you, Grandad."

"Love you too, my boy. Love you too."

It took me a while to gather up all the gear for the lake and get it into the back of the truck. With the cooler stocked with drinks and sandwiches from The Backyard, I make a split-second decision to swing by the Kettle and Kiln for a couple of iced coffees.

I have a few minutes before I need to head to Ellison's, so I pull a U-turn and head toward the shop. It's still pretty early, but the lot is surprisingly full as I park and hop out. With a spring in my step, I make my way toward the door, my body feeling lighter than it has in weeks.

Images of Ellison in a bikini flash through my mind as I take a step inside and inhale the rich coffee aroma. I wave my hand in greeting at Karina who nods as she hustles behind the counter making coffees and filling orders like the magician she is.

A woman at the table to my right laughs and shakes her head, her glasses catching the light at just the right angle to grab my attention. The line moves forward, giving me a better view of her face, her name easily coming to me now that we have an interview scheduled for next week.

I'm just about to look away when the man she's sitting with looks up, his eyes locking on mine, a mixture of irritation and fear in them.

His eyes.

No fucking way.

Arden must notice the shift in her tablemate's demeanor because she looks up at him, her lips tipping down as her gaze follows his until it lands on me.

Coffee forgotten, I stalk my way across the room, standing every inch of my six-foot-three frame, towering over Evan Fucking Mills as he sits across from a woman who looked familiar to me but I couldn't previously figure out why.

A woman who has the same eyes as her father—*and Ellison.*

She has a sister?

"All the shit you put her through and you were hiding a god damn *family,*" I seethe, my voice low and menacing as I make the obvious connection. "You're a fucking disgrace." I snort but it lacks all humor. "And to think I've been striving to earn your respect all these years. You can go to hell."

Belatedly I can hear him excuse himself from the table as I push out the door and into the parking lot, sucking in a lungful of air as I will my head to stop spinning.

"Montana, stop." His voice is close and I whip around fast enough to force him to take a step back.

"You've got a lot of nerve—"

"It's not what it looks like." My eyebrows are somewhere in my hairline, and Evan notices because he holds his hands up and adds, "Okay, it's not *exactly* what it looks like."

"She has your eyes. Ellison's eyes." My voice breaks and I don't even care. "How could you do that to her?"

"I didn't know. I didn't know any of it. Arden contacted me a couple of months ago after she'd taken the job at the *Blackstone Gazette*. Her mother disclosed information to her that Sherri Ann had been involved in forcibly paying off and covering up the pregnancy. It's messy, but I didn't cheat on either of them. Arden asked for a paternity test. We're waiting for the results to confirm,"—he swallows—"that she's my daughter."

"That's some story."

"I wish it was sensationalized but it's not. I'm living in some god damn daytime movie, and if I screw up even *one* thing, my entire world is going to come crashing down around me. I'll lose everything."

"Always so concerned with money—with your *image*." I spit the last word out like a curse, because that's what it is.

"It's not like that."

"Bullshit! Ellison's whole life you've waffled between

indifference, her having to earn your affection, and down-right cruelty."

"You don't understand…"

"No," I say, taking a step into him, "*you* don't understand. I picked up the pieces every single time. Every time you let her down, every time you let her mother belittle her and make her feel like she wasn't good enough. And still I trusted you to take care of her when she left for Savannah. I let you chase me away because what could I do?" I throw my hands out to the side before dropping them down. "Believe me when I say that *nothing* has changed. I would have married Ellison at eighteen, and you can bet your life that I'll be marrying her just as soon as she lets me."

He drags a hand down his face, a weary sigh escaping him, but I can't find it in myself to feel bad.

"Believe it or not, I don't want to fight with you. I don't want to hurt my daughter." He clears his throat. "Either of them."

"Did you only come here for Arden? Or did you actually come for Ellison? Because I've been supportive of her nurturing the relationship she has with you, but I'll end that real quick if she's just an afterthought. You failed at protecting her, but I won't."

"I had to protect her!" he barks but I'm too wound up to care.

"I don't believe you. You isolated her and stripped her of her childhood. You did *everything* you could to tear her down." He opens his mouth to speak but I rush on, "But you know what? She's resilient and so fucking strong and she made it—she made it in spite of you. And I'll do everything in my power to make sure she has everything she could ever want. You never treated her like a princess, but I sure as hell will treat her like a queen," I say as I yank open the door of my truck.

"Montana—"

"You have one week to tell Ellison. Everything. You tell her about Arden and you tell her about what happened after she left for college." I point at him, my voice breaking again. "You tell her why you stole the last ten years from us."

"Please, just—"

I shake my head. "No. You tell her. I'm giving you this one courtesy, not because you deserve it but because *she* does. She deserves her father to man up and face his past—take responsibility for his actions. You have one week, Evan, and it's the last time I cover for you."

Without another word, I get into the truck and peel out of the parking lot, dust kicking up around Ellison's father as he stands there watching me drive away. He doesn't seem as big as he did growing up—no longer invincible.

He's just a man and everything I promised myself I'd never be.

32

ELLISON

Montana's truck pulls to a stop in my driveway, the back end kicking out a little as he takes the turn faster than normal before parking. Tension radiates from him as he climbs out, and I don't wait. Pushing open the front door, I race down the porch steps and launch myself into his arms.

He grunts as he staggers backward but catches us just as quick, my legs wrapping around his waist as he crushes his mouth against mine.

It's heated and sloppy and desperate all at once. I want to ask what's wrong, but something tells me I don't want to know.

Not yet.

Not when today's supposed to be about us. But I can't help it.

"Do you want to talk about it?" I ask panting against his lips, my heart in my throat as I wait for his response.

"Not yet. I want to go to the lake and strip your bikini off you and fuck you against the waterfall."

The whimper that escapes is involuntary because *Lord do I want that*, so I tease, "Well, I bought this one for you."

His eyes flick to my cover-up then back to my eyes, mischief now replacing the stress in his expression when he arrived.

"Are you ready?"

"Yeah, I just need to grab my bag." Cupping his face, his stubble biting into my palms sends a delicious shiver down my spine even though I'm trying to be serious. "Are you sure you're okay?"

He turns his head and places a lingering kiss on my palm. "All I need is you, Eddie. Now let's get that bag so I can get you naked."

Montana squeezes my ass, and I squeal as he carries me back up the stairs, not letting go as he finds my bag inside and then closes the door before walking us back to his truck.

It's silly, really, but it makes my heart nearly skip a beat at the way he's lookin' at me, carrying me around like he never wants to let me go.

"You're such a goof." The words are light and breathless, and his smile matches my own.

"Yeah, but I'm your goof." He kisses my nose and then maneuvers me and the bag inside the truck before walkin' proud as a peacock around the hood to get into the driver's seat.

"Nobody's More Country" by Blanco Brown blasts from the speakers as soon as the engine roars to life, making me shimmy in my seat as I sing along.

Montana grabs my hand, linking our fingers before bringing our joined hands to his lips where he places a sweet kiss on my knuckles. We're mostly quiet as we take the winding roads to Cedar Lake. It's been a lifetime since I've enjoyed one of Tennessee's most beautiful and secluded wonders.

It's a bit of a hike and not easy to get to but it was *ours,* or at least it had been. That thought sours my stomach, forcing me to turn in my seat.

"Did you bring other girls here?"

Montana chuckles. "Call me a romantic, but I always knew you'd come back to me." He winks and I roll my eyes even as my cheeks heat. "And even if you hadn't—this has only ever been our spot."

"You knew I'd come back?" I ask because sometimes it feels like a dream being back here.

He lifts a shoulder and lets it drop, his eyes still on the road. "I had a hard time believing our story stopped when you left for college. I mean I know it was more complicated than that but…"

He lets the words hang between us. He doesn't elaborate and neither do I. Up ahead, the road veers off, the trees getting thicker, and Montana slows as pavement is replaced by dirt under the tires.

A couple of cars and trucks are parked in the lot, the path to the main waterfall well-worn and loved by locals and tourists alike.

Sharing a secret smile, knowing we won't be joining them, we gather our stuff and wait patiently until the coast is clear before turning the other way and dodging the brush and moving toward our spot.

It's so quiet, the farther we get from the crowd, the only sound coming from the rushing water, the birds flying above, and me huffing and puffing like I've never exercised a day in my life.

"You gonna make it?"

"Shut it, Max." He laughs and I shove him enough to

make him laugh harder as he takes off ahead of me down the makeshift trail. We walk a while longer before the trees open up to reveal a place so beautiful my heart swells in my chest.

The earthy tones of the rock shelf are magnificent as the water cascades over it before landing in the crystal-clear pool below. The teal color of the water is almost unnatural —a true sight to behold—and one that never fails to take my breath away.

I know the water is colder than the pool at my childhood home, but that thought is secondary to Montana dropping his gear onto the ground and ripping his shirt over his head.

"Stop starin' at my ass."

"Never." I grin like the Cheshire cat as I gawk at him, sweeping over his body. My gaze is more salacious with every flex and ripple of muscle. Shaking his head, he looks at me over his shoulder, his cheeks the slightest shade of pink.

"Your turn." His voice is husky as he watches me set down my bag and inch my cover-up higher over my thighs, then my hips—acutely aware of every intake of breath and groan Montana makes. By the time I toss the gauzy white fabric onto the cooler, the man is practically panting, the bikini top pushing my breasts up and out for his enjoyment.

But there's more.

Montana eyes me like I'm his next meal, the black barely there fabric accentuating exactly what the expensive price tag promised. Bending forward, I grab the sunscreen from my bag and stand slowly.

"Can you put some on my back?" I ask sweetly, my expression full of faux innocence as I turn, pulling my hair to the side, my bottom lip caught firmly between my teeth.

"Holy hell," Montana curses under his breath before

dropping to his knees behind me and palming my bare ass cheeks. He growls, alternating between squeezing and peppering my skin with kisses, his stubble sending shocks of electricity straight to my core.

I'd been half out of my mind ordering this bathing suit, somehow being in a push-up top and a skimpy thong bottom more nerve-racking than skinny-dipping.

"Spread your legs and put your hands on the cooler," he rasps, and I don't argue because I'm getting exactly what I'd hoped for the moment he pulls my bottoms to the side and licks up my slit.

Gasping, I arch my back as his hand comes down on one cheek, the flesh stinging before his palm is rubbing and kneading the undoubtedly pink skin.

"Wider, El, show me what's mine."

Whimpering, I let my feet slide out a little more, his growl of approval making me wetter with each passing second.

"I love that this is all for me."

"What are you gonna do about it?" I taunt even though I'm the one completely exposed to him, my body too primed for his touch to be self-conscious. There's not a whole lot I wouldn't do for Montana Greene in this moment, and instead of being terrified, it has my heart pumping faster as I push back toward him.

An offering.

A plea.

A cry of desperation rips from my lungs a second before his mouth covers my pussy, his tongue and lips relentless as his fingers spread me—tormenting me as he feasts. My core clenches with my impending orgasm.

"Ohmygod, ohmygod, don't stop," I chant, my knuckles white as I grip the edge of the cooler before I shatter, my knees practically buckling as little dots dance behind my eyelids. I whimper and writhe as Montana's tongue thrusts inside me, my walls clenching around him as he fucks another orgasm out of me.

It's never been done before—not like that—not by anyone.

This time my knees do buckle and Montana pulls me down against him, letting me cling to his muscled body as I start to come back to mine.

"You hungry?" he asks and I look up at him in disbelief. "What? I asked if *you* were hungry." He smirks and it's downright wicked. "I already ate."

33

MONTANA

"Knock it off if you don't plan on doing anything about it," I grumble into Ellison's hair as my arm tightens around her waist. Her sexy little ass pushes back against me like a quick tease before she's spinning to face me.

She's been insatiable all week. My restraint had snapped at the waterfall, that scrap of fabric she'd called a bathing suit making it impossible to resist tasting her sweet pussy before sinking into all that tight heat over and over again.

We can't get enough of each other, and I am not complaining.

"I've been begging to do something about it since I got here, Max. You know I'm nervous about the first day of school tomorrow," she whines a split second before her lips land on mine in a bruising kiss that she commands with every lick of her tongue. My palm finds the curve of her ass and I squeeze, digging my fingers into her flesh and pressing her tighter to my body.

I'm tired—but never too tired for this.

Her teeth nip at my bottom lip before she's forcing my head back to kiss the underside of my jaw and down my throat. My chest heaves as she slides over me, traveling lower, her mouth hot and wet on my skin until she's settled between my legs.

"You gonna let me take these off you?" she asks, the words sounding innocent—but it's all an act. Her breath ghosts over the head of my dick through the fabric, causing it to jump and me to groan.

"Yes."

Humming, she hooks her thumbs in the elastic waistband and drags the tight cotton slowly over my hips, nipping and tasting me without really touching.

It's maddening.

And addictive.

And she's definitely going to pay for it.

"Is this for me?" Ellison asks coyly, taking my dick in her hand once she's finally gotten me naked and laid out for her.

"Yes." The word is hoarse as it leaves my throat, my pulse pounding in my chest as she strokes me. I feel exposed and vulnerable and completely at her mercy.

I feel owned by Ellison Mills.

"You've been so good, haven't you? I've been dying to taste you, Max." She had me last night. And the night before but that hardly seems relevant when she's been using my body to take her mind off this new chapter in her life.

"Fuck, baby." My hips jerk off the bed as she licks up the entire length of my cock. "*Fuck. Fuck. Fuck.*"

"Mmm, that sounds sexy, Max." She purrs as her tongue drags along the veins before her lips wrap gently around the head, teasing the underside and licking precum from the slit.

God damn this woman.

"Ellison." I moan her name as I grip her hair lightly, desperate for something to hold on to.

"Not this time." She bats me away, her gaze wicked as she looks up at me. "Grip the headboard. I want to see you all stretched out for me." She pulls her shirt over her head, and I watch as it falls somewhere beside her. Ellison's full, round tits mock me, and my arms flex as I grip the headboard tighter.

"I'm gonna break this thing if I can't touch you," I say through gritted teeth, but she just shrugs, her breaths rising and falling with the motion, her pretty pink nipples peaked and taunting me.

"I'd say that'll be a hell of a compliment." She winks and then drags her chest over me before settling back between my legs. My eyes squeeze shut and I pray for control even as she taunts me with her mouth, her hands...her whole fucking body.

The headboard slams against the wall when her lips start to devour me. The movements are slow—intentional—and so fucking maddening as she licks and swirls her tongue, pulling off just a little before taking more of me until the head of my dick hits the back of her throat.

She hums, one hand squeezing and massaging my balls while the other wraps around the base, stroking me so good my eyes roll back and I curse.

I want to fuck her mouth. I want her gagging on my dick as she moans around me, her tits bouncing and swaying until I come so hard I black out.

"Not yet, Max."

"You're too fucking good, El—it feels too damn good." She hums her approval and I grip the wood, the bite of it the only thing keeping me grounded. Sweat dots my hairline as every muscle in my body flexes under her touch.

"Are you going to come down my throat?" she says, pulling off long enough to taunt me.

"Jesus, yes." The headboard rattles again. "Please, baby."

Her eyes are molten as she sucks me harder and deeper until I can't hold on anymore. My orgasm rips through my body, the magnitude of pleasure beyond everything I've ever felt as my vision blurs and she swallows around me.

My chest heaves but it doesn't matter—I need her.

And I need her now.

Sitting up just enough, I grab her arms and haul her up my body until my mouth crashes over hers. She gasps as one hand grips the back of her neck and the other dives under the sheer fabric of her panties to grip the perfect globe of her ass.

"I need you out of these," I say as I drag the material as far as it will go with her pressed against me, "and sitting on my face."

***

ELLISON

MONTANA KISSES me one last time before hauling me up his body. His muscles bunch and flex and my mouth waters again like I didn't just have him coming down my throat a couple of minutes ago. His breath is hot against my core, and I want desperately to lower myself down so he can take control of me the way I had with him.

Watching him surrender to me had been the ultimate high and something I hadn't been able to put into words until this very moment. Things like empowered—emboldened—come to mind. Being with Montana has always been about more than just the chemistry and lust pulsing between us, but finally being able to act on it is practically euphoric.

It is the way I know without a doubt that I could ask for anything and he'd give it to me without hesitation. I'd definitely been asking for it at the waterfall. But I'd never been able to do that with anyone, romantic or otherwise, and the idea that I could *ask* for the things that made me feel good is something I'm still trying to reconcile.

"You're not nervous are you, Eddie? I had you bent over and spread wider than this just the other day," he says as he leans up and swipes his tongue against my slit. I moan, my cheeks heating as I stare down my naked body to the absolute hunger in his eyes.

"Course not," I say even though I can hear the slight tremor in my voice.

"Mmm, then be a good girl and let me help." His voice is soothing—confident—and I nod, grateful for his willingness to do this for me even though I don't know how I feel about his use of *good girl*.

Do I like it?

Am I a *good girl*?

Does his sayin' it low and growly turn me on?

I can't dwell on it too long though because his rough palms grip my hips, his skin against mine a delicious contrast as he pulls me slowly down to meet his waiting lips. His stubble tickles the inside of my thighs right before he sucks my clit into his mouth.

I gasp and he holds me tighter, forcing me to buck against his glorious assault. Montana groans, his fingertips kneading my ass cheeks as he licks at me before thrusting his tongue inside me. He moves and grinds me against his face, his beard and hands and mouth all taking part in the pleasure building between my legs.

It's hot and messy, and I love every second of the way he's staring at me with a wildness he only ever gets when we're together.

"Do that thing to my clit again," I pant and he does, sucking and rolling the tiny bud and teasing the hell out of me. I gasp and moan and writhe against him, his palm coming down hard on my backside once—*twice*—and I shatter.

Montana's tongue is relentless until I'm nothing more than a whimpering mess, my throat hoarse from chanting his name over and over for giving me the best orgasm of my life.

"Think I can make you come again?" He grins, his face absolutely covered in *me.* Somewhere in the recesses of my brain is the little voice that says I should be embarrassed— that this was wildly unladylike and I should be ashamed for demanding my own pleasure.

But the look on Montana's face and the way my heart skips a beat at the sight of him under me forces all the doubt back into the box where it belongs. This moment was for me —us—and I won't let anything stop me from enjoying it.

"I think I might need a minute," I say wryly, and he chuckles as he moves me carefully until I'm lying beside him.

Lacing my fingers with his, I note all the scars—new and old—that mark him and think not for the first time how well we fit together.

"I needed that," I say honestly without taking my eyes from where his thumb brushes back and forth against mine.

"Your mouth on my cock?" he asks sarcastically. "Baby,

anytime you need to let off some steam, I'm more than at your service."

"I was thinking more about your face between my legs and your tongue in my pus—" His mouth slants over mine in a kiss that's as sweet as it is possessive. It's marking and I am *so* here for it.

Pulling back, his chest heaving, he stares at me. "Since when do you talk like that?" My mouth opens and closes, the uncertainty his words spark in me making me want to rethink my answer. He growls, his hand gripping mine as he slides my palm down his chest, over his abs, and lower before we're both gripping his erection. "You did this."

"Is that a bad thing?" I ask, completely mesmerized by the way he grows harder as I stroke him. *You did this.*

Hell, yeah, I did.

My grin is wide and cocky, and he grunts as he shakes his head and pulls my hand off him.

"God damn, you're trouble." The words hold a fondness that has my heart swelling and butterflies swarming in my belly.

"But you said I was a *good girl.*" I bat my eyelashes at him, and he gives my ass a quick slap, startling me and forcing me to rock against his thigh nestled between my legs. I moan and he snickers.

"Brat."

"You like it."

"I do."

"I've never been able to ask for what I want." I swallow as I look up at him through my lashes, sincerity replacing the teasing. "I like knowing I can do it with you." Instead of answering with words, Montana takes me in a sweet, exploratory kiss before pressing his forehead to mine.

"You know I'd do anything for you," he rasps, and

because the emotion between us is too heavy, I plaster on a smirk.

"That's what I'm counting on."

"Aaand, the moment's gone," he says, feigning annoyance, but he knows...knows exactly what I need.

Rolling his eyes, he climbs out of bed then hefts me naked onto his shoulder. Squealing, I fight against his hold—my fight instinct at the ready as he takes a bite on one ass cheek and spanks the other.

"Now *this*,"—he spanks me again—"is a bitable ass."

"Put me down, Max," I bark but there's no force behind the words—just a whole lot of heat pooling between my legs as he carries me into the bathroom.

"That make you wet, Eddie? I bet it did." Flipping on the shower, he closes the curtain before setting me on my feet, making sure to drag me down the entire front of his body in the process. "You're gonna be in a minute." His lips twitch at his joke, but I can't take my eyes off his mouth and the things it did to me. "Should we check?"

"Yes."

"Yes, you're wet? Or yes, we should check?"

"Both," I rasp as I grip his wrist and draw it down my stomach much the same way he did to me in bed. He follows my lead and lets me impale myself on his finger, moaning as I rock against him, searching for more.

"Fuck, that's hot," he groans as he starts pumping his hand in time with my hips before pulling back and spinning me toward the shower. The sound of his palm against my backside is muffled with the running water, but it doesn't mask the way I feel him absolutely everywhere. "Shower. Now."

"But—"

"I didn't stutter, Eddie. I want you soapy and wet with your tits in my mouth as you come all over me."

"Well then, I'd hate to make you wait."

Muttering under his breath, Montana swats at me again as he follows me under the spray, and just like he said, it's the best shower I've ever had.

34

ELLISON

"Hey, I just need to stop over at my dad's real fast and then we can head to dinner," I say without looking up from the text I'm trying to send.

"Can we do it tomorrow?"

Stashing my phone in my purse, I put my hand on his forearm and try to infuse as much understanding into my voice as I can muster. "Look, he just has something for me to sign for the bank. He asked me to come over this week, but you know how crazy this first week of school has been."

He nods and gives me a small smile as he weaves through Blackstone Falls toward my childhood home which my father has been living in after negotiating with the she-devil. I don't know the terms and I don't want to. I've let her calls go unanswered, choosing my happiness for once.

Because I've never been happier.

The first week of school has been a dream, the kids full of excited energy that has filled my heart with so much joy it nearly burst.

Cal and I have set up a standing lunch date three times a

week when our schedules allow it, and I'll most likely be hidden in my classroom on the other days.

"It looks like he has company," Montana says as the house comes into view. "We can come back."

"It's probably a lawyer; I'll be quick, I promise." I kiss his cheek as soon as we're stopped, unclipping my seatbelt and opening the door.

"Ellison, wait…" he says as he scrambles out of the truck after me. I'm already on the porch and about to tell him how ridiculous he's being when the door swings open.

Montana curses under his breath as I stare open-mouthed at the woman before me. She's my age with auburn waves and glasses that hide big brown eyes, the light making the gold flecks pop.

Eyes just like my father's.

Just like mine.

"Ellison?" My father's voice sounds like it's coming through a tunnel, panic evident on his face as his gaze bounces between us.

"What in the actual fuck is going on?" I snap, my voice rising with each word.

"I'm just going to…" the woman says, but I shake my head and force her back inside the house, Montana hot on my heels as we pile into the entryway, the door closing behind us with an ominous click.

"Talk," I snap at my father.

"We didn't want you to find out like this," he says, and the laugh that bursts from my chest is borderline hysterical.

"Tell me you're dating her and I will—"

"I'm your half sister," she blurts out, surprising herself as much as me by the look on her face. "The results came back this week confirming it."

The results came back this week confirming it.

The words run on a loop in my mind. How long has everyone known?

"Arden contacted me when I was still in Savannah. She's the reporter I mentioned."

My mouth opens and closes but no words come out.

Mentioned.

Yeah, he mentioned it all right—just left out a crucial piece of information, the bastard.

I have a sister.

And she's obviously around my age.

What the fuck is going on?

"I'm so sorry you found out this way," Arden says. "I've had longer to come to grips with it and—"

"You're sorry?" My voice is practically hysterical. "You didn't do this to us,"—I motion toward my father—"he did. And what the hell, Dad? I have a sister and you never told me?"

"Ellison," he starts but I shake my head.

"You just—believe me?" Arden asks, her lips parted, her eyes wide and glassy like this wasn't something she'd really considered coming here.

"What? Of course I do; you look just like me." And she does. Our resemblance is uncanny, but more than that, just seeing her has already started to heal so much of my heart that was broken from my childhood. There are so many things I want to say—to *scream*—so much time wasted when I could have been loving my sister and feeling not as alone in the world.

"It's the eyes, right?" Montana says, and I turn to glare at him before facing my *sister.*

"Do you have your phone on you?" I ask hoarsely and she nods, opening it and handing over the device without hesitation. A strange sense of comradery hits me, like maybe she gets it too. She's trusting me with a heart as fragile as my own, and I make a silent vow to protect it—to protect us.

With shaking fingers, I enter my name and number before sending myself a text and handing it back to her.

"I'm not mad at you, but I don't want to start like this." I swallow and she nods, relief on her pretty face even as her eyes fill with tears.

"We'll be okay," she says with a half smile and just enough hesitation that I can't stop myself. Taking a step, I reach out and wrap Arden in a hug, her arms instantly returning my fierce embrace.

I don't know how long we stand like that, but all too soon she's pulling back, her smile wavering. I miss her already.

"I'll call you," I whisper, and she nods before squeezing my hand and letting herself out of the house.

Tension-laced silence fills the cavernous room. It feels suffocating, and there's nothing I want more than to run screaming from here and never look back. To catch up with Arden and leave this mess with our father for another day.

But I can't. I can't spend my whole life running—hiding —not being myself.

"She contacted me in Savannah," my father says, breaking the silence. "I told you I'd fallen for another woman—had plans to break things off with your mother for good. Monroe didn't know she was pregnant when I told her things were over. Your mother and I were married not long after, and when Monroe came to tell me about the baby, she got your mother instead."

And your mother is worse than we thought.

His words from his first night in town slam into me, and the thought of what my mother said to that poor woman makes me sick.

But still...

"Did you know?" I turn on Montana, the last twenty minutes coming back in a rush. "Did you know about this?"

It's the eyes, right?

"I saw them at the coffee shop the day we went to the falls."

"What?!"

Montana's face is hard and unyielding and he looks at me and then my father. "I gave him a week to tell you, because this"—he waves his hand toward the door—"should come from him. Like the other thing."

My father's expression is murderous, his hands fisted at his sides.

"We're not doing this now," he murmurs, the warning clear in his tone.

"What other thing?" It's a whisper, but I can tell by the way that both men flinch that they hear it, as if they'd forgotten I was even in the room.

"Don't—"

My father's objection is silenced when Montana says, "After you left for college, I went and asked your father's permission to marry you." He turns and looks at me, his expression still hard. "Told him I'd support you while you went to school. That I'd go there or wait for you to come home. That I wanted nothing more than to build a life with you."

"You were too damn young to understand," my father snaps.

"And I would have waited!" Montana roars. "I would have waited till she was ready, till she finished school. I would have followed her anywhere."

"You were already married to the farm!"

"You had no right!" I yell, startling them both. "You stole

the life we could have had—being with him is all I've ever wanted. But you *moved* to Georgia after me and forced me into a life you knew made me unhappy. And *you*," I seethe, turning on Montana, the anger mixed with hurt. "You just gave up? Just like that? You let me push every damn boundary—said yes to me no matter how crazy the idea. You took the blame over and over but—"

"He's your *father,* Ellison. You can't understand that level of rejection."

"*I can't understand*? I was devastated. You stopped talking to me, and I wondered for years what I had done *wrong.*" A sob punctuates the last word as Montana's jaw tics, his hands clenching like he's trying not to reach for me.

"It's not like you chased me down either. I was fuckin' heartbroken, El. I just wanted to be with you—be worthy of you—and you stayed away. You didn't come for me either. What was I supposed to think? My whole life I was told I wasn't good enough for you—and that just confirmed it."

My father curses under his breath as he drags his hands down his face, but I ignore him.

"Then you didn't know me at all! What about what I wanted? No one gave me a say in my own damn life!" Anger races through my bloodstream, tears rolling down my cheeks as I think of the way it had all played out. My parents had moved to Savannah, and Montana had stopped talking to me. I'd wanted to go home, and they'd put a stop to that too.

"Ellison," my father tries, but I don't want to hear it.

Montana hadn't come for me and I hadn't gone to him and we were just kids but now?

"Like they would have let me anywhere near you." Montana points a finger at my father.

"But you didn't even try and you carried on with your life—"

"Don't you dare finish that sentence," he says, wiping a hand over his mouth. "You were with Blake for *years*, Ellison. Another man in your god damn bed—"

"And what? The revolving fucking door in yours?" I'm not proud as the words leave my lips and Montana blanches.

So does my father.

I'm being unfair. We both are.

"What the hell was I supposed to do?" His voice is quieter now. "You came back to Nan's funeral belonging to some other man, and I couldn't fight, El. I just needed to be back in your world—to have whatever small piece of you I could as I buried my grandmother, took over the farm, and became the sole caretaker for my grandfather. It was all too much."

"I told you about Blake," I say, even as the guilt squeezes the air from my lungs.

"Listen, you should know..." my father starts again but I can't hear anything over the blood pumping in my ears.

"I bided my time and I waited—did everything I could to help you find yourself again. But I won't sit here and act like all of that didn't fuck me up too. That I couldn't god damn breathe without you here—that I took on every task, every responsibility till I lost myself to the land because it's the only thing that's never let me down."

I gasp, his words slicing through me. "And I always let you down? I've never wanted to hurt you, but you kept my sister from me, and that day we..." My eyelids slam shut as the perfect day is tainted with secrets and revelations and deception, both innocent and not.

"He should have told you," Montana whispers, his eyes full of unshed tears.

"We were waiting for the results and you had school..." my father tries but it's futile.

"We both screwed up and now...we need a couple of days to cool off."

"I don't need a couple of days," I challenge because the prospect of being without him—of losing him—makes me physically sick.

"I do." His Adam's apple bobs with the admission, and my hand flies to my mouth to suppress the sob that wants to escape. "I want to be ready and I want to do this right, and I want you to be with me because you're in love with me and not because it's comfortable. I would've married you at eighteen, Eddie, or when you graduated from college. I would have married you the second you stepped foot back in Blackstone Falls because you've always been it for me." He takes a step forward and brushes a piece of hair behind my ear. "I would still marry you today, but I'd rather it be tomorrow when you know without a doubt that growin' old is what you want with me." Montana presses a lingering kiss against my forehead as I choke on a sob. "I'll leave the keys in the truck so you can drive home, and I'll get it later," he says quietly as he takes a step back and then another. "All I've ever wanted was to be good enough for you—just make sure that I am."

"Max," I plead but it's no use.

The snick of the door is worse than if he'd slammed it, my heart completely obliterated in my chest as I whirl toward the man who's been quieter than not as my entire world has imploded.

"What the hell did you do?"

35

MONTANA

It's been a long time since I walked the path from the Mills's home to mine. It's different than I remember but familiar all the same. My breathing is ragged, even to my own ears, and I know it's got nothing to do with trekking through the still present heat.

I want to strangle Evan Mills with one of those pretentious neckties he wore back then for creating the shitstorm of the century. I know Ellison was projecting her emotions onto me more than she was accusing me, but it hurt all the same.

The longer the words were hurled back and forth, the harder it was to ignore those teenage emotions I'd buried deep in the recesses of my soul. I am a grown man, but standing in that house took me back to that night. I know we were young, but my love for her had run through my body as surely as the blood in my veins.

And that hasn't changed.

It never would.

My boots are heavy as I climb the porch steps, barely registering how I'd gotten here. Grandad's eyebrows climb up his forehead as I give him a nod and move past him toward my room. I can't talk about it—not right now.

My body collapses face down on the comforter, and I don't hold back the muffled outburst at smelling Ellison's perfume on the fabric.

Rolling onto my back, I stare at the ceiling, my phone vibrating in my pocket forcing my eyelids to squeeze shut as I wrestle the device from where it's sandwiched between the denim and the bed.

Groaning, I swipe open the group message and pray for patience.

VIENNA: I cannot believe you!

ASPEN: I already booked my plane ticket

> MONTANA: No one is gettin' on a plane

> MONTANA: How the hell do you even think you know something?

ASPEN: I can't hear you they're starting to board

> MONTANA: I swear on Nan's pot roast you better not be getting on a plane

VIENNA: Then why don't you reassure your favorite sisters why we shouldn't come home when you told us that Ellison Mills would not break your heart?!

ASPEN: And that we had nothing to worry about

MONTANA: Seriously—what the hell?

ASPEN: We have spies everywhere

VIENNA: You left with Ellison for dinner, went to her dad's, and now you're home instead of at said dinner

VIENNA: Looking miserable and heartbroken

MONTANA: Nothing is wrong

VIENNA: No one believes that lie

ASPEN: Seriously what is the matter with you big brother?

DRAGGING my hand down my face, I take a couple of deep breaths and relax the grip on my phone. If I could launch it across the room right now I would, but then they'd really get on a plane, and I don't have the mental capacity to endure that right now.

VIENNA: STOP IGNORING US!

MONTANA: Stop yellin' at me

ASPEN: Stop making us yell!

MONTANA: I am fine. Ellison is fine. We had a disagreement.

ASPEN: Who needs to apologize? It's you, isn't it?

VIENNA: I dunno…she's got some rich lady baggage

MONTANA: That South Carolina air is really getting to you, isn't it?

VIENNA: Love is always in the air—it's Love Beach

VIENNA: (gif of a beach)

ASPEN: She's not wrong though…

MONTANA: Y'all need to stay out of it.

VIENNA: Too late

ASPEN: We just want to help

VIENNA: No one deserves their HEA like you do, Montana

MONTANA: What the hell is HEA?

ASPEN: Happily Ever After…

MONTANA: Why not just say that?

ASPEN: You're seriously uncool sometimes

MONTANA: I'm gonna take that as a compliment

VIENNA: Please don't

MONTANA: Can y'all just trust me that things will work out in their own time?

ASPEN: But we need to know if we can ship the two of you or if we need to kick her to the curb

MONTANA: Are you on a boat?

VIENNA: (gif of I'm on a boat video)

VIENNA: We need to know if we're team Montana + Ellison = Forever or if we need to hate her

MONTANA: You never get to hate Ellison okay?

ASPEN: That's not how it works. She hurts you, she's toast

MONTANA: You leave her alone. She's been hurt enough in her life and if things don't work out with her—y'all will be nice and supportive and NICE

VIENNA: I hate being nice

ASPEN: No you don't that's me

VIENNA: Oh, that's right

ASPEN: But you love her don't you?

MONTANA: Of course I do. Now, promise me.

VIENNA: I hate that promise

MONTANA: Please?

ASPEN: I hate it more when he says please. I'm picturing the puppy dog eyes.

VIENNA: That's the worst

MONTANA: Say it

ASPEN: Promise.

VIENNA: Promise big brother.

I LET my phone drop down beside me and close my eyes, a headache creeping into my brain.

Buzz. Buzz. Buzz.

JENSEN: Are you okay?

MASON: Shit man—after all that nice stuff I said about forever and stages of love and life

JENSEN: Too soon man

MASON: Shit sorry

MONTANA: Do I even want to know how you fools know something even happened?

ARCHER: Probably not

ARCHER: But also are you okay?

BODHI: I held them off as long as I could

THAT LAST MESSAGE has the ghost of a smile gracing my lips. The levity is appreciated.

JENSEN: I'm the sheriff—I know everything

ARCHER: Your sister texted Bea

MONTANA: Figures. Traitors—both of them.

ARCHER: They're just worried about you and so are we

MONTANA: You can't be that worried it's been like an hour

MONTANA: And we're gonna be fine

JENSEN: Want me to ticket her dad? Jaywalking? Failure to stop at a stop sign?

MASON: Blackstone Falls has a Jaywalking statute?

JENSEN: Of course it does, don't be
ridiculous

> MASON: Well, then you must be writing
> tickets all day because I saw at least fifteen
> chickens swerving all over the downtown

> ARCHER: Jamison's cows too

JENSEN: Stay out of it

> ARCHER: Just tryin' to help

BODHI: Grandad just took the ATV outta the
barn—I'll keep you posted

> MASON: You just want out of this message

BODHI: I have no idea what you're talking
about

SIGHING, I put my phone down again and scrub my hands
over my face. Bodhi will make sure Grandad is safe, and
even though no one said it, I know they'll make sure Ellison
is too.

Because right now it can't be me, and somehow that
hurts most of all.

36

ELLISON

I stab the small trowel into the bag of potting soil again and growl only a little when I get more on the patio than the pot. This was supposed to be relaxing, but so far, I think the only thing happening is that my blood pressure keeps going up.

It's nearly eight at night, but the sun is still up and I needed the distraction. I hadn't stayed long after Montana had left me with my father. It was a miracle I was able to drive the truck home with the tears streaming down my face.

Dad hadn't had a lot to add and what he did I hadn't wanted to hear—he owed Montana those words anyway. Part of me understood, could grieve with him on the years lost and the things he wished he could change. But my father's deception was something I didn't know if we'd ever recover from. The dominoes had been set, one right after the other, quietly added to for years. They'd sat precariously for so long it was like they'd been forgotten.

But the events today had sent them tumbling, the catalyst a woman with my eyes and tear-stained cheeks who I already loved with my whole heart.

My phone dings and I look at the screen, wiping my soil-covered hands on my shorts before picking it up.

> BLAKE: Your mother is on a rampage more than normal—just wanted to give you the heads up

> BLAKE: Also, did you come back to Savannah for something and not tell me? I could have sworn I saw someone who looked just like you the other day.

I SNORT because no doubt Arden had landed on my mother's doorstep looking for answers. I wish I could have been a fly on the wall for that—my own need to confront the woman who had given me life sparking anger in my belly.

> ELLISON: She's my sister

> ELLISON: Well, technically half sister

> BLAKE: Your WHAT?!

> ELLISON: It's a long story

> BLAKE: That I need immediately

ELLISON: Soon. I have to fix things with Montana first.

BLAKE: I thought you were trying to get away from the drama not add to it

ELLISON: You're hilarious

BLAKE: I know that's one of the things you love about me

ELLISON: Debatable

BLAKE: I feel like I need to see this for myself

ELLISON: You're always welcome here

BLAKE: Think Montana would agree?

ELLISON: He'll like you once he meets you

BLAKE: Debatable

ELLISON: Brat

BLAKE: That's a given

BLAKE: You owe me a phone call once things settle down

BLAKE: I have QUESTIONS

ELLISON: Yes dear

> BLAKE: Take care of yourself and I'll let you
> know if I hear anything else about your
> mother

> ELLISON: Thanks, I definitely owe you
> for that

> BLAKE: I'm glad you said it

I SNORT and toss my phone aside, trying to wedge the plants together without making more of a mess.

The sound of an ATV cuts me off as another slew of curses bursts from my mouth. Sighing, I drop the trowel and wipe my hands on my shorts before standing as Grandad pulls up to the cottage and lumbers over to me, a reusable shopping bag in his hand.

"Does Montana know you took that out for a spin?" I ask even though saying his name physically hurts.

"Ah, I see you're also enjoying this beautiful summer evening," he says with a chuckle as he eyes my dirt-stained clothes and steers me toward the patio chair. He waits for me to sit before taking his own, his eyebrows inching up like he thought I'd put up more of a fight.

But I don't have it in me—not today.

Pulling two bottles of soda from the bag, he twists off the top before handing one to me, the glass still cold against my hand, and I smile.

"You know I only ever drank these here."

"Why?"

I shrug. "I guess I aways thought they tasted different. Like after a long day's work this was the ultimate reward—tasted colder and more refreshing than just picking it up at the store. I've never been able to replicate that feeling anywhere else."

He nods but doesn't say anything for a while, both of us lost in our own thoughts—mine most likely spiraling faster than his.

"Do you think he should be the one to apologize?" Grandad says slowly. "Or is it you?"

Opening my mouth, I'm about to respond when something stops me, a lot of somethings. I'd been so wrapped up in my own world and my own grievances with my family. I'd been relying on Montana to help shoulder the burden—be my knight in shining armor.

But did I ever try to be his? Had I always just assumed he was invincible? Like he was strong enough to withstand the darkness of the world I'd grown up in?

He's your father, Ellison. You can't understand that level of rejection.

"I don't know," I say finally, and Grandad nods before turning to look at me. His smile is soft, understanding, and I feel the fragile curtain I'd hung start to fall under his kind eyes.

"I hate seein' my two favorite people so upset."

"I know, Grandad, but—" He waves me off and I swallow the half-hearted excuse I was going to give him.

"Montana told you about goin' to see your daddy?" he asks and I nod. "It was a long time before he was ready to talk about it. Years. He turned to the farm, working the land, building a legacy away from prying eyes. Just waiting to be ready."

"Ready for what?"

"For you." He lets the words hang between us. "Didn't think it'd take this long though."

"He pulled away and it hurt. I was away at school and

missed him so damn much. I wanted to transfer home but..."

But my father wouldn't hear of it and now I knew why. To reaffirm the point, they'd bought a house close to campus, my mother demanding weekly dinners. I'd never felt more isolated—if driving me and Montana apart was the end goal then it worked.

"I know, Dolly. And my heart hurts for both of you. Montana's always wanted what Nan and I had. Married my sweetheart when she turned eighteen. I'd dropped out at sixteen to work the farm, but it wasn't such a big deal back then. Learned what I needed to right here,"—he waves his hand around—"and married my girl the second I was able. My grandson has always wanted that for himself; wanted it with you."

"I would have married him," I say on a watery laugh. "I would have married him the very same day."

He nods but reaches over and takes my hand, a seriousness etched into the lines of his face as he says, "I have to believe things happen for a reason." I open my mouth again but he just shakes his head. "When Nan passed, I was ready to go right on after her."

"You owe me a good ten or *fifteen* years, mister," I choke out and he chuckles softly.

"I know, Dolly. But when you get to be my age, the years of your life you spent by someone's side far outweigh the ones that you don't, and I lost a part of me I'll never get back."

"I'm so sorry I stayed away. I loved you both so much and I never came home." The words are choked as I scoot my chair closer to wrap my arm around his and lay my head on his shoulder.

"We knew you loved us and how hard it must have been

for you to stay away. She looked forward to your weekly call —loved teachin' you the things she loved." His voice is tight, a shuddery breath escaping as he says, "I have to believe there's a reason the good Lord didn't see fit to take me too."

"You're not allowed to go until our kids are at least in college, maybe after."

His body shakes with silent laughter, and I lift my tear-filled eyes to see his staring back at me. "I don't need to live long enough for you kids to have to wipe my ass."

"We still need you," I say, swallowing hard. "*I* still need you."

Pressing a kiss to my forehead, he whispers, "I know, Dolly, I'm not goin' anywhere," before pulling a container out of his bag and setting it in front of me.

"You got an apology tour in there too?" I joke, my heart both heavier and lighter since he arrived.

Chuckling, he removes the lid and I snatch a cookie and shove it in my mouth before he's able to grab one for himself. It's *so* good. The butterscotch is decadent and the perfect complement to the light, chewy texture.

Grandad hands me another before taking one and sitting back in his chair with an amused expression.

"Did you know that Montana takes the blame for me gettin' the tractor stuck?"

"You do it on purpose," I say without question because there isn't a piece of equipment that he couldn't run, fix, or create in all the years I'd known him.

"I do."

"Why?" It's exactly the kind of thing I'd do just to see Montana all growly with his hands on his hips trying to hide that *she did it again* smile.

"Because he lost you, Dolly. He lost his spark, and most days I don't know where he ends and the cotton fields begin.

You made him live, and you brought out that little bit of wild that always simmered under the surface with him. He's the most like himself when he's tryin' to keep me out of trouble—has to call the Thayer kids to come help and he gets to be himself for a while."

"But he takes the blame for it and..."

Grandad's bushy, silver eyebrows climb his forehead as I let that sink in. Montana had been taking the blame for me for years. To this day, our high school still thought it was his idea to paint 1, 2, 3, and 5 on pigs and release them on the football field our senior year.

He'd gotten detention for a week and community service after. I did his hours right alongside him even though he never ratted me out. Everyone thought I was just being a good friend.

Boy, if they only knew.

I felt guilty, but he just laughed it off saying I was his favorite kind of trouble and that he lived to see me wild—he still does.

"I owe him an apology."

"I reckon you both do," Grandad says as he stands from the chair. "Should I leave those?" he asks, pointing to the half-full container of cookies, and I nod.

"Definitely. I'm gonna be stress eating those while I figure out what to do."

Grandad chuckles and shakes his head. "It's nice having you home, Ellison. Wasn't the same without you."

"Ugh, stop making me cry," I grumble as I get up and hug him tight, burying my nose in the collar of his shirt that forever smells like his aftershave.

Halfway to the ATV, he stops and looks at me over his shoulder. "How long should I expect him to be moping around?"

I bite my lip to contain the smile trying to stretch across my face. "At least a day or two. I'm going to have to make him good and mad if this is gonna work."

"I'll leave it to you then. I have to go check on Patches before turning in."

"Oh, hold on," I say, running inside and coming back with the keys to Montana's truck. "Tell Mason and Bodhi to bring this home to him since they're your protection detail tonight."

"Damn kids," he grumbles but takes them and meets Mason in the driveway, saying something to make the kid chuckle before starting up the ATV and heading home.

My heart squeezes because it's where I should be going.

And I will.

But first I need to show Montana what he means to me, not just now but always. The smile that spreads across my face is real and bright as an idea starts to take shape.

Poor guy has no idea what's about to hit him.

37

ELLISON

"Mornin', Max," I say cheerfully as I push off the driver's side door of his truck with a smile I hope is bright and shining and not at all like the nervous butterflies taking up residence in my belly.

He pauses midstride, his hand tightening around his coffee cup as he stares at me, the dark circles under his eyes mirroring my own.

"I'm not ready to talk to you," he says not unkindly as he swallows hard and blinks at me.

"That's all right," I say even though I hate it. "I can wait but this can't." I thrust the navy blue hat at him that I dug out of the bottom of the closet. Crocheting with Nan had been one of my favorite things even though I'm still terrible at it.

There were a handful of blankets with uneven lines out there that I'd donated.

I'd been working on this hat when she'd passed away, and I'd never been able to finish it—just moved it with me here to Blackstone Falls.

"It's hot out," he says as he eyes the winter hat in his

hand. I can't guarantee it'll fit right but also that's not the point.

"You can never be too prepared," I say with a smile. "Besides, did you know Nan taught me how to crochet?"

"Uh, yeah. I remember," he says as his thumb moves back and forth over the soft weave. "Pretty sure I have a scarf that ought to match this." His brow furrows, and if I wasn't dodging a minefield, I would reach up and smooth the crease with my thumb then rub between his eyes hard enough for him to laugh and push me back a step.

"I've gotten better though, right?" We both look down at the hat and I fight my smile. "Maybe I'm still a little rusty."

"I know what you're doing,"—I open my mouth to speak but he holds up the hat to silence me—"but I'm not ready. I'm mad and I'm pissed...and I'm fuckin' hurt, Ellison."

I hate the way he uses my real name, and I hate the way his warm, brown eyes are pleading with me to just let it go.

"I'm so sorry, Max."

"I don't want to say something I can't take back, Eddie."

"Then you can listen, okay?" I say with more bravado than I feel. "Because I'm sorry I never told you that you're my favorite part of every day. That I want to crawl inside you and feel your heartbeat sync with my own because being a part of you is all I'll ever need. You've been my champion since the day we met, and you were right to call me out because I haven't been yours, and I'm so damn sorry, baby."

"El." My name is a choked whisper, his fingers tight around his mug like he's doing it so he won't reach for me.

"Just tell me I can make it right—because my plan is epic," I add and smile when his lips twitch. "And I need you to know there's no *good enough* with us. You're the only one I'll ever want, Montana Greene. You're the other half of my beating heart and a thousand times more patient with me than I deserve."

"I'm sorry I didn't fight harder. For you. For us."

"I think Grandad was right. There's a reason it took us so long to get here, and I promise I won't mess it up, all right?"

"Yeah," he murmurs as his expression softens.

"Good. You get *one* day."

"What?"

"One. Day." His Adam's apple bobs as I start backing away. "One day and then I'm coming for you. And get ready, Max, because when I'm done there won't be a single person within a fifty-mile radius who doesn't know you're mine."

"That's an awful big promise, Eddie," he says evenly, the twitch of his lips his only giveaway. My heart swells in my chest even as I keep my expression light.

"No risk, no reward, and you, sir, are the *ultimate* reward."

Winking, I don't wait for his response, just turn and try to keep one foot moving in front of the other. He wanted time and he's got it.

One day.

Now it's time to put my plan in motion—just as soon as I make this phone call.

"You knew," I say as I pace the hardwood floor of the cottage. The words are accusing because I already know the answer. I just need to hear her say it.

My mother scoffs. "Of course I knew. What kind of wife would I be if I didn't know each and every one of my husband's indiscretions?"

"You weren't together. You *trapped* him using me as an excuse."

"I did what I had to do."

"What about Montana? The farm?"

"Is there a point to this?" she asks, her tone bored, the sound of her manicured nails clicking against the phone like she has a million better things to do besides talk to her daughter.

Part of me isn't surprised.

But the other is downright furious that I let myself be tied to them for so long—tied to *her*. I've been a puppet on a string my entire damn life but not anymore.

My father and I would survive this, but my relationship with my mother ends today.

I might not have had the words for it back then, but I knew something was wrong. They weren't happy and loving and I *knew* I never wanted to be them.

But this...there are no words for this.

She's a monster—diabolical—and in the end, we've all been casualties in her scheme to ensure she'd always have power and prestige.

"Did he love her?"

"Does it matter if he did? I took care of a problem, kept my family together, gave you the privileged life our name deserves."

"I have a *sister*!" I bark into the phone, the plastic case digging into my hand the longer I talk to her.

"*No,* you do not."

"Yes. I. Do." I punctuate the words because if there's anything that's worth it in this world, it's finding the people you love and love you in return.

"You're being ridiculous. That *woman*—"

"That *woman* doesn't deserve your disdain. *She* is a

victim and so is her daughter. You don't get to judge them. Either of them."

"You have no idea what I've done to keep this family together."

"You did it for yourself and you did it for nothing."

"Ellison!" Her voice is shrill but not quite panicked. She's outraged I have the gall to talk to her like this, but she's not heartbroken—not over me. "You can't just throw your life away." She seethes like it's a personal affront that I don't want to be in her world.

"My *life* is Montana Greene. My life is with him, and I would rather be poor and happy in Blackstone Falls with my best friend than—" My voice cracks and I have to swallow down the lump in my throat.

"Than what?"

"Than be like you."

"I gave you *everything.*"

"No, you did everything for yourself. The only thing you ever did for me was to stay in Blackstone Falls so I'd have a home to come back to when I was finally free of you. Good-bye, Mother."

Without waiting for a response, I push the end button on the screen and let my phone fall to the counter, the tears immediate as they roll down my cheeks. But I'm not crying over losing her.

I let the tears fall as I purge the most toxic relationship in my life. I cry for the little girl who'd never known love or affection and the woman who grew up to finally realize a person like that doesn't deserve the title of mother.

The tears fall for me, for Arden and Monroe, and they even fall for my father who sacrificed decades of his life to a loveless and remarkably cruel marriage. Healing will take time, but I deserve the lightness in my heart—we all do.

38

ELLISON

The knock on my door is expected but still makes my heart hammer in my chest, my body already wrung out from the phone call with my mother. Turning the knob, I open it, the woman's expression one that most likely mirrors my own.

Arden James.

My sister.

"I brought cake," she says, holding up the box. "I didn't know if it was too early for wine, and I was too nervous to drink any more coffee."

"Is it chocolate?" I ask on a choked laugh.

"Is there any other kind?"

"No," I agree as we stand there, both nervous as excitement pings tentatively between us. "Is it weird that I missed you?"

"Only if it's weird that I missed you too."

Placing the box on the counter, I wrap my arms around the woman with the eyes like mine who I've always longed for but never knew why. Grandad had talked about a piece of him dying with Nan, but my heart had never been whole because I'd been waiting for her.

Had she always missed me? Had she felt the ache of loneliness that I'd worn like a second skin my whole life?

"I love you," she whispers as her tears land on my shoulder. "I loved you even when I didn't know you existed."

"I love you too," I say, the words coming on a sob as I hold her tighter, completely unafraid of this moment and what it means. "And I know, because I felt it too."

Pulling back, she laughs as she pushes her glasses up into her hair, the lenses fogged up as she swipes at her eyes.

"I think it's time for cake," I say, taking her hand and leading her to the breakfast bar. Grabbing two forks, I hand her one as she opens the cardboard lid, stamped with The Poppy Seed, the bakery in Clementine Creek.

We're quiet as we take bites of the decadent layer cake, the entire scene almost comical as if I am looking in on it rather than experiencing it.

"Evan didn't know," Arden says finally, a bite of cake suspended on her fork. "I asked my mom a lot over the years about him, but I never got far. She'd been on her own and took the money from Sherri Ann to support me." Arden's smile is sad. "She wasn't proud of needing it."

"He loved her."

"I know."

"I think he still does," I confess and she nods.

"I think he does too."

"Are you staying here? In Blackstone Falls?" She doesn't answer right away, her fork slicing through the layers of chocolate.

"I'm...I'm not sure. I guess it depends."

"On what?"

"On you, a little on Evan, and a little on my mom."

"I don't want you to leave. Like at all. And I mean, you have a job here already—seems silly to just up and go already."

She laughs and tips her head from side to side. "It's been a lot getting here. The buildup and then the blowup," she adds wryly before sobering. "I'm sorry about the way you found out—that was never my intention."

"Things with our father are complicated. They always have been, and it's going to take a long time before I can forgive him. That's on him not you."

"I still hate the way it happened though."

"I'm not sure it could have happened any other way honestly." Grabbing two glasses, I fill them with milk, handing one to Arden before setting mine on the counter. "Is...is your mom mad at me?"

"Definitely not," she says without hesitation. "She'd actually like to meet you when or if you're ready."

"Really?" A feeling of hope blooms in my chest.

"Really. She's amazing and she'll love you." She doesn't say *just like I do* but it hangs between us all the same.

"Well, I'm looking forward to meeting her."

"And things with your boyfriend, are they okay?"

"They will be—a lot of that is on me though. I mean on Dad too. But Montana and I will be okay; I'm gonna make sure of it."

Tilting her head to the side, she stares at me. "How are you going to do that?"

"I'm pulling out all the stops." I grin. "Wanna help?"

Worrying her bottom lip with her teeth, she nods. "Yeah, I think I do."

"I BROUGHT WINE!" Bea says as she wraps me in a one-arm hug as she crosses the threshold into the house. "This requires wine, right?"

"So much wine," I confirm as she pulls back, Archer hovering in the entryway. "If I hug you, does that make it worse," I start while motioning to his shuffling feet and the blush creeping up his neck, "or is it like ripping off the Band-Aid because I've known you almost my entire life?"

"I have no idea," he says, exasperated even though he can't fight his smile.

I squeal and launch myself at him hard enough for him to stumble back and grunt from the impact. Bea's laughter behind us has the exact effect I was going for as Archer shakes his head and laughs too.

"See? Isn't this easier?"

"What? Being tackled by a kindergarten teacher moon-lighting as a linebacker?"

I snort as I accept a glass of wine from Bea and shake my head. "We're practically family with you bein' Montana's cousin and all."

Archer rolls his eyes but it's more fond than annoyed. "It's hard to say no to that guy."

"Hard to say no to who?" Arden asks as she walks in the room, her hair pulled up into a messy bun on the top of her head.

"No way," Bea gasps as there's a knock at the door, and Archer's hand reaches for the knob without looking as his gaze ping-pongs between us. "I knew you looked familiar. I can't believe I didn't figure it out sooner!"

"Hey everyone. Oh holy hell, there's two of you!" Cal exclaims as he crosses the threshold, unceremoniously dumping the bags in his arms onto the floor before moving to stand in front of us. "Well, this is a plot twist if I ever saw one." He nods and looks around. "Oh, I'm Cal; your host is terrible."

Archer snickers and I shove Cal, making him laugh before properly introducing everyone in the room and explaining my plan.

"Do you think it will work?" Because I desperately want it to work. I need it to work.

"You're the only one who makes him smile like that," Archer says firmly as he holds my gaze. It's unwavering as my heart threatens to beat out of my chest.

"He smiles a lot," I try, but it's weak and I hate that I need the reassurance—need him to say again that it's *me* Montana needs.

"It's been my experience..." Bea cocks her head to the side and he blushes as he looks at her. "What? It's limited but I do have some."

"Of course you do, baby," she says teasingly before blowing him a kiss. He narrows his eyes and even though his face is scarlet, I can still feel the tension bouncing between them.

"What I mean is," Archer says while returning his attention to me, "the guy is perpetually happy. There's not a lot that derails the person he puts out into the world, and few people know the guy who's under all that. He's humble and quiet,"—he points at me—"but you've always known that version of him."

He doesn't say anything else and he doesn't have to. I've taken those moments with my best friend for granted. I'd traded the possibility of something more for stability. I'd taken every smile and laugh and selfishly tucked it away.

Montana had taught me how to climb trees and throw a football. He'd doubled down when I told him Owen

Sanders had been my first kiss in the hallway outside the gymnasium and I didn't see what all the fuss was about.

He hadn't taken too kindly to that. Montana had cursed and muttered under his breath the entire way home from school, dragging me deep into the cotton field and away from prying eyes.

And then my best friend had kissed me breathless.

He'd kissed me like I'd seen in the movies and he kissed me like he could have done it forever. He'd been smug afterward, like any other sixteen-year-old boy who'd left a girl panting from making out, but I wasn't mad because he'd shown me exactly what the fuss was about.

But that kiss was the only thing I had to keep me warm at night—the only thing I had to make it through the day.

Archer looks around the room at the rolls of paper, bottles of paint, and brushes littering my living room and sighs. "And now him smilin' at you means I'm doing arts and crafts."

"Have I mentioned how handsome you are lately?" Bea says with a grin.

"Y'all are too cute," Cal says, placing a hand over his heart, and I can't help but giggle.

"Yeah, yeah,"—Archer waves me off—"just show me what we're doin' so I can pretend like I'm not getting arrested tonight."

I gasp. "I am offended you'd even say such a thing." He snorts and Bea looks on amused. I'm about to retort but decide against it and just shrug as I hold out my wineglass. "To the things we do for family."

"To family," Arden says, and my heart grows three sizes because I've finally created the family I'd always wanted. A sister I'd missed my whole life and friends who came just because I needed them—it was more than I could have ever imagined.

Bea clinks her glass enthusiastically against Arden's and then mine as Archer takes a sip from his water bottle, Cal already refilling his glass after a single toast.

Scrolling through my phone, I find a playlist, and the first beats of "Make Me Want To" by Jimmie Allen fill the room as we all break off to our respective corners and get to work.

With any luck, this will be a story worth telling for years to come. But for now, I just have to make it to tomorrow.

39

MONTANA

I've barely made it through the day, my back aching from pushing myself to drown out the noise in my head. Descending North blares through the speakers, the rock band justifying the hurt, anguish, and fury I've been holding on to.

It has been the soundtrack to my life on and off for years, but thinking it was all behind me makes this new wave of heartbreak that much worse.

The setting sun bounces off a shiny new SUV as it follows the gravel drive toward the house. It doesn't belong.

It never has.

And he never will.

It'd be easy to slink back into the shadows, to hide myself away and wait for him to leave, but a bigger part of me doesn't want to give Evan Mills the satisfaction of being able to hightail it out of here without a word.

If he wants to talk, we can talk.

For Ellison's sake.

Moving slowly, I close the distance, Evan rounding the hood and meeting me in the middle.

It's almost *poetic.*

"Evening," he says, his voice quiet but determined, so I nod as he looks around. I can't imagine what he's thinking. In all my years of knowing him, I don't think I've ever seen him this casual—so *normal.* "You've done a lot since we've been gone."

"Had nothing but time," I say and watch as his lips press into a firm line. We stand like that a moment before he turns toward me and speaks.

"My wife, soon to be ex-wife, was friendly with the former mayor around here. I don't know if you remember him."

"I do," I say, my voice even because there's not a soul in Tennessee who doesn't know what that man did to one of our own. It took years, but justice had finally been served.

Evan nods. "A total bastard." I grunt before he goes on, "But he had influence. Small town or not, he made a reputation for himself in certain circles."

"Why are you trying to rehash this? He's in prison—has been for a couple of years now."

"But he wasn't when y'all were eighteen."

I feel the color drain from my face as I will my legs to hold me under the weight of that single sentence.

"I knew you loved my daughter, Montana, and I knew you weren't going anywhere. Hell, I was hoping we'd be able to start over and I could support you the way you both deserved. I could see the way things had shifted between you two that summer." Clearing his throat, Evan shoves a hand into the front pocket of his jeans. "I told Sherri Ann as much in the days before Ellison left for college."

"And?"

"And she threatened the farm." He motions out toward the land before letting his arm drop back to his side.

"Inspectors. Grants. Funding. Legislation. Ordinances." His tired eyes meet mine. "And that was only the beginning." He doesn't mention her illegal plans although I'm sure they're just as cold and calculating as the woman herself.

"We could have fought it if we'd known. We could have—"

My retort dies on my lips as he shakes his head because maybe we *could have* fought but we wouldn't have won. Not in Grandad's lifetime and not in time to send my sisters to college.

"I thought maybe you'd keep doing what you were doing while she was in college—being friends and maybe a little more—but then you came to see me." He blows out a shuddery breath. "I couldn't let it happen, because I knew she'd say yes."

He doesn't have to say Sherri Ann would have lost her shit over that announcement and would have unleashed hell on my family. I'd like to think that if he'd trusted me with that information back then, that I would have been able to have Ellison and protect us both.

I'd been just a kid with love in my heart and the need for reassurance that I was worthy of his daughter.

But I hadn't been reassured—I'd been gutted.

He'd been unusually cruel that day, the words almost menacing and giving life to all the fears I'd kept at bay since I first learned her name.

"I'm sorry, Montana. I haven't always been a good man. I won't stand here and say I made all the right choices or that I didn't take the easy way out in my life. Every single one of my days is filled with regret, but I'm trying."

"How's that goin' for you?" I ask wryly, making the corner of his mouth twitch with the barest hint of a smile.

"So far, not good." It's an understatement and we both

know it. "But I would rather work for Ellison's forgiveness, for Arden's, and for yours until I'm old and gray than live another moment in the past. I'm sorry, Montana. I'm sorry I took so much of the time you could have had with Ellison, and not that you need it, but you have my blessing and you always have. I just hope that you'll both let me witness what comes next."

I stand there in the driveway of my family's farm—my legacy—my *home,* and not for the first time I'm thankful for the simplicity of it all. I'm humbled to do what my father and grandfather have done and generations before. The man in front of me has wasted half his life just trying to keep his head above water. At first glance, I would have said that time had been good to him just living without a care in the world.

But the stress lines around his eyes and mouth tell a different story.

He looks exhausted and, more startlingly, sincere.

My heart spasms in my chest with an emotion I'd rather ignore. I hurt for him and I hate it—hate that he warrants my sympathy. But more than that, it's reassuring that I hadn't totally misjudged him. Even at his worst, I'd some-how, inexplicably, always harbored a sort of empathy for Ellison's father.

"Have you talked to Ellison?"

"A little after you left yesterday and again this morning. I'm trying to give her some space."

"But not too much."

"Not too much," he agrees with a lift of his shoulder. "Unless she tells me to get the hell out, I'm in Blackstone Falls to stay."

"And Arden?"

"That will take more time. I'd like to apologize to

Monroe, but I'm not sure she's ready to see me or if she ever will be."

"One thing at a time, I guess." I hold my hand out as I say the words. Evan's mouth presses into a line again, but this time it's to hold back the emotion written all over his face. Glassy eyes meet my gaze as his hand clasps mine, his grip firm and steady.

A lifeline.

But now, it's me offering it to him, not the other way around.

"Thank you," he whispers before clearing his throat and saying the words again.

"I won't let you hurt her again—hurt us." I sigh. "I'll give my life to make her happy. I need you to do the same. She deserves it."

And so much more.

"I envied the way you could so freely love her."

"Show her now."

"I will." He hitches his thumb toward the car. "I don't want to keep you any longer, but maybe next week, if you're free, I can take you and Ellison out to dinner? I'm still trying to get ahold of someone at Sundown Realty so I can find something a little more permanent. I will sell the house as soon as the ink is dried on my divorce."

My lips twitch at the mention of Sundown Realty, and now would be the perfect time to tell him all about the ways Archer and I had launched ourselves into such a lucrative business.

But I won't, not today.

"Maybe you can take over the lease at Ellison's cottage," I offer as casually as I can because mad or not, I'm still gonna get my girl tomorrow.

"I'll ask her."

Nodding, we walk in silence to his car, and I shake his hand once more before he waves at Grandad sitting on the porch.

"Evening, Hal."

Grandad returns the wave from the rocking chair, a small black lump of fur in his lap. "Evenin'." His eyes sparkle as his gaze bounces from Evan to me and down to the cat. "Told you she'd come back."

Evan chuckles and I just shake my head because between the love of my life coming home, her father, her half sister, and more than a decade's worth of angst put to rest—why wouldn't my grandfather's beloved cat return?

Sure, stranger things have happened, but nothing in this moment comes to mind and I'm okay with that. I feel lighter than I have in a long while and I'm ready—ready to finally get my girl and make it forever.

40

MONTANA

Waking before my alarm, I try to keep the smile from breaking out over my face.

It only lasts a couple of seconds but I can't be mad. I thought a lot about Ellison and what I want from her.

With her.

After talking with her father, I'd taken the time to strip away all the noise—the fear and excuses—of why I couldn't go after my girl. The list hadn't changed since I was sixteen, but I sure as hell have—and so has she.

Hearing her tell me to *get ready* had my dick getting all kinds of ideas.

But more than that it was the way she'd squared her shoulders, the way she didn't back down, and the way I *knew* she'd make good on her promise today.

"Get ready, Max, because when I'm done there won't be a single person within a fifty-mile radius who doesn't know you're mine."

That woman...

I'm ripped from my musings by a wet snout and tongue up the side of my face, Hermie's body vibrating with happiness as he tries to decide whether he wants to get up on the bed or just continue to assault from his perch on the floor.

"C'mere, you mutt." I laugh, grabbing him around the middle and hoisting him onto the mattress. He stumbles a little in the blanket but is otherwise unfazed and recovers quickly, tongue hanging out and tail wagging. "Grandad already let you out?"

Hermie barks and I laugh as he pounces on me before rolling onto his back and rubbing along the quilt my Nan made for me in high school. I'd pulled the gray and turquoise monstrosity from the cedar chest yesterday after Ellison had gifted me the asymmetrical winter hat, the nostalgia hitting me full force.

A sharp whistle sounds from the kitchen, and Hermie scrambles off the bed in search of my grandfather—my cue to face the day. Shaking my head, I throw back the covers and shuffle toward the bathroom for a quick shower, going through the motions, my mind running wild with thoughts of what she has in store for me. For us.

I half expect to see her in the kitchen when I come out of my room, but aside from Grandad putzing around, there's nothing out of the ordinary.

"Mornin'," Grandad says, his eyes bright with excitement and I smile, a swarm of butterflies making a home low in my belly. "If I was you," he says as I help myself to coffee, "I'd probably head on over to the barn. Feed the horse."

"I'll definitely do that," I say and he nods, squeezing my shoulder as he goes to sit at the table.

"Good luck, Montana," Celeste says, coming into the kitchen and placing a kiss on my cheek. "If all goes well, you bring everyone over for dinner."

"Everyone?" I ask, surprised.

She nods. "I'm countin' on a celebration."

That makes two of us.

I tell her as much, and with a steadying breath, I take a step out onto the porch. I pause, giving myself a minute to get my head on straight before descending the steps and going to find my girl.

Rounding the side of the house, coffee mug in hand, I pull my ballcap down low over my eyes to block out the rising sun.

"Montana Greene."

Coffee sloshes out over the lip, my name being shouted over a megaphone enough to have my blood pumping a little faster in my veins. There's no missing Ellison's voice or the way it wavers slightly.

She's nervous, which is good, because so am I.

"Lookin' good this morning, Max," Ellison says through the megaphone, and my gaze finally snaps up to meet hers as my boots eat up the distance between us. Her hair is swept up into a messy bun on the top of her head, and she's wearing a white crop top that shows off a band of tan skin I want to get my hands on and cutoff jean shorts that are frayed from wear—not a store.

Her cowboy boots are loved to perfection, but I can't take my eyes off her long, tanned legs that had been wrapped around me just a few days ago.

"Eyes up here, Max." My gaze flashes to her, and she smirks as I roll my lips inward to hide my smile. I don't bother tryin' to hide what she's doing to me below the belt —there's no point.

She knows she's hot as fuck.

"You're up early, Eddie," I say when I've gained enough composure to not sound like I've eaten a handful of gravel with my coffee.

"Wanted to start the day off right," she says with a smirk I can't help but return.

"I've got a question for you," she says, putting the megaphone on the ground next to her as a homemade banner unrolls from the hayloft, Archer and Cal waving and grinning like fools as I read the words painted in large pink letters.

Will you Marry Me?

"El?" My lips part, my eyes slowly moving from the sign down to meet her gaze.

"I like that we've always just been us, and I want to spend the rest of my life bein' what you need. A partner and a cheerleader, a lover and friend."

"Best friend," I amend, making her smile.

"Best friend. I want to be your wife, and I want to give you babies and help Grandad get the tractor stuck so you can come rescue us. I want early-morning coffees and sneaking moments in the barn. I want a lifetime with you, Max, because that's how long I've loved you. I love you, Montana Greene, and even though I didn't get to marry you at eighteen,"—she pulls a ring from her pocket before dropping to one knee—"I hope you'll marry me now."

"Hell yes, I'll marry you," I say on a laugh before hauling her up and swinging her around.

"The ring!" she squeals but I don't stop—I can't—not until my hand is tangled in her hair and my lips are slanted over hers.

Cheers erupt from around us, and I pull my mouth from Ellison, taking in our friends and family—everyone we love offering congratulations as I give Ellison my hand so she can slide on the smooth gold band.

"I love you, Ellison, and I'm damn proud to wear your ring."

"That's my boy," Grandad says, tears welling in his eyes as he takes Ellison's and my hands in his wrinkled ones. "You've made Nan and me so proud." His hands shake as he presses something into my palm, the moment so much bigger than an engagement.

"We love you," Ellison murmurs as she places a kiss on his cheek, his eyelids falling closed as a single tear slides down his face.

My breath catches in my lungs as I stare down at the ring in my hand.

Nan's ring.

"Grandad." His name is just a whisper as Ellison gasps.

"She'd want you to have it." He looks between us. "Both of you."

"Marry me?" I ask, not able to make a speech as eloquent as hers, but there will be time for that later.

"Yes, please."

With a little laugh and shaking fingers, Ellison holds out her left hand and I slide the antique ring into place. It's perfect.

"And we love you too!" a familiar voice yells a split second before my sister Aspen throws her arms around me, Vienna squeezing in next to her, enveloping us in a group hug.

"Oh my God, y'all are making me cry, and this mascara isn't waterproof," Vienna complains.

"I told you to borrow mine," Aspen snaps back but it's all in jest.

"What in the world?" My question is directed at Ellison, but it's my father who answers.

"Think we'd miss our son getting engaged?" His smile is warm and he nods toward Ellison who beams at him.

"Good thing he said yes, huh?" Vienna asks as she pulls Ellison in for another hug.

I snort because there wasn't a chance in hell I was sayin' no. Not today and not any other day.

"Hey y'all!" Celeste yells as a laugh burst from my lips. Even from across the crowd I can see the winks she throws my way, and I just shake my head because Ellison thought of everything. "Supper is at five o'clock so don't be late!"

Cheers erupt around us as I untangle myself from my family before pulling Ellison against my chest, her hands fisting my shirt as I kiss her again like every person I know isn't watching—her father included. He might be shuffling his feet along the periphery of this celebration, but he's here and that feels right too.

"Behave yourself, Max." She pants, her back arched, and she presses her body against mine in a way that has me completely out of my mind for her.

"That's not what the sign says," I murmur back. "And now we got all these people here with you lookin' like you do." My hands find her lower back when all I want to do is grab her denim-covered ass, squeezing it tight as I drag her up my body. I want her legs wrapped around my waist because there's just something about havin' her cowboy boots digging into my back that makes me lose it a little more.

"I thought the sign came out nice," she teases. "And if we hurry, I bet you can get three, *maybe* four orgasms out of me before it's dinner time."

"Then what are we waiting for, Eddie?"

41

ELLISON

The knock on my door has my back straightening and my requisite kindergarten teacher smile in place before I even look up. I love my kids, but they usually go for a much less subtle entrance.

Cal's eyebrows are somewhere in his hairline as he leans against the doorjamb. "Wow, that was some transformation from resting bitch face to reigning queen of *one, two, three, eyes on me.*"

"Why are we friends?" I say as I chuck a marker from my rainbow pencil cup at his head and miss.

Laughing, he retrieves it from the hall and holds it out for me. "Because we had no choice and now it's too late to go back."

I shrug and accept the marker as he leans against my desk and crosses his arms.

"Don't you have some finger painting to get to?" I tease because Cal has become one of my favorite people, and my life is exceptionally more exciting with him in it.

"It is honestly shocking people think we're so nice."

"Right?" I say dramatically even as we share a smile.

We're a couple of months into the school year now, having survived harvest season and all that goes along with it. My engagement ring—Nan's ring—sparkles, and my heart squeezes in my chest just like it does every time I look at it. Montana said he would've gone and gotten me something different if I wanted, but I couldn't dream of wearing anything else. A love like theirs had been timeless, just like ours would be.

"No shotgun wedding this weekend?"

"No," I sigh. My father and I had been working slowly on rebuilding our relationship, but it was taking time. My mother was still dragging her feet with the divorce proceedings, ensuring that he remain miserably attached to her for as long as possible. I didn't want that hanging over him when he gave me away—I didn't want her to have any part of this new chapter in our lives.

And even though I was upset with the delay, I knew Montana was right when he said I'd regret not having my father walk me down the aisle.

As long as he continued to put in the work.

We'd had a couple of family counseling sessions both with and without Montana, and it felt good—affirming—to know that he was willing to fight for me even as the rest of his world crumbled around him.

"Are you headed out?" Cal asks, and I glance at the clock and nod before powering down my computer.

"Yup, I have plans for my stud of a fiancé."

"I don't want to know."

"You really don't," I confirm as I gather my bag and hoist it onto my shoulder, my expression wolfish as Cal rolls his eyes.

"I really need to get laid," he grumbles, following me out into the hall.

"That would require you to make an effort."

Aghast, he motions down his body. "Effort."

"Yes, but you also have to go out and meet people or use one of the apps collecting dust on your phone."

"That's not a thing." He sniffs as he pushes open the front door, the weather still hot for the fall.

"Well, you're not gonna meet anyone only hanging out on game night."

He scowls and I give him a quick hug when we stop in front of my car. "You're gonna find someone who's right for you." Throwing my stuff onto the passenger seat, I add, "Even if it's just right now."

Chuckling, he shoos me with his hand. "Go and engage in enough debauchery for the both of us."

"Oh, I plan on it." I wink and slide into the car, blasting the air conditioning as I navigate my way out of the parking lot and onto the road.

MONTANA

"YOU DIDN'T SAY anything about leavin' the house," Ellison whines immediately upon getting in the truck.

"We're still grabbing dinner. We just need to stop over at Sundown Realty for a minute."

"Why? I thought we could get takeout and eat naked in bed." She pauses. "Wait, did something happen at the cottage again? Dad didn't mention it," she asks, frowning. Evan had moved into the cottage not long after Ellison and I had gotten engaged, and she'd officially moved in with me.

It was a happy *coincidence.*

"No, I just keep forgetting to drop off the receipt for the

part I had to buy," I say easily, referring to the leak under the kitchen sink that Evan had called about a week ago.

Ellison doesn't say anything, and I'm thankful as we pull into the lot that Archer's truck is already parked, the lights on inside.

"Come on, I think Bea is inside still."

She huffs but otherwise doesn't complain as she gets out without waiting for me to open her door. I chuckle as I snag her hand, lacing her fingers with mine as we walk toward the building.

"You should have fed me first," she hisses and I chuckle, planting a kiss on her forehead, opening the door to Sundown Realty and letting her walk in ahead of me.

"Surprise!" Bea yells, a massive grin on her face.

"Um, what?"

Archer hands out beers because while this normally calls for champagne, it's really not our style.

"Welcome to the family!" Bea singsongs while Ellison holds up her left hand, awkwardly pointing at her ring with her bottle.

"This isn't enough?"

I snicker, taking her hand in mine. "Welcome to the Sundown Realty family."

"We own it and we just closed on a bunch of properties closer to Nashville," Archer clarifies when Ellison continues to stare at us.

"We're celebrating!" Bea says while doing a little dance.

"Can we go back to the part about you owning it?" Ellison asks as she looks around.

"Montana and I needed a way to ensure we'd never lose the farms—this is it," Archer says.

"All of it?" she asks, her gaze locking on mine.

"Yes."

"All the signs and the cottage and the renting of my parents' house?"

"Yes, and only the four of us know," Archer confirms.

"Why?" Ellison asks, her brow furrowed. "Why the secrecy?"

Archer's lips roll inward as his cheeks heat. "We're just two guys who never wanted to leave the county, and a lot of people see that as a lack of ambition."

"They can fuck right off," Bea huffs, making Archer grin and pull her against him.

"We'll never have to worry about losing our legacies. And I needed to make sure I could give Grandad everything he needs," I say. "We're the underdogs."

"Well, I'm proud of you." Ellison squeals as she launches herself at me. "Both of you, truly, this is incredible."

"Is it weird how unaffected they both were?" Archer asks as he looks from Bea to Ellison and back again.

I shrug. "I think it means we picked the right ones."

"I do have a question though," Ellison says, looking up at me. "Why didn't you rub your success in my dad's face? The signs are all over town, so you have to be doing well, right? And now into Nashville?"

"Better than well," I admit. "It's made us a lot of money, but we did it for the financial security of our future. I'm proud of what we've done but I did it for me—not him. Besides, I like knowin' I won in the end." And Evan isn't so bad these days.

She smiles as I drop a kiss on her lips because winning her has always been the ultimate prize.

We finish our drinks, talking and laughing before closing up the building and stepping out into the parking lot.

"Y'all celebrating without me?" Jensen says, climbing

out of his car and looking around. "What are y'all doin' here anyway?"

"Date night," Ellison says easily and Bea nods.

"Wanna come?" I ask because it seems like the polite thing to do.

"Yeah, as fun as that sounds..."

His voice trails off as a dark sedan pulls up behind Jensen's cruiser and parks, a gray-haired man slowly climbing from the driver's seat.

"Evening, Sheriff," he says with obvious recognition, and Jensen closes the distance toward him.

"Hey, Dennis, how are you?" The two men shake hands and I watch as Dennis swallows hard, unease churning in my gut.

"Good, good, but..." Seeming to remember some semblance of professionalism, he straightens and pulls out an envelope from inside his suit jacket, "Jensen Kade?"

"Yes."

"I'm sorry, son. You've been served."

EPILOGUE

ELLISON

"Well, hell, Max," I say as I fan my face with my hand and saunter into the office. "You look mighty fine back there." Montana is perched like a king behind the large wooden desk that's been in here as long as I've known him.

We'd played in here growing up, pretending to oversee a kingdom. We just never imagined how true it would be.

Montana is so much a part of the land—the outdoors—but he looks just as at home in here with his forearms flexing on the worn surface as he stares at me.

He's sexy in the fields.

But this version fits him too.

"You're home early," he drawls as he sits back in the black leather chair, causing it to groan under his weight.

"I missed you."

He grins. "How much?"

I lick my lips and his gaze drops to my mouth as mine raises to the cowboy hat hanging on the hook beside his head.

"Depends if you wanna wear that for me?" I ask as he

turns his head and pulls the hat down and places it on his head. It fits perfectly, worn in from years of being out in the sun on the hottest days in Tennessee.

"Didn't know this would make you so hot." He gives me a devilish smile. "I would have started wearing it a long time ago."

Smiling, I move between him and the desk, leaning my backside on the edge of the wood as he moves his legs to accommodate me. The dark wash denim stretches against his muscular thighs and my mouth waters—the man truly is a vision.

His posture is relaxed as he watches me, but the pull between us is undeniable. Leaning forward, I duck under the brim of his hat, my hands cupping his face as I take his mouth in a slow kiss, savoring each and every swipe of my tongue against his.

He tastes like mint, and even though he's been working all day, he still smells like cedar from the bar of soap in his shower. It's divine and I can't help but snag his bottom lip between my teeth as I drag my nails down his chest and over his abs.

He groans, his body flexing and bunching under my touch.

But I want more.

"I want you out of this dress," he rasps against my lips, but I can only smile in return. He can have me any way he wants.

But not right now.

"Later," I reply as my fingers work open the clasp on his belt before moving to the top button of his jeans. "Right now, I'm busy."

He snorts but hisses out a breath as I pull the zipper

down and free his dick with award-winning efficiency as I drop to my knees in front of him.

"I got all day, baby," he drawls right before I wrap my hand around his length and stroke him the way I know he likes.

Montana's eyes cut to the door I left open, his jaw clenching as my lips wrap around the head of his cock. His hand grips my ponytail as if he thinks he can dictate anything about this situation—as if I'd let him do anything but hang on and enjoy the ride. I suck harder and he exhales heavily as my tongue traces over his velvety skin before taking him as far as I can.

"You have no idea how badly I want to fuck up into that pretty pink mouth of yours." His eyes follow my free hand as it dips below the hem of my dress. "Are you..."

His question trails off and I moan around him as my fingers tease up and down the silky fabric covering my slit.

"Show me, baby. Show me your pretty wet—"

Footsteps land hard against the floor of the barn, the sound echoing with each step. My pulse quickens, and the potential to get caught has my blood burning hot in my veins.

Pulling my mouth off the angry head of Montana's gorgeous length, I grin. "Act natural, Max."

"What the fuck are you—" he starts, but I'm already shimmying backward under the desk, sliding his chair with me, the movement throwing off his ability to right his jeans before I've sucked him into my mouth again. "God fucking dammit..."

"Bad time?" a familiar male voice asks from the doorway, and I can't help but smile before stroking Montana slowly with my hand. My movements are as coordinated as they can be in the tight space, but I love everything about this.

"A little busy."

"Need me to come back? It will only take a sec."

"Make it quick," he says, the words measured, and I can only imagine the amount of control he's exerting to appear normal.

"The, uh...goats,"—Bodhi clears his throat as I tease the underside of Montana's cock with my tongue—"we had to move them to a different pen. They busted out of there—"

"Little fuckers," Montana snarls and Bodhi snorts. "But you know it's not your job to take care of it, right?"

"It's not a big deal. Keeps me busy. Just need more material to repair and reinforce the fence so we can move 'em back and keep 'em secure before you start getting calls from the neighbors."

Montana nudges me with his boot—most likely as a warning to stop—but the audacity in that one little motion has me swallowing him down as far as I can take him. His big strong thighs cage me in, applying pressure, in hopes of being able to gain the upper hand.

It's like he has no idea who he's dealing with—and just to remind him, I do it again.

And again.

"You sure you're okay?" Bodhi asks, and Montana forces a chuckle before assuring he's fine and asking Bodhi to let him know if there are any other issues.

It's only when the footsteps fade to almost nothing does Montana push back enough to look at me, my lips still wrapped firmly around him.

"You are in so much fucking trouble; get out here," he growls and grabs me by my biceps, forcing me to release his dick with an audible pop.

"Trouble for what? I—"

Like a man possessed, Montana bends me over, my chest

pressed against the cool wood of the desk. He's hiked my dress up and pulled my panties to the side before I even have time to blink, and all I can do is moan as I feel him push against my entrance.

I'm soaked and I know he can feel what our little game did to me.

He swears again before slamming inside me with one hard thrust. I gasp and he does it again—pistoning into me with such ferocity my knuckles are practically white from gripping the edge of the desk.

"Just wait until I spank the shit out of you later." The words are a threat whispered against my ear as he punishes me harder and faster, his fingers digging into my hips as my orgasm rips through every cell of my being.

I come on a silent scream as I shake and writhe with every wave of pleasure, perspiration coating my skin as Montana grunts and spills inside me.

"I'm gonna be dripping out of you for hours." His hips rock against my ass to punctuate his words, and all I can do is whimper.

I may have won the blow job battle, but he owned me in the orgasm war.

Sliding out of me, Montana stays true to his word and only rights my panties. They're soaked and probably ruined, but it was so incredibly worth it I will gladly sacrifice them as tribute—and honestly every other pair I own if it gets me a reaction like today.

Propping myself up on one elbow, I look back at Montana over my shoulder and grin. "Same time tomorrow?"

"You're going to be the death of me."

"You say the *sweetest* things to me, Montana Greene," I tease, standing as I turn to face him and patting his chest.

His hand covers mine, his expression still filled with a lusty haze and complete and total adoration.

"I'm still spanking your perfect ass tonight."

"Wear that hat and I'll let you do anything you want."

"You have yourself a deal."

THE END

Thank you so much for reading Feels Like Falling! Get a sneak peek at Montana and Ellison's wedding on the next page!

BONUS EPILOGUE

ELLISON

THE NEXT SUMMER

"Five minutes everyone!" Bea sing songs as she twirls around in her knee length, eggplant colored bridesmaid dress.

"Are you nervous?" Cal asks as he comes up and stands behind me, meeting my eyes in the mirror.

"Not even a little."

He snorts and shakes his head but honestly, what could be better than finally getting to marry Montana Greene?

"You look stunning." He says and this time, his eyes are glassy as he reaches for my hand and squeezes. The dress is light and simple, more bohemian than traditional with peasant sleeves, cut outs that wrap around my sides and a high slit in the layered, flirty skirt.

It's perfect and so very *me*.

A throat clears behind us and I look to find my father in the doorway, shifting his weight from foot to foot.

"Is everything all right?" I ask and he nods before tugging on the lapels of his suit jacket.

"I was hoping to talk to you for a minute."

"Of course." I say, giving Cal's hand another squeeze before stepping away.

My father's smile is genuine and adoring as he bends to place a kiss on my cheek.

"You look beautiful, El."

"You look very handsome yourself."

"I uh," pulling a black velvet box from his pocket, he gives me a sheepish smile, "I got you something and you don't have to wear them but –"

He opens the box to reveal the most stunning set of vintage sapphire earings. My mouth drops open because they're almost a perfect match to the detail in my engagement ring.

Nan's engagement ring.

"Dad, these are beautiful," I manage, already taking the diamond studs I'd throw in earlier and placing them in Cal's magically waiting hand. He winks and then moves away again.

"I took a picture of your ring to a jeweler in Nashville I found – told them that you wouldn't want something so *traditional* for your wedding."

"These are perfect, thank you."

My heart swells with affection for the man who had worked tirelessly to mend our relationship since returning to Blackstone Falls. He'd taken to spending time at my house, helping Grandad in the garden, manning the grill and showing up for Montana and I over and over again.

He was constantly trying and so was I.

"It's time." Bea says quietly and I smile because *this is it!*

My father offers me his arm and I take it, following my bridesmaids and Cal as we descend the stairs to the main floor.

Montana had been adamant that we wait to do this until my father could be a part of it – that I'd *want* him to be a part of it. In exchange, I'd asked him to replant the field of sunflowers so we could get married in front of them.

So we could say our vows in a place where love had been given so freely.

So beautifully.

So Nan could be a part of it too.

Stepping out into the sunshine, I tilt my face up and smile as a light breeze blows the tendrils framing my face around.

Hi Nan.

I smile, the words a silent acknowledgement, because I *feel* her here. The thought settles my nerves as we walk towards where rows of chairs are filled with friends and neighbors.

Montana's friends.

And now mine.

Aspen, Bea, and Auden stand across from Grandad, Celeste and Cal at the top of the aisle, a beautiful sunflower in their hands from the field.

I accept the first from Aspen, hugging her tight before adding it to my bouquet as she then goes to take her place at the front. I repeat the ritual with each of them, Grandad offering me two – one for him and one for Nan.

The tears are inevitable as I hug and thank each one of them for being with me just today but always.

Turning towards my father, I watch as he takes a burlap ribbon from his pocket, tying it around the base of the bouquet and then looping the remaining length into a bow.

A gesture that makes me smile because he'd asked Celeste to show him the best way to tie it. And he'd practiced so he wouldn't fumble today.

My heart swells as he smiles triumphantly at me, once again offering his arm. I take it and look up, my breath whooshing from my lungs as Montana eye's lock with mine.

Lips parted, he wipes at his face with the back of his hand and I can't even make a joke because emotion clogs my throat as I walk towards the man that will be my husband in a matter of minutes.

Montana's sister Vienna stands at the top of the aisle, ready to officiate our nuptials because apparently it's her thing now. She beams at me as my father and I stop before her and Montana.

"Who gives this woman away?"

"We do."

An echo of voices sound around me and I choke back a sob. My father, Grandad, Celeste, my bridesmaids and Cal, Montana's groomsmen including Mason, Bodhi, Jensen and Archer and half the attendees all say the words together and my heart soars.

I'd spent so much of my life in this town trying like hell to fit in as a child, and still as an adult, but these people had become mine – my friends and neighbors.

My family.

"What do you say, Eddie? You ready to do this?" Montana whispers, his eyes glassy and his lips curved up in little grin.

"I'm ready, Max. Now and forever."

Thank you so much for reading Montana and Ellison's story!

Want to stay in touch? You can find me here!

Want a look at the inspiration for Ellison and Montana?
Check out their **Pinterest** board Here!
Listen to their **playlist** Here!

———

Preorder Jensen's book, Unexpectedly Falling here!

———

Turn the page to read the first chapter of Archer and Bea's
happily ever after in Secretly Falling!

SECRETLY FALLING (CHAPTER 1)

ARCHER

"Excuse me, that's my table."

Startled, I spin around so fast I nearly drop the box of Mason jars in my hands as I come face-to-face with the prettiest girl I've ever seen. My brain helpfully registers that observation which engages my defense mechanism—silence.

Her hair is light brown and pulled back into a ponytail, and while I don't go out of my way to meet women, I definitely *would* have noticed this one if we'd crossed paths before.

But we haven't.

Not that seeing her before this would have helped me in this moment, but it would have been nice to have time to preemptively panic before this morning.

I swallow and will myself to do anything other than catalog every freckle on her face, but nothing happens. I'm frozen to the worn gym floor and wonder for the hundredth time why I agreed to this winter festival in the first place.

Peeking up at me though thick brown lashes, the kind

that are natural, she waits for me to speak—as if I need more time.

I don't.

Because it's me, and pretty women render me speechless.

Vying for an out, I frantically look at the number at the corner of the table and try and rack my brain for the email I read last week.

"Hey man," Jake Booker says as he comes up next to me with a smile, "you're right over there next to me." Equally relieved and annoyed at his arrival, I grunt a "thanks" to him before nodding to the woman in front of me.

Turning faster than a wet dog in a truck bed, I hightail it toward the table Jake indicated and try to force my lips upward as his wife, Cheyenne, gives me a bright smile and an enthusiastic wave. There'd been a time when I'd been *tempted* to ask her out, but that ship had long since sailed and I am happy, and still somewhat surprised, to have them both as friends.

Friends.

That was a weird concept too, but I was trying. I was friendly enough with most people and just left it at that. I didn't mind the quiet and I didn't mind being alone. People came to my farm for the quality my family had provided for generations—the quality I still provided.

Which was why I'd been forced into this indoor market event. Setting the box top full of canned pickles and jellies on my table, I blow out a breath and try to calm my nerves. Despite the chilly February weather outside, I can feel a bead of sweat rolling down my spine. It has less to do with the weather and more to do with the woman across the room, but I'm choosing to ignore that.

"She's still starin' at you," Jake says under his breath.

"Who?" Cheyenne asks while she pops up on her toes to peer behind us.

Lord have mercy.

"Stop doin' that," I hiss, and Jake chuckles as Cheyenne's blue eyes go wide.

"You like her?" she whispers back, and I can feel the heat climbing up my neck, my cheeks turning an embarrassing shade of red a moment later.

"How can I like her? Y'all were there. I only saw her for like a minute and I couldn't even talk to her," I lament as "That's Why I Love Dirt Roads" by Granger Smith starts playing overhead. I love this song and I can't even enjoy it as I replay the last ten minutes over and over.

"You know damn well *time* doesn't mean anythin' when you find *the one,*" Jake says without taking his eyes off Cheyenne.

I open my mouth with a rebuttal to his declaration, but I'm wasting my breath with these two. Jake had known the moment he saw his wife that she was special, and he'd tell anyone who stopped long enough how he convinced her to finally go out with him.

"You know..." Jake starts but I hold up my hand.

"I don't need your help," I grumble even as my heart starts beating faster in my chest. Jake chuckles, and I want to hate him with his dark hair, full beard, and country star good looks that give him an uncanny resemblance to Jordan Davis, but I can't. He means well, and it's not his fault I'm so completely inept at social interaction.

"But Archer," Cheyenne starts, "she's watchin' you. You gotta go talk to her!" Cheyenne's blonde hair bounces around her shoulders as she shifts from one foot to the other, her excitement plain on her face as she stares from me to the woman across the room.

I narrow my eyes at her, remembering that she'd been just like me before Jake came and swept her off her feet.

We'd both been painfully shy. I still am, which means there's a better chance of a shark attack in our little Tennessee town than me walkin' over like Fred Astaire to talk to a beautiful woman.

I swallow hard. "I'm gonna go grab the rest of my stuff from the truck."

"Hey, watch out for—"

Jake's warning doesn't come fast enough as I turn and walk straight into the petite frame of the woman who already has me tied up in knots.

Shit.

Want the rest of Archer and Bea's story? Get it Here!

ACKNOWLEDGMENTS

I'd like to start by saying thank you to my husband for keeping me grounded through this journey. We'll always be better together.

To my family for their complete and unwavering support and enthusiasm. I couldn't ask for a better cheering section.

To K. Powers – there are truly no words. Thank you for bringing my vision to life and for knowing me better than I know myself. It is an honor and privilege to work with you – it's a dream come true.

To Atlee for holding me accountable even when I didn't want you to – you're a rockstar and I'm so thankful to have you in my corner. To Lindsey, thank you for pushing me to be better and being the good cop to Atlee's bad cop – you girls are the best! And thank you both for humoring me and telling me I'm pretty.

To Nicole for loving my lasagna recipe and the forever friendship we've forged. I'm so thankful we get to walk this path together.

To Jenna for being my writing partner and forever keeping me focused. Thank you for never giving up on me and staying up past your bedtime to make sure I make my deadlines. To Nicki for being my sounding board and loving me through every stage of my process.

To Carolina for enduring the chaos with me. To J.

Hutchison for all the late night sprinting and making me write even on the days I didn't want to.

To my author and book friends turned real friends and the writing community (there are so many of you!) – your support has been overwhelming and I am truly humbled. Thank you for being on this journey with me.

To the HEA Babes - y'all are the best and I'm so very thankful for you!

To my ARC/Street Team – I still can't believe I have one of those – thank you. You showed up and went above and beyond for me, y'all are the best!

To my Books, Babes & Bombshells – you make me ridiculously happy!

To the readers who took a chance on me – thank you. I'll never be able to say it enough. You've already exceeded my wildest dreams.

To the Anns of Happily Editing Anns – you're the real unsung heroes of this adventure. Thank you for walking me through hours and hours of editing – those side margin notes are gold. To Gina who nurtured my passion for writing – thank you for seeing my potential – I hope I always make you proud.

To my cheering squad who never let a day go by without kind words of encouragement or that swift kick to get me going – you're the absolute best! You know who you are and I love you more than words.

ABOUT THE AUTHOR

Alexandra Hale is a small town girl living with her family in Upstate New York. She routinely runs on caffeine, dry shampoo and thrives on procrastination.

A lover of all things romance, Alexandra finally began putting pen to paper shortly after graduating college. An unobtainable dream has slowly become a reality with the love and support of her friends and family and the romance community.

She currently writes steamy, small town romance with a dash of lighthearted fun and happily ever afters that will make you swoon.

Want to stay in touch?
Connect with Alexandra here!

ALSO BY ALEXANDRA HALE

Blackstone Falls

Secretly Falling

Feels Like Falling (Blackstone Falls Book 1)

Preorder Unexpectedly Falling

Add Unexpectedly Falling to your TBR (Summer 2024)

Clementine Creek

Back in the Country

Making it Country

Home in the Country

Out in the Country (A Standalone Novella)

Playing it Country

Christmas in Kiwi Country (A Clementine Creek Novella 4.5)

Forever in the Country

Loving it Country (A Newsletter Freebie)

Love Beach

Summer With a Brother's Best Friend (June 2024)

Merry with a Brewmaster (November 2024)

Magnolia Point (Man of the Month)

Watermelon With You? (August 2024)

Ironwood (TBD)

Staged (An Ironwood Crossing Novel, Book 1)

Made in United States
North Haven, CT
31 May 2024